A Pilgrimage of Whispered Truths

A Steamy Romantic Whodunit on the Virginia Coast

By M. Jayne LaDow

For Julia Grey, who taught me to question, to wonder, and to write with honesty. Your lessons endure in every word I put to paper.

I miss you.

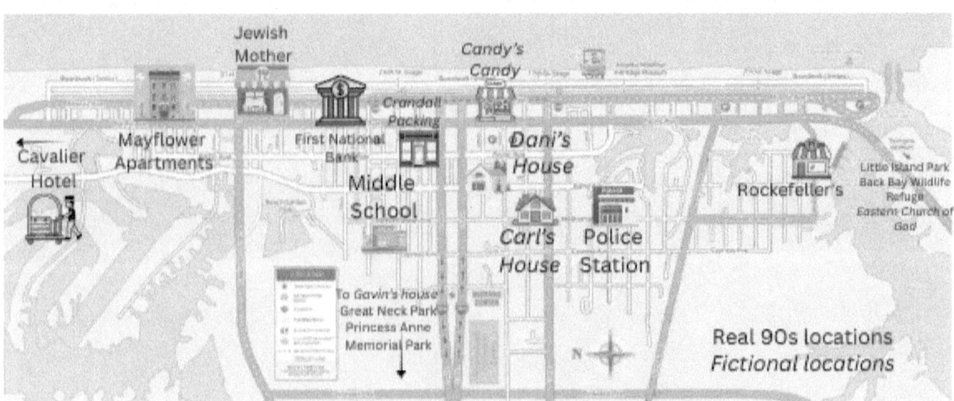

Virginia Beach, VA 1997

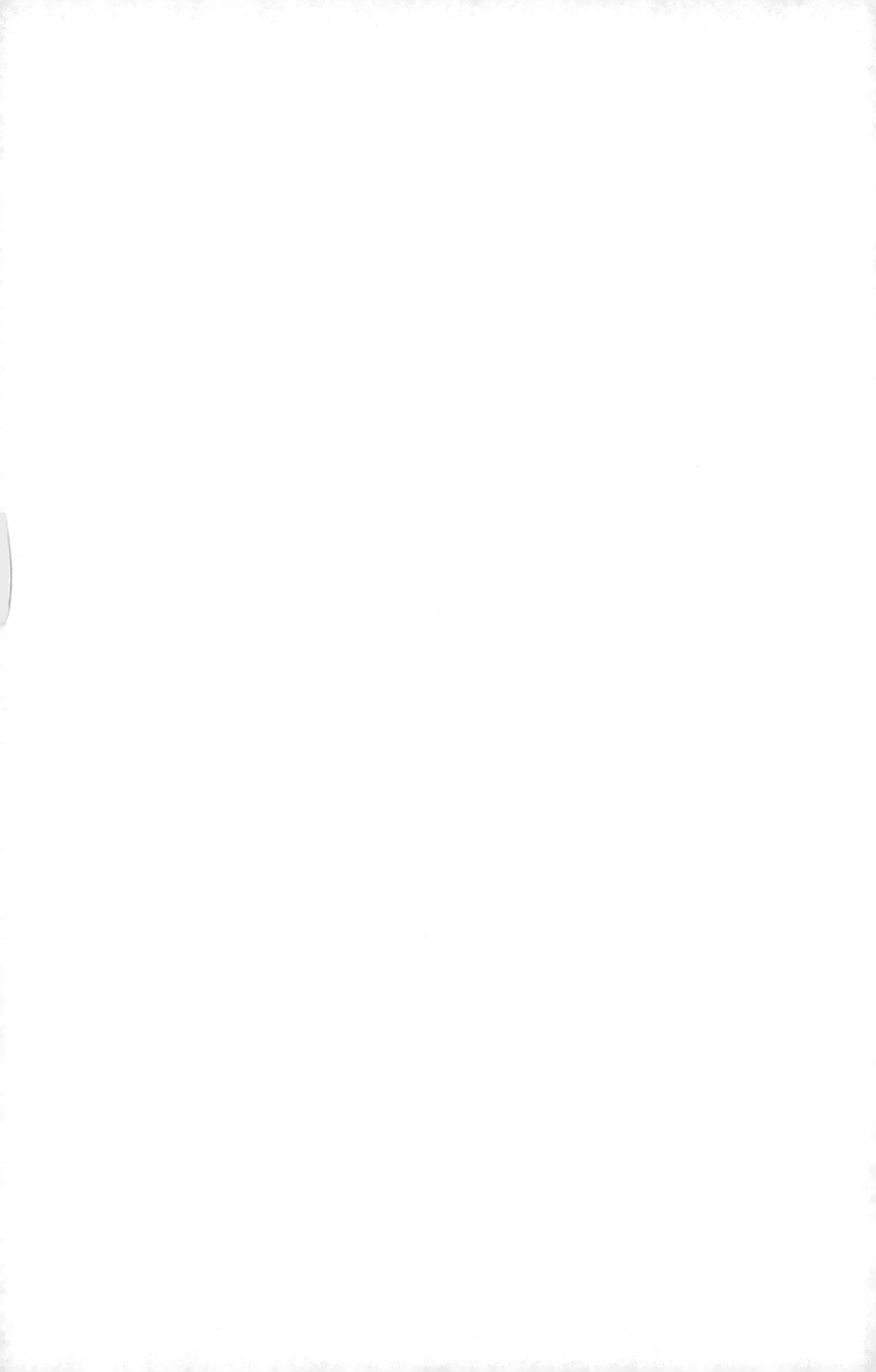

Prologue

Allegheny County, Virginia, November 1, 1986

The church burned like a sacrifice. Flames clawed at the steeple, swallowing the cross first, as if Heaven itself had turned its face away. The stained glass wept molten color. Charred beams split like ribs, exhaling the soul of the sanctuary into the night sky.

He watched from the roadside, hands clasped loosely before him the posture of prayer learned long ago. Smoke curled around him like incense. To those who glanced his way, he appeared a man in mourning: a pillar of faith brought low by tragedy.

They saw only what he wanted them to see.

Deacon. Treasurer. Shepherd. A middle-aged man, kind, a little slow to speak, a little too fond of sweets. No family of his own, just the church. The sort who remembered birthdays, cried during baptisms, and made his quiet loneliness look holy. A man trusted with spare keys and whispered confessions. A man no one would ever suspect.

He wore each title with the solemnity of ritual. He bent his head in prayer.

But today, on All Saints' Day, even the venerated ones had forsaken their vigil, leaving nothing but empty shadows in their stead.

He had destroyed Holy Covenant Baptist Church from within slowly, methodically, like termites in the pews while the sheep of Oakville, Virginia, smiled and nodded, mistaking his hunger for holiness. He knew how to make piety look honest, how to turn guilt into gold.

He could have walked straight out of Chaucer, relics and all *Radix malorum est cupiditas*, and all that.

Accounts shifted quietly. Insurance policies drafted under the names of companies that never existed. Donations rerouted, laundered, sanctified with forged signatures and seals pressed from dust and age. The books always balanced if you knew which set to open, and which to keep locked behind the vestry door.

And now, the fire. The final sacrament.

Behind him, someone sobbed. Someone else lifted their hands to heaven. The air reeked of smoke and scorched hymnals. A siren wailed in the distance, slow and solemn as a processional.

"Such a loss," a voice murmured beside him.

He did not look. "God's will," he replied, his voice like velvet.

The east wing collapsed, and the fire leapt high, ecstatic, unrestrained.

He turned then, his coat catching the wind like a preacher's robes in revival. "I'll help rebuild," he said softly, as if to the ashes themselves. "With all I have left."

And then: "But first... I must go out of town for a bit."

The lie tasted sweet.

His car waited at the end of the gravel road. The engine was still warm, the trunk already packed.

Behind him, the bell tower fell, groaning like something ancient and betrayed. A single bell tolled as it died. Once. Just once.

He smiled faintly, reaching into his coat pocket, fingers brushing the charred edge of a small, warped object: a fragment of stained glass, sharp against his skin. Red, like blood.

He had pulled it from the grass, still warm. A warped souvenir of melted faith and misplaced trust.

A relic.

It would rest beside the others, tokens from other sanctuaries, other flocks, other towns that never saw him coming.

He kept them in a narrow, velvet-lined box, tucked away in his luggage. Small enough to hide.

Not for God.

For himself.

Chapter One

Virginia Beach, Virginia, May 14, 1997

Danica Jones tapped her pencil against the edge of her worn wooden desk.

"All right, class, let's keep going with The Canterbury Tales. Last night, you were supposed to read the prologue to The Pardoner's Tale. Can anyone tell me what a pardoner is?"

Outside, a gull screeched, thin and distant, through the open windows. The spring breeze carried the scent of salt and wet grass, laced with a thread of honeysuckle from the overgrown fence beside the teachers' parking lot.

High in the tall oak behind the school, a faded red kite fluttered where it had been caught for over a week, tangled like a secret no one had claimed. Dani watched it twist in the wind before scanning the room, absently tucking a strand of her dark brown, shoulder-length hair behind her ear. It held a bit of a wave, always threatening to frizz in the coastal humidity.

Room 212 wore its age like an old cardigan, patched in places but still comfortable. The paint was chipped around the doorframe, the linoleum tiles dulled by decades of shoes. Book posters lined the back wall in various states of curl, and a crooked "READ" banner sagged above the chalkboard. The corner bookshelf was messy, littered with books and magazines tossed every which way.

Over it hung a vintage class photo from 1952 that Dani had found in the supply closet her first year and never quite had the heart to throw away.

Only two hands were raised, as expected.

Mark, the ever-eager know-it-all. He would either become a tenured professor or a professional brown-noser.

The other belonged to Taneika, brilliant but solitary. She already wrote better literary essays than most college freshmen.

Dani let the silence stretch a moment longer, hoping for a surprise. Her warm brown eyes flicked from desk to desk, amusement glinting behind them. The easy curve of her smile lingered, even when her students didn't answer right away.

But the final bell was fifteen minutes away, and the room had begun its quiet drift toward dismissal, eyes on the clock, minds already elsewhere.

"Ashley?" Dani asked, her tone a gentle nudge. She'd read enough of the girl's writing to know there was something sharp beneath the quiet.

Half-slouched in her seat, Ashley had one arm stretched across the desk, the other absently twisting a strand of long black hair. At the sound of her name, her eyes flicked up, guarded.

She blinked. "Um, I'm not sure," she said, her voice barely rising above the soft rattle of the old A/C unit grinding beneath the sill.

Dani knew that look, the tilt of the head, the wary eyes, the voice gone small, as if it didn't want to be noticed. It wasn't laziness; it was camouflage. She'd mastered it herself in classrooms just like this one, a long time ago, when her father's moods swung sharp and sudden and it was easier to live unnoticed.

Ashley didn't need to be called out. She needed to be seen.

Maybe nothing was wrong. Maybe it was just a spring afternoon, a restless body and a head full of things more interesting than medieval literature. Or maybe it was something more.

Dani had learned not to assume, but she also knew when a kid was trying not to be watched.

She offered a small, encouraging nod. "That's all right," she said. "Let's walk through it together."

Ashley nodded, looking relieved. Dani made a mental note to talk to her after class, not to scold, just to check in. Teaching wasn't only essays and vocabulary; half the job was reading the silences.

She turned her gaze back to the class, wondering not for the first time how many secrets a roomful of twelve-year-olds might be keeping right beneath her nose.

"Ms. Jones, I know!" Mark blurted, nearly launching himself from his chair with the force of his enthusiasm.

A chorus of groans drifted across the room like the sigh of an old house settling in the wind. Even Taneika rolled her eyes. Dani caught it and filed it away. The kid was smart and hardworking, but middle school politics were a minefield. Being too clever, too fast, too eager could make you a target. She'd keep an eye on that dynamic, too.

"All right, Mark," Dani said, stifling a sigh with a small smile. "Enlighten us."

He sat up even straighter, if that were possible, and launched into his answer like a miniature professor at a podium. "A pardoner worked for the Church in medieval times," he declared. "He traveled around selling pardons to people for their sins."

His tone was precise and practiced, as if he'd rehearsed in front of a mirror, possibly more than once.

"Right." Dani nodded, folding her arms and leaning lightly against her desk. "But how does Chaucer's pardoner… bend the rules?"

She let the question hang in the air like bait. This was the moment she always looked forward to, the instant when a spark might catch and someone would connect the dots. She watched the room, scanning for any flicker of recognition.

Silence settled over the classroom like dust.

A few students shifted in their seats. Someone coughed. Outside, the gull shrieked again, offering its own commentary on the lack of participation.

Dani glanced at the clock. Nine minutes until the bell. The tide was already going out on their attention spans. She sighed inwardly with quiet resignation. She loved this work, but there were days when teaching felt like throwing breadcrumbs into a storm.

A chair creaked. Brian raised his hand, fingers hesitant at first, then steady. The room stilled, curiosity rippling through the class.

"Uh… I think he's lying to people and stealing from them," he said, his voice low but certain, as if testing the weight of his own knowledge.

Rumors always clung to Brian: strange late-night visitors, unmarked packages, whispered disappearances. Nothing ever confirmed, just enough to make people wary but careful not to cross the line. Unconventional, sure. Private, definitely. Not openly unkind.

Whatever the truth, his mind worked like a quiet engine, always running deeper than the surface. Dani made sure he knew she saw it.

"Great answer, Brian. And if he's stealing, how does he get away with it?"

"No one questioned it," Taneika responded, "because he was from the Church."

"Yeah," Ben smirked, "no America's Most Wanted back then."

That cracked the class wide open. Seventh-grade laughter is a strange, contagious sound—half shriek, half bark, entirely uncontainable.

Dani let it ride for a moment, then raised her voice over the noise.

"Okay, literary detectives-in-training," she said, half teasing, half serious. "Tonight's assignment: write a paragraph on what makes The Pardoner's Tale funny and what message you think Chaucer was trying to send. Bonus points for spotting anything suspicious."

A rustle of papers and the screech of chair legs filled the room.

"Any questions?" she asked, knowing full well the answer.

No hands. Of course not. No one wanted to be the one to delay escape.

"All right then," Dani said, stepping aside as the tide of students swept toward the door. "Have a good afternoon. I'll see you tomorrow."

The sudden noise was deafening. Books slammed shut, backpacks unzipped and zipped with frantic energy, and voices rose in bursts of laughter and mock arguments. Students hollered over one another about forgotten math homework, plans to meet up at the spring dance, and, of course, teasing remarks about who was going with whom.

Endless middle school theater.

Dani leaned against the edge of her desk and watched them spill out into the hall like a tide breaking through a dam. She loved their energy, truly, but God, it could be exhausting.

She couldn't blame them. The weather was gorgeous, the surf was up, and summer vacation loomed like a promise just a month away. Even she found herself longing for long mornings with no bells, no copy machine jams, no arguments over who had stolen whose notebook.

The oceanfront sparkled this time of year, and Dani never forgot how lucky she was to live and work so close to it. Twenty-one miles of coastline, fresh seafood on every corner. But beneath the salt air and sunny charm, there was something else, something most vacationers never noticed: a quiet, persistent sense that the town had been built on shifting sand.

Not just literally.

Back in the '60s and '70s, developers had rolled in like a second tide, sweeping away charm and wilderness to make room for the hotel strip. The skyline changed. Concrete swallowed dunes. The crash of waves gave way to the hum of traffic, and an ocean view became something you had to buy.

Sure, the beach was still public. But to reach it, you had to feed the meter and run the gauntlet of souvenir shops, sunburned tourists, and overpriced lemonade, unless you were one of the lucky few who lived or worked nearby.

Like Dani.

Her school, one of the city's oldest buildings, sat just six blocks from the water, close enough to smell the salt on the breeze, close enough to flood when the tides rose too high, when hurricanes rolled in and the storm drains choked.

Sometimes, after class, she walked down to the boardwalk and let the wind pull the day from her shoulders. The ocean always cleared the static left behind by too many voices, too many questions. Maybe she'd go today.

The thought of that cool, briny breeze was tempting.

Still, as the last student's voice faded down the hallway, Dani lingered at the window a moment too long. The classroom, once buzzing with life, settled into a silence that felt too complete.

It raised the hairs on her arms.

"Ms. Jones, please report to the office. Ms. Jones, please report to the office."

The announcement snapped through the classroom like a slap. Mrs. Haley's voice, flat and tinny, crackled from the ancient speaker above the door, then fizzled into silence.

The quiet that followed was louder than before.

Dani exhaled slowly. Of course.

She flicked off the lights. Some part of her had felt it building all day, like pressure behind her eyes, like the hush before a storm broke.

Chapter Two

At the far end of the long, quiet hallway, Dani gently closed her classroom door.

The corridor stretched ahead, leading to the main hall, where the office sat just across the intersection.

From the open door of the neighboring science classroom, Dot's teasing voice floated into the hall. "What'd you do this time, Danica?"

"We'll see," Dani replied, peeking into the room. "If I'm not back in fifteen minutes, send a rescue team."

Dot grinned with the easy confidence of someone who'd taught middle school science for over three decades. Her short, swept-back gray hair, skinny legs, and round belly gave her a familiar, unbothered charm. She and Dani had hit it off immediately and had been on the same team for nearly ten years.

"Rescue? Nah," Dot said with a wink. "You're on your own, kid."

Danica smirked. She'd been teaching for twenty years and had turned forty-three last April, definitely not a kid. But Dot called everyone "kid," even the principal, so she let it slide.

Her small heels tapped steadily against the tiled floor as she hurried down the corridor. The walls were a patchwork of student artwork, flyers for the upcoming dance, and wrinkled notices begging for library books to be returned.

But the closer she came to the front office, the more the colorful clutter faded, replaced by a heavy stillness. A familiar prickle crawled up her spine, a warning she couldn't name.

Just beyond the glass doors of the office stood a man.

Her first thought was sharp and clear: he didn't belong here.

Her second, even more certain: he was trouble.

Middle-aged and heavyset, he wore his long gray hair loose and greasy, hanging past his shoulders in tangled waves. A scraggly beard, patchy with brown and gray, clung unevenly to his jaw. His clothes carried a musty scent. The old flannel shirt with fraying cuffs, heavy jeans, and brown, scuffed boots looked like they hadn't seen sunlight since the mid-1980s.

With rigid arms crossed, he stared through the glass as if daring Dani to come closer. His dark eyes dropped to meet hers.

She slowed instinctively, then reached for the handle and opened the office door.

The front office smelled faintly of copier toner and the lemon cleaner the custodian used. A long counter divided the reception area from the inner offices beyond.

The man didn't move. He just stood there, his eyes tracking her with an unsettling, measured calm. Up close, he loomed at least six inches taller than her five-foot-seven frame, his presence as heavy as the boots planted on the linoleum floor.

She glanced toward the front desk, where Mrs. Haley sat behind her typewriter, working with calm precision. The older woman didn't look up, but her eyes flicked briefly toward Dani, then back to the screen. One hand moved subtly to the large black telephone beside her, resting there, not dialing, but ready.

Relief flickered. Whatever this was, she wasn't walking into it alone.

Squaring her shoulders, Dani met the man's eyes. In her twenty years of teaching, she'd handled hallway fights, a raccoon trapped in the ceiling tiles, and a furious PTA mob with a bullhorn. She could handle this.

"Are you Ms. Jones?" No hello, no attempt at civility. His voice was like gravel, sharp and accusatory.

Her stomach gave a small, involuntary twist, but her voice stayed calm and even. She fixed her expression into her best teacher poker face.

"Yes, sir," she said evenly. "What can I do for you?"

"You can explain why you're forcing my nephew to read this religious propaganda," he snapped, jamming a dog-eared paperback of The Canterbury Tales an inch from her nose.

His fingers were grimy, nails chewed to the quick.

The cover of the book was smudged with fingerprints.

"It's all in here, priests, pardoners, sermons, damnation. You think I don't see what this is? Indoctrination. You're pushing medieval Catholic garbage on impressionable children. Teaching religion in school is against the law, so what you're doing is illegal, Ms. Jones." He spat the last word, sharp and wet. His breath carried the sour tang of old coffee.

His eyes blazed not with conviction but with the erratic, ritualistic fury of a man who measured every gesture, every word, as if casting judgment.

Dani felt her jaw tighten. She'd faced down plenty of angry parents, ones who wanted to ban books, rewrite the curriculum, or shield their kids from uncomfortable truths.

But this felt different. Fanatic.

Still, she didn't flinch or step back. She held his gaze, steady and calm, letting the silence stretch just long enough to make it clear she wasn't afraid.

"Mr.?"

"Rendell," he snapped, slamming the book onto the office counter with enough force to curl its corners. His glare sharpened, daring her to challenge him.

At the desk, Mrs. Haley lifted her head. Her hand slid to the phone's receiver as Dani asked evenly, "Mr. Rendell, which student did you say was your nephew?"

"Brian Fenz." His voice rose, sharper now, as he jabbed a finger toward her. "Teaching him this trash is a crime. You're poisoning his mind, Ms. Jones, just like the rest of you so-called educators who think you know better than parents."

Danica didn't react. She didn't shift her weight or even blink as he ranted, his words spiraling into something more frantic, more accusatory.

"I bet you think you're some kind of enlightened teacher," he sneered, his tone caught between mockery and menace.

"Always pushing them, making kids think for themselves. Opening their little minds... as if that gives you power, as if it changes anything." He stepped closer, the book clenched in his fist like evidence in a trial. "Too bad the truth doesn't fit your little agenda."

"Mr. Rendell, I assure you, the lessons I've taught on The Pardoner's Tale focus on the literary and cultural significance of biblical allusions and themes," Dani said carefully, keeping her tone even.

Her pulse thudded beneath her collarbone.

It wasn't the first time a parent had bristled at a text, but this was different. He wasn't asking for clarification, he'd already chosen his enemy.

All she could do now was hold the line, stay calm, and hope logic might succeed where empathy clearly wouldn't.

Rendell's eyes narrowed, his mouth twitching with the weight of his next accusation. "Dress it up however you like, literature, critical thinking—I see it for what it is. Lies. You think you're better than the rest of us, hiding behind your degrees and lesson plans as if they make you untouchable, as if you're some kind of priest dispensing truth."

Then, with a sudden shift, his voice dipped, almost pitying. "You're leading them off a cliff and calling it education."

Dani stayed still, her expression unreadable, though tension knotted low in her stomach. This wasn't a parent seeking dialogue.

This was a man looking for a target.

His insult landed harder than she wanted to admit, but she didn't let it show. Her stance remained steady, her gaze unwavering. His words were meant to rattle her. She wouldn't give him the satisfaction.

"The lessons on The Pardoner's Tale examine the literary and cultural role of biblical allusions and themes," Dani said, folding her hands tightly on the counter to keep them from fidgeting. "The curriculum was developed by the city to be respectful and aligned with educational standards."

She nodded toward the dog-eared paperback, still creased at the chapter in question. "Many works of classic literature reference religion not to mock it, but because it was central to the worldview of the time. Chaucer wrote from within his own world. That's why The Canterbury Tales is studied." She paused, forcing her breath to steady.

Rendell's shoulders remained taut, his jaw locked. He hadn't come here to listen; he'd come to accuse.

And the way he gripped that book, as though it were proof of some moral crime, sent a thread of unease crawling up her spine.

He didn't want context. He wanted confession.

Still, Dani kept her voice calm. "No one is being taught to reject or ridicule faith. The purpose of the lesson is to understand how literature reflects the complexities of the time it was written. That includes religious influence, both sincere and satirical."

But even as the words left her mouth, Dani knew they weren't landing. He wasn't here for nuance. No explanation, no curriculum citation, was going to make The Pardoner's Tale less offensive to the story he'd already written in his head.

Rendell's nostrils flared, jaw tight, bracing for another outburst.

Then something shifted. The fire in his eyes wavered, flickering like a candle in the wind. His chest rose sharply, then sank, the rigid line of his shoulders slackening. Something inside him had unraveled, a hidden thread snapping.

When he spoke again, the venom was gone.

His words came slower, tighter not defeat, more like exhaustion, or the low simmer of something waiting to ignite.

"Ms. Jones," he said, voice low, "children shouldn't be taught to question religion. Teaching it insults those who believe in the will of God. And it confuses the children."

Dani met his gaze evenly. "Teaching literature isn't the same as teaching belief," she said. "And questioning isn't the same as rejecting."

She softened her tone, but not her conviction. "Children are smarter than we give them credit for. They can hold a story in one hand and their faith in the other."

She let that settle, then added carefully, "It's not about telling them what to think. It's about showing them how to think for themselves. That's my job."

The room held its breath, silence prickling at the edges.

"Brian's a thoughtful young man," Dani continued. "He asks meaningful questions and backs up his ideas in his writing."

Rendell's mouth twitched. His jaw worked.

"I don't need him bringing those questions home," he said, voice edged with something brittle. "I'm already having a hard enough time with Brian's fa" He cut himself short, blinking hard, as if the word had slipped free before he could snatch it back. His jaw locked. "I just don't need more arguments. Not right now."

Then his eyes flicked toward the door.

Dani caught it. He'd said too much, and he knew it. Father? Family? Farm?

She wished he'd finished the thought. Whatever it was, this was bigger than a grumpy uncle arguing Chaucer.

17

"I can prepare an alternate unit for Brian," she said slowly. "But I'll need written permission from his parent or guardian."

"That's no problem." His reply was too fast, too loud, the sound itself trying to hold the world at bay. He dug into his coat pocket and pulled out a battered ballpoint pen. Its barrel was cracked, the white plastic stained with years of use. Faded navy script spelled out Eastern Church of God, the ink rubbed nearly away.

"Are you Brian's legal guardian?" The question wasn't a formality anymore. It was a thread, and if she pulled it, Dani had the sinking feeling something tangled would unravel.

Rendell blinked, caught for a fraction of a second before the scowl returned.

"He's staying with me. While his parents are out of town."

She didn't buy it. Out of town was too vague.

Too practiced. Her instincts, sharpened by years of navigating evasive parents, pressed hard on the brakes.

"I'll give them a call tomorrow," Dani said evenly. "Do you have a number I can use to reach them?"

Her tone stayed calm, but the warning behind her eyes was deliberate.

She didn't trust him, not his evasiveness, his wild swings between fury and retreat, and certainly not with Brian's safety.

Rendell's eyes narrowed to slits. "There's no need for you to go digging, Ms. Jones." His voice cracked on her name.

The anger was still there, but fading, smoke now, where fire had been.

"You'll get your note Monday. I'll make damn sure of it."

Dani took a measured step back. The air in the room felt stretched thin. She needed to end this.

"All right."

She opened the door before he could speak again, the metal handle cool against her palm. The hinges groaned softly, breaking the silence.

She stepped aside, making it unmistakably clear the conversation was over.

He followed, slow and heavy-footed, the soles of his scuffed boots dragging against the floor with each step.

Almost as an afterthought, he muttered, "May God be with you." His voice was low and hoarse, each word dragged out as though it scraped his throat on the way out. The syllables dropped like stones, soft in volume, sharp at the edges.

It wasn't a blessing. It was a warning. Not a prayer for her safety, but a promise.

Chapter Three

The phone began ringing just as she reached the landing in front of her apartment door. Her keys jangled as she fumbled with the lock, trying to balance the bags of groceries in her arms.

"How does she always know the exact moment I've got my hands full?" Dani murmured with a tired smile as she nudged the door open with her shoulder and stepped inside, catching the phone just before the answering machine clicked on.

"Hi, Mom… of course I knew it was you. You're right on time," she said, affection threading through her voice despite her exhaustion. "Listen, can I call you back in a little bit? It's been a long day, and I've got groceries to put away before the ice cream melts."

She hung up with a soft sigh, already picturing her mother perched in the sunny kitchen on Martha's Vineyard, tea in hand, worrying that her youngest daughter was alone and that she was too far away to do anything about it.

They talked often. Her mother needed that connection, and, if she was honest, so did she. Even when the timing wasn't perfect, the love behind the calls never wavered.

Dani closed the door, dropping her keys into the ceramic bowl by the entrance. The second-floor apartment, part of a remodeled beach house six blocks from the ocean, was small but welcoming. Sunlight filtered through gauzy curtains, casting golden patches across the worn hardwood floors.

A tall bookcase leaned slightly in the corner, crammed with literature anthologies, teacher's guides, and dog-eared mysteries and romances. Across from it sat a faded corduroy loveseat, its cushions sunken in the middle and a crocheted throw draped over one arm. A mismatched armchair stood nearby, its legs a little uneven, propped up by a folded magazine.

A low coffee table held a half-burned candle, a World's Greatest Teacher mug, and a stack of lesson plans marked up in red ink. The kitchenette, visible from the living room, featured teal cabinets and a small two-seater table pushed against the wall, where a lone houseplant leaned dramatically toward the window.

From below came a chorus of barks from Mrs. Caster's three plump corgis. Her landlady was kind and spoiled the dogs with treats all day long.

Setting the brown paper bag on the kitchen counter, she moved through the familiar motions, placing milk in the fridge, cans in the cupboard, and fruit in the wire basket by the window. Lost in thought, the scene from that afternoon's conference replayed in her mind.

What a pompous blowhard, she thought, placing a box of cereal into the pantry with more force than necessary. Brian's Uncle Rendell. His logic had twisted and bounced through so many contradictory avenues that she could hardly keep track. Had his anger come from some rigid religious conviction? Possibly—but it hadn't felt righteous. It was too sharp, too personal, like a knife disguised as a sermon. Then again, maybe he was offended by Chaucer? But that didn't make sense either. He owned a well-worn copy of The Canterbury Tales, its margins scribbled with notes.

Maybe he was an atheist or one of those smug agnostics who believed faith of any kind had no place in public discourse.

If she let them, her thoughts would spiral, looping back over the conversation continuously, like a scratched record stuck in the same bitter groove. She hated that she always did this, picking at conversations until the edges frayed. A habit born from too much anxiety and a lifelong instinct to make sense of what didn't sit right, as if clarity might soften the sting.

Closing the pantry door with a soft click, she took a deep breath, counting to four like the therapist had taught her. Her thumb traced the edge of a chipped nail, a nervous habit she barely noticed anymore. Something that kept her anchored when her mind started to drift too far.

Enough, She told herself, letting the thought settle like a stone dropped into still water.

She glanced at the clock on the wall, nearly five-thirty.

Reaching over, she flipped on the radio beside her bread machine, and a burst of George Jones's He Stopped Loving Her Today filled the kitchen with twangy country before fading into the evening news brief. Dani leaned against the counter, rubbing her temple absently as the announcer took over.

The familiar voice filled the room, smooth and calm, with just the right hint of warmth. Dani found herself smiling faintly. There was something oddly grounding about Gavin Larkhurst's voice; it settled into the space around her like sunlight through a kitchen window—unnoticed until it wasn't there.

She'd never seen his face. He was just a voice on the radio, tucked behind static and station jingles, a man reading headlines and local events. Yet somehow, she'd been tuning in to him almost every day for months. Not out of habit exactly, more like ritual. A quiet, dependable ritual.

She wondered, not for the first time, what he looked like. Was he older? Younger than he sounded? Did he smile when he spoke, or was that just something her mind added, a trait she assigned to the warmth in his tone?

It was silly, she told herself. He was just a voice on the airwaves, a local anchor with a good cadence, part of the background noise of her day.

"...and now, the local headlines." Gavin's voice shifted into a brisk, measured cadence.

"A fire broke out this afternoon at the Eastern Church of God in Virginia Beach. Fire crews responded quickly and were able to contain the blaze, but the sanctuary and church offices sustained significant damage. At this time, authorities have not determined whether the incident was an act of arson or connected to a series of similar church fires in the Hampton Roads area. This marks the third church fire in the past five years."

Danica froze, one hand resting on a loaf of bread she hadn't yet tucked away.

Eastern Church of God, the name echoed strangely.

The pen Carl Rendell had pulled from his pocket. The name of the church was printed on it.

She frowned, her eyes drifting toward the window, where dusk had begun to gather at the edges of the sky.

Church fires....

Gavin Larkhurst continued, "In other news, volunteers are still needed for the upcoming Clean Up the Bay Day next Saturday. Organizers hope to make this year's event the biggest turnout yet in its six-year history. If you'd like to pitch in, give us a call at 555-1050 for more details on how to get involved. This is FM100 WKNS, Country's Best Music. I'm Gavin Larkhurst. Stay tuned, we have all your country hits coming your way after the break."

Dani turned off the radio, muting the clatter of jingles and chipper ads that followed the news. Blowing out a breath, she took out a can of cat food just as two furry shadows padded in from the hallway.

"There you are, you tubby monsters," she said, softening despite herself. "Big day of napping and judging humanity from the windowsill?"

The larger of the two, a smoky gray named Shakespeare, leapt lightly onto the counter to sniff the empty grocery bags. His tabby companion, Lady Rosalind, made a slow circuit around Dani's ankles.

"All right, all right, you're not here for small talk," she murmured, stepping around the half-unloaded groceries. She crossed to the cabinet beneath the sink, pulled out two mismatched ceramic bowls, filled one with dry food, and opened a small can of salmon pâté with a satisfying click for the other.

The moment the lid peeled back, Shakespeare dropped to the floor with a thud, while Rosalind's meow turned insistent.

"Yes, I know. I am scandalously late." She set the bowls down on their feeding mats and watched as they moved in with ravenous grace.

Dani moved into her bedroom, already tugging her green school dress over her head. She tossed it carelessly into the laundry basket, slipped out of her flats, and let her bare feet touch the cool floor. She pulled on a well-worn James Taylor T-shirt and loose cotton shorts, comfortable armor after a long day. The wire-rimmed glasses stayed perched on her nose; she never took them off unless she was asleep or in the shower. Contacts felt like too much work for someone who spent most of her life behind books and whiteboards.

In the bathroom, she paused before the mirror, gathering her hair into a low ponytail. A few stray strands slipped free, framing her temples. Her brown eyes met her own gaze clear and steady, but tinged with fatigue.

As she wiped the makeup from her face, Dani felt the quiet truth settle in. Her body wasn't the same one that had walked the brick paths of her college campus: lean, quick, full of restless energy. At forty-three, she was still learning to live with softened curves and a slower pace. She wasn't drop-dead gorgeous, never had been, but she liked her face: the gentle slope of her nose, the way laughter crinkled the corners of her eyes.

Wandering back into the kitchen, she opened the fridge, mentally assembling a salad, romaine, grape tomatoes, half a cucumber, a few stray olives. She pulled items out one by one and began to rinse and chop with automatic rhythm.

The phone rang.

She dried her hands on a dish towel.

"Hello?"

"Hooray! You're alive! I heard that guy yelling in the office and thought I should check," Dot Swan replied, her voice bright and nosy, with just enough concern to make it real. "You okay?"

Dani sighed and dumped the lettuce into a bowl. "That was Carl Rendell, and he came in ready for battle. Accused me of indoctrinating his nephew. Claimed the story we read mocked Christianity."

"Oh my God," Dot said. "Wait! Rendell? I taught a Carl Rendell my first year, way before your time. I remember him because he was a total rage goblin."

"Sounds about right," Dani huffed a laugh. "You've got a connection to everyone near the oceanfront."

"Yeah, yeah. I should be the mayor," Dot muttered. "So, what happened?"

Dani reached for the vinaigrette and gave it a good shake. "He stormed in like he was on a crusade, raving about morality and corruption. Said the book was disgusting."

"He hasn't changed a bit," Dot said dryly.

"Did you hear about the church fire?" Dani asked, folding her arms.

"I did," Dot replied, fanning herself with a magazine. "Heard it on the radio from that sexy-voiced Gavin Larkhurst. I swear, that man could read my grocery list and I'd still get goosebumps."

Dani didn't smile. "Carl had a pen with the name of that church on it. Probably a coincidence," she said, though her voice lacked conviction.

"It's the fourth church," Dot said, her voice lower now. "It led the six o'clock news. First was St. Jude's, a white Catholic church in

Chesapeake. Then Greater Elm Baptist over in Portsmouth, a Black congregation. Third was that little Presbyterian chapel in Norfolk. And now this one, Eastern Church of God in Virginia Beach." She paused. "You know, they were the ones who fought so hard to bring prayer back into the schools."

"The Eastern Church of God was the one that petitioned the school board about putting prayer back in school?" Dani asked, brow furrowed. "I don't remember that."

Dot nodded. "They're the reason we added the moment of silence last year."

Dani glanced out the kitchen window. The sun had dropped below the horizon, and darkness was filtering in. Downstairs, the landlady's dogs gave a soft bark.

She pictured Rendell's face again, his gray hair and unkempt beard, the wildness in his eyes, and that final parting shot: May God be with you. Not a comfort. A warning.

"You still there?" Dot asked.

"Yeah. Just thinking." She gave the salad a quick mix and grabbed a fork.

"Well, don't think too hard. You've already had a day. I don't want to keep you."

"Thanks for calling, Dot," Dani said quietly.

"Anytime. I'll see you tomorrow."

"Good night."

She hung up, the salad bowl cool in her hands. Then, finally, she sat, fork in hand, and ate, slowly and quietly, her mind still circling like a whirlpool.

Minutes ticked by until Dani finally picked up the phone, dialing her mom back.

Balancing the phone between her ear and shoulder, she took a bite of her salad. "Hey, Mom. I've got my salad, and you have my full attention now."

"Thanks for calling me back," her mother said. The line was a little staticky, coming from thirteen hours north in Massachusetts. "I saw something on the news about a church fire down your way. Fourth one in five years, they said?"

Dani sighed and popped a piece of pepper in her mouth. "Yeah, it was on the radio earlier, too. Eastern Church of God, not far from here."

"That's terrible. Is it racially motivated?"

"I don't know, Mom. I'm sure there will be more news as they have a chance to investigate."

Her mother was quiet for a beat. "Eastern Church of God. It sounds evangelical."

"Maybe. They were loud at school board meetings two years ago, made a big push to bring prayer back into the classroom. The board added a daily moment of silence during the morning announcements to appease them."

"People can be so reactive when it comes to religion," Mom sighed.

Dani stared at her hands, the weight of her mom's words pressing on her chest like a stone. She wanted to tell her about Carl Rendell and the way he'd cornered her in the office, how his voice had shaken with anger when he accused her of mocking his religion.

But she didn't.

Telling her mom would only worry her. No matter how old Dani got, her mother still saw her as her baby, a child to protect, not an adult who could handle ugly confrontations.

And Dani knew exactly what would happen if she said anything: the frantic questions, the late-night phone calls, the well-meaning spiral. She'd been through it before, in college, when the panic attacks first started and therapy became a lifeline.

She was better now.

But she'd learned a hard lesson about which things to say out loud and which to swallow quietly.

Dani gave a dry chuckle as she sat down at the table. "You and me both."

"Still planning to help with that beach cleanup next weekend?" her mom asked, changing the subject.

"Yeah, I think so. It'll be nice to get outside and get my hands dirty."

Her mother's voice warmed. "Just be careful, sweetheart. Don't stretch yourself too thin. You know how you get."

"I'm fine," Dani said. "It's only Wednesday, but it's been a long week. Seventh graders, you know how it is."

"I do," her mother replied fondly, her voice warm and steady. "And for what it's worth, I think you're doing more good than you realize."

Dani could almost picture her mom on the other end, sitting at the kitchen table, one eye on the clock to make sure the call didn't run long and rack up the charges.

A soft thump sounded beside her as Shakespeare leapt from the floor onto her lap, rubbing his head against her arm. She scratched under his chin.

A second later, Roz piled on. Dani gave her a slow stroke along the back as she wormed in beside her sibling.

How could she explain to her mom that sometimes doing good didn't feel so simple?

She couldn't. So instead, she said, "Thanks, Mom. I'll talk to you soon."

Hanging up, she patted the cats until the silence of her apartment pressed in, the questions whirling through her mind again.

Why had Carl Rendell come to see her?

How was he connected to the Eastern Church of God?

She needed to let it go. Move on. She didn't have all the answers, probably never would, and puzzling over the questions wouldn't change a thing.

Chapter Four

Thursday crept in with a whimper. Clouds hung low, thick and brooding, pressing against the school's aging windows as if they, too, wanted to be anywhere else. The hallways echoed with sluggish footsteps and half-hearted greetings, exam dread, and the distant pull of summer break tangled together in a haze of apathy.

Dani trudged into her classroom with a travel mug of lukewarm coffee and a stack of handouts. Her usually bright posters, grammar puns and inspirational literary quotes, looked faded in the dim light filtering through the rain-streaked glass.

During class, she ran through the motions of the vocabulary drill, her voice steady but her mind elsewhere. The students mirrored her mood: heads propped on hands, notebooks open but filled with half-hearted scribbles.

Beneath her practiced calm, Dani's thoughts kept circling back to Brian and the conversation that loomed like storm clouds on the horizon. She didn't want to upset him, but the thought of him staying with Rendell had kept her up all night.

Dani straightened a little as the final period began. Her advanced English class always brought a different kind of energy; this group usually lifted her spirits. They were curious, quick-witted, and often challenged her in the best possible ways.

Discussions could veer unexpectedly into philosophy or contemporary politics, and more than once, their insights had surprised her into reevaluating a text she thought she knew inside and out.

The students filtered in with familiar chatter, backpacks slumping to the floor as they took their usual seats. Outside, the first few drops of rain tapped against the window, soft but insistent.

"All right," she said, infusing brightness into her tone. "Let's pick up where we left off with participial phrases. You'll be working in pairs or groups of three. Your job is to write at least five original sentences using participial phrases effectively. Be creative. Surprise me."

She moved between the rows of desks as the students got to work, the low hum of conversation beginning to rise. Damp air drifted in through a cracked window. Her eyes swept the room and found Brian Fenz seated near the back, his face neutral, maybe even a little wary. He'd chosen to work alone today, which was unusual for him. Normally, he paired off quickly, especially with Jonah or Clara, who shared his dry sense of humor.

Dani hesitated, pretending to shuffle papers while stealing another glance in his direction. He wasn't writing, just sitting, shoulders hunched slightly, as if he knew she was watching him.

She drew a steadying breath and walked over, her heels clicking on the linoleum floor, her heart ticking faster with every step.

She stopped beside his desk, bending down and keeping her voice low and even.

"Brian," she said gently, "could I speak with you for a moment?"

Thunder rumbled faintly in the distance as Brian glanced up.

"Did you bring the note from your parents to school today?" Dani asked, keeping her tone light but her eyes steady.

His brow furrowed. "No, Mrs. Jones," he said quietly, eyes darting up to meet hers before dropping in uncertainty. His posture shifted not with guilt but with the awkward stiffness of confusion.

Dani tilted her head slightly, studying his reaction. He didn't look evasive, just genuinely puzzled.

She folded her hands in front of her, smiling.

"Brian, I spoke with your uncle yesterday about giving you some supplementary work, so you wouldn't have to read The Pardoner's Tale. I need a note verifying your parents' permission to do that."

Brian's eyes widened. "Ms. Jones, I don't know... I mean..." He shifted awkwardly, his face flushing deep red. "I haven't seen my uncle in a couple of weeks, and my parents didn't say anything to me yesterday."

Dani's stomach tightened. If Brian hadn't seen his uncle in weeks, then who was he staying with? Her mind whirred, trying to reconcile what Rendell had said with what she was hearing now.

Softening her voice, Dani asked, "Okay, well... when will your parents be back in town, so I can call them?"

"My mom's home all day." Brian hesitated, looking even more uncomfortable now, his fingers tugging at the hem of his t-shirt. "Am I in trouble?" he asked, barely above a whisper.

"Oh, Brian, no," she said with a smile. "Why don't you join Jonah and Claire to finish the assignment?"

Relief flooded the boy's face, and without another word, he made a beeline to his friends, sliding into the seat beside his classmates.

Dani felt a bit like Alice tumbling through Wonderland. Nothing made sense, and every conversation seemed to twist itself into one of the Mad Hatter's riddles. Logic bent in impossible directions: If Brian wasn't staying with his uncle, and hadn't even seen him in weeks, then why had Rendell come to the school at all? What was he trying to prove? Or hide?

The questions spiraled faster than she could untangle them, each answer leading to more uncertainty.

Now wasn't the time to chase riddles. She had a room full of students waiting for her to teach.

But as she drifted between student groups, nodding absently at sentences riddled with dangling modifiers and misplaced participles, her attention was only half on the grammar. Her mind still circled the questions that wouldn't let go.

What was Rendell trying to accomplish by coming to school?

If Brian wasn't staying with him, why had Rendell interfered?

It felt as impossible to unravel as Lewis Carroll's infamous riddle: Why is a raven like a writing desk? Stubbornly answerless.

Relieved to see that most of the class hadn't forgotten everything Dani had taught them, she noted that only a few of the grammar rules seemed a bit hazy. After clarifying a couple of common pitfalls, she reassured them, "Don't worry, there'll be more days of practice before you see a quiz on this."

The mood in the room lightened slightly.

"Now," she continued, moving to the front of the room, "take out your homework."

There was a rustle of paper and backpacks unzipping.

"We're shifting gears a bit. You were to write a paragraph on what makes The Pardoner's Tale funny, and what message you think Chaucer was trying to send."

Mark's hand shot up, eager to share his thoughts. "The tree with the gold under it represents greed," he said, his expression serious.

"Good, Mark. But how does The Pardoner's Tale use this symbol to make the story funny?" Dani asked, guiding him toward the humor in the tale.

Mark hesitated, thinking for a moment. "Well, I guess it's funny because the men think they can cheat death, and instead, they all end up killing each other over a pile of gold."

"Exactly!" Dani said, her eyes lighting up. "The humor comes from how absurd the situation is."

Ben raised his hand, ready to jump in. "It's funny because they're so focused on the gold, they forget what's really important. They end up dying for money."

Dani nodded. "Their greed is so overwhelming that they don't see the obvious consequences right in front of them. And that's the dark humor in the story, how their own actions, driven by greed, lead to their deaths."

Ashley chimed in, her voice barely louder than the rustle of notebook pages. "And the old man who points them to the gold is also kind of funny. He tells them to go find Death, but it's a set-up."

Dani's head tilted slightly in surprise. Ashley had barely spoken during their last discussion, avoiding eye contact and shrinking into her hoodie when called on. Now she was volunteering. It wasn't much, but it was something, a flicker of confidence. Dani was determined not to let it slip by unnoticed.

"Good point, Ashley," Dani said, nodding. "The old man's advice is funny because it's part of the trap. It's as if he's in on the joke, guiding them to their doom without them realizing it."

Mark added, "The old man's advice is funny because it's part of the trap. It's as if he's in on the joke, guiding them to their deaths."

"Who's the real villain in the story?" Dani asked, shifting gears.

Laura raised her hand. "It's the Pardoner. He's a jerk."

Dani smiled. "Fair. But remember, he's not the one living it, he's telling it. What's Chaucer's purpose?"

"Money," Nick said.

"Do you think that's the only reason writers write, Nick? Chaucer's making a point, too."

"With satire," Mark added.

"Exactly. He preaches against greed while profiting from it. That contradiction, that's satire."

The room buzzed.

"So, if greed itself is the antagonist," Dani pressed, pacing slowly, "what does that tell us about the way the story works?"

"They betray each other," Mark said.

"Right. And what drives all their decisions?"

"Greed," Ashley whispered.

Dani smiled at her. "Yes. And the way they behave ruthless, ridiculous, impulsive, what does that make the story feel like?"

Taneika grinned. "Kind of funny, in a messed-up way."

"Exactly. Chaucer uses humor to slip in a truth bomb. So, what's the bigger point?"

Ashley raised her hand again, hesitant but steady. "That greed leads to destruction?"

"Good start." Dani nodded.

Taneika glanced at her notes. "That people are their own worst enemies when they let greed control them?"

"Perfect. And the Pardoner himself, warning against greed while wallowing in it, what's that called?"

"Irony," Mark said.

"Bingo." Dani grinned. "So, we've got irony, dark humor, and a timeless message: *Radix malorum est cupiditas.* Unchecked greed corrupts and destroys."

Ben groaned theatrically. "Why is there always a bigger point?"

The class chuckled. Dani let herself laugh too. "Because authors are sneaky. They make us laugh, then sneak in the truth."

The students bent back over their paragraphs. Pens scratched. Rain tapped the windows. When the bell rang, Dani collected their papers, stacking them with a thud that seemed louder than it should have in the sudden quiet.

At her desk, she yanked open the bottom drawer and flipped through folders until her fingers landed on the parent contact list. She hesitated at Brian's name.

This wasn't just a disagreement over curriculum. Rendell had pulled her into something deeper, murkier, something that didn't add up.

She carried the list into the hallway, detached from the end-of-day chaos around her. In the lounge, the silence felt heavier than the noise outside. Once, this room had been the school's nerve center, cluttered with couches and gossip. Now it was sterile, blank walls, a flickering computer, and a lone grimy phone.

She lifted the receiver and dialed the Fenz household.

On the fourth ring, a polite, impersonal voice answered: "You've reached Amanda, Jacob, and Brian. Please leave your name, number, and the time you called."

Dani waited for the beep. "Hello, this is Danica Jones, Brian's English teacher. I'm calling to follow up on a concern that was raised by Carl Rendell regarding our current unit on The Pardoner's Tale. I just wanted to check in and confirm whether you're comfortable with Brian continuing in the discussion. If you could give me a call back at the school tomorrow, I'd really appreciate it. Thank you."

She hung up gently, though unease gnawed at her. An angry confrontation, a student caught in the middle, none of it sat right. But the final bell had rung. For now, there was nothing else she could do.

Chapter Five

The bass thudded against Dani's chest before she even stepped inside the gym. Already regretting the heels that had seemed like a good idea twenty minutes ago, she wove through the chaos, waving to fellow teachers. Strobe lights pulsed over clusters of students doing their best impressions of dancing while chaperones circled like wary sharks. The Yearbook Dance had barely started, and Dani already felt like the night was two hours too long. Still, her presence was expected. Volunteering wasn't optional, not with Mr. Herring, the principal, calling it an "excellent way to connect with students outside the classroom." In reality, he hovered near the refreshment table, hands clasped behind his back, bobbing his head stiffly to the beat in an effort to look engaged. Like his fishy namesake, his round, close-set eyes and puckered lips gave him a perpetually startled look, and his slicked-back silver hair only added to the aquarium effect. It was hard to take advice about "student engagement" seriously from someone who looked like he belonged in a tank.

All around, students clung to their friend groups. Girls wobbled in heels, boys in wrinkled button-ups orbited the edges of the gym. Some clutched their yearbooks like security blankets, while others had already collapsed against the wall, scribbling glittery messages in loopy cursive. Dani stood just off the dance floor, arms loosely crossed, watching with the bemused detachment of a chaperone.

"Ms. Jones!" a girl in a sparkly blue dress called, hustling over with her yearbook. "Can you sign mine?"

Dani smiled, taking the book. "Only if you promise not to judge my handwriting."

"Only if you don't write 'Have a great summer' like everyone else."

"Deal." Dani crouched and scrawled a quick note:

You brought energy and laughter to class. Don't ever lose that. Ms. Jones

Another student appeared, a lanky boy with braces and nervous energy. "Ms. Jones, can you settle an argument? Is this a slow song or a fast song?"

Dani tilted her head. Everlong by the Foo Fighters hovered in that ballad-gray area: technically a slow song, but fast enough to confuse the rhythm-impaired.

"My advice?" she said, smiling. "Just sway and hope no one's watching."

He nodded solemnly and dashed back to a knot of boys daring each other to approach nearby girls. A trio of seventh-grade girls from her class passed by, giggling, one of them carrying her three-inch heels in one hand.

"I told you those heels were a bad idea," Dani called after her.

"They were so cute, though," the girl shot back without slowing.

The music shifted into something louder and thrashier, a remix with a beat that could punch through drywall. A small pack of eighth-grade boys started jumping in time, arms flailing.

Dani winced and strode toward them before a mosh pit could form. "Hey! This is a school gym, not a rock concert."

They froze mid-flail, grinned sheepishly, and scattered toward the refreshments.

Mr. Herring materialized at her side, wide eyes blinking rapidly behind wire-rimmed glasses.

"Ms. Jones!" he yelled over the noise. "Don't let the boys get out of hand."

"Yes, sir," Dani said.

"What? Did you just invite me to surf?" His eyes widened further. "That's highly inappropriate. I am your boss."

Dani shook her head, but he nodded to himself, satisfied he'd handled the situation with dignity. Then he pivoted and floated back to the refreshment table, still bobbing stiffly to the beat.

Dani sighed and resumed her post, resisting the urge to roll her eyes. Apparently, enunciation was now a professional hazard.

An hour slipped by in a hazy blur. Students drifted on and off the dance floor, new clusters formed, old ones dissolved, and the music never stopped pounding.

Across the way, Dot stood behind a folding table like a sentry, short silver hair swept back off her face. Her glasses perched on top of her head as she slid a wooden ruler down the crinkled log of yearbook pre-orders.

Deciding to take a break, Dani headed over, wincing as Nirvana rattled her ribs.

Dot leaned forward, waving the ruler toward her. "Can I ask you a favor?" she shouted.

Dani grinned. "Only if you promise not to whack me with that thing."

Dot gave the ruler a sweet little wag. "No promises. Can you take over for a minute? My feet are killing me."

Sliding behind the table, Dani scanned the list, careful not to smudge the ink. A few students lined up, some bouncing impatiently on the balls of their feet, others clutching wrinkled bills like lifelines.

"What's your name? Did you pre-order?" she asked the first girl.

Beside her, Dot collapsed into a chair with a grunt. Kicking off her sensible-but-still-punishing heels, she dug into a tote bag and produced a pair of thick frog-print socks. She tugged them on without ceremony, slipped into battered brown Birkenstocks, and let out a sigh loud enough to cut through bass-heavy pop.

After Dani sold a few more yearbooks, Dot leaned closer. "I was thinking about Carl Rendell. Always shooting his mouth off when he didn't know what he was talking about."

Dani looked up, surprised. "You must've had him your first year. How do you remember him that well?"

Dot snorted. "I taught him two years in a row. Failed him once. Should've been twice, but he squeaked by. Always in trouble. I went to high school with his mama. She was at her wit's end with him from the moment he was born."

Dani shook her head. "Do you know everyone in Virginia Beach?"

Dot shrugged. "I either grew up with them, taught them, or taught their kids."

"Did you know Carl was related to Brian Fenz?"

Dot's eyes narrowed. "No. That poor child."

"Rendell told me Brian's staying with him while his parents are out of town."

Dot gasped. "I hope it isn't for long. I'd hate to think what a man like Carl Rendell could do to a sweet kid like Brian."

"You don't think he'd hurt him physically?" Dani asked.

"Physically? No." Dot's lips tightened. "But Carl knew how to drive teachers insane. There's no telling the emotional damage he could inflict."

The unmistakable opening bars of The Electric Slide sent squeals and laughter ripping through the gym. Students surged onto the dance floor, forming jagged, wiggly lines as they tried to sync with the beat.

Dani and Dot stepped toward the crowd, ready to intercept any elbows or accidental collisions. Laura spotted them first.

"Ms. Jones! Mrs. Swan! You have to dance with us!"

Dani held up both hands, smiling but shaking her head. "Nope! I'm just here to supervise!"

Too late. Laura and Ashley each grabbed an arm and dragged her into the line. Cheers rose. A few kids clapped.

"Ms. Jones knows the moves!" a boy shouted.

And she did. Suddenly, she and Dot were stepping left, clapping, pivoting, laughing despite themselves.

Dani tried to remember the last time she'd done this dance, a wedding in '92? Maybe '93?

For a few minutes, she let her concerns dissolve into the beat, the lights, the shuffle of dozens of feet mostly moving in the same direction. It was near the end of the song when Dani noticed a man in a police uniform pulling Dot off the dance floor. He looked to be in his early fifties, stocky, with buzz-cut hair and a badge clipped to his belt. Dani vaguely recognized him as one of the off-duty officers who rotated through school events.

No one else seemed to notice. As Dot disappeared through the side doors, the DJ launched into another track, *MMM* Bop by Hanson, and the girls squealed in approval.

Curious, Dani thought about following them, but the gym was hot, and she was thirsty. She drifted toward the concession stand, eyes on the hallway, and poured herself a cup of flat soda. The sugary fizz clung to her tongue.

She'd barely taken a sip when the officer reappeared.

"Ms. Jones?" His voice was low but firm.

Without waiting for an answer, he turned and walked out of the gym. Dani hesitated for half a beat, then tossed her soda and followed.

The music faded behind her, replaced by the soft echo of their footsteps on polished tile. He stopped outside the art classroom, the door slightly ajar, and pushed it open with two fingers.

The room smelled of drying paint. Pale fluorescent light fell over easels, stools, and scattered half-finished projects. Dot sat on a tall stool near the front, arms locked across her chest, one foot tapping against the rung.

"Inside," the officer said, holding the door for Dani.

Her pulse quickened as she stepped in. She glanced between Dot and the officer. "What's going on?"

According to his nameplate, he was Officer Tate. He closed the door with a soft click.

"I happened to overhear you and Mrs. Swan earlier," Tate said, his gaze shifting briefly to Dot before fixing on Dani. "You were talking about Carl Rendell?"

Dani stiffened. "Yes. Why?"

"He's wanted for questioning in connection with the fire at the Eastern Church of God," Tate said, arms folded across his chest.

Dani straightened. "We heard about it on the news."

Tate gave a curt nod. "Rendell's tied to that church. Hasn't been answering calls. Neighbors say he hasn't been home in days. My captain's put out a notice any intel, sightings, we log it."

Dot shifted on the stool, arms tight across her chest. "He came to the school Wednesday to yell at Dani."

Tate angled toward her. "You were present?"

"I was nearby," Dot said. Then, after a pause, "I actually taught Carl. Years ago. He was here in '54 or '55. Smart, intense, disruptive. Always testing boundaries, looking for a fight."

Tate's eyes narrowed. "You knew him well?"

"As well as any teacher could. Enough to know silence didn't mean calm. I knew his mother too back in high school. She raised him alone, but he was often too much for her."

Tate jotted notes quickly, then turned to Dani. "You spoke with him directly on Wednesday?"

"Yes. Around three-thirty, right after classes let out. He was angry about a reading assignment. Said it mocked his religious beliefs. Wanted his nephew to have a substitute text while staying with him."

"Did he give the boy's name?"

"He's enrolled here, in my class. But if you need specifics, you'll have to go through the principal."

"Did Rendell mention how long the boy would be with him?"

"No. Only that the parents were out of town."

"Did he seem… off? Nervous? Angry? Carrying anything unusual?"

"He was furious," Dani said. "He had an old, battered copy of The Canterbury Tales, the book we were studying. His hands were greasy, fingerprints smeared on the cover."

Dot nodded. "I heard him yelling all the way down the hall. Mrs. Haley, the office manager, told me later she almost called the police."

Tate paused, then slipped his notepad into his pocket. He handed each of them a business card. "If either of you hear from him, contact Detective Marcus Gates at Second Precinct."

"We will," Dani said, accepting the card. A chill settled in her chest. Had she been the last person to see Carl Rendell before he disappeared? Was he truly suspected of burning down the church?

Tate thanked them and left. The door clicked shut behind him.

Silence stretched between the two women, louder than anything Dani had heard all night.

Dot pressed her lips thin, then tried to joke. "I didn't think tonight's dance would turn into a crime scene."

Dani nodded, forcing a smile she didn't feel.

It felt like something had begun, and it wasn't going to stay quiet for long.

47

Chapter Six

Dani woke late on Saturday morning to warm, golden sunlight spilling across her bed. She lay still for a moment, staring at the ceiling as the past few days churned in her mind, the tense, bewildering meeting with Carl Rendell, the interview with Officer Tate, and the nagging sense that something was off about Brian's family.

No one had called her back on Friday, though she'd left another message before heading to the dance.

But today would be different. For once, she would let the questions and worries rest. Her body needed sun, her mind needed peace, and her heart needed a friend.

She reached for the phone on her nightstand and dialed Chanice's number by heart.

"Beach day?" she asked, skipping the hello.

"Girl, yes," came the instant reply. "I'll swing by soon."

An hour later, Chanice pulled into the driveway with her usual burst of energy, honking once for flair.

Dani grabbed her beach bag and met her outside, both of them already laughing about nothing in particular. Side by side, they fell into step, flip-flops slapping against the sidewalk.

Pacific Avenue buzzed with weekend color. Shops spilled onto the pavement, food stands perfumed the breeze with sugar and sunscreen, and music pulsed from the Coastal Edge Surf Shop, weaving together with the crash of waves and children's laughter.

"God, I've missed the beach," Chanice said, slowing to eye a rack of sun hats outside a boutique. "Remember that summer you were going to bartend to make ends meet?"

Dani groaned, embarrassed and fond all at once.

"Oh my god, until I dumped two margaritas on those tourists."

"You were terrible," Chanice said with a snort. "But charming. That's probably the only reason they didn't fire you on the spot."

"They just stopped scheduling me," Dani admitted with a grin. "Passive-aggressive mercy."

Chanice nudged her shoulder. "You've always had a way of landing on your feet, even mid-disaster."

"Maybe," Dani said softly. "But lately, it feels like I'm landing more sideways than anything."

"Well, sideways still gets you to the beach," Chanice shot back. "Come on, I want a spot close enough to hear the waves, but far enough not to get splashed by toddlers."

Dani laughed and followed her across the boardwalk and into the sand, already feeling the weight she'd been carrying grow a little lighter.

The beach was busy but not crowded. Families huddled under umbrellas, couples stretched out on towels, and kids darted in and out of the surf.

A few teens lingered near the ice cream stand, debating flavors and flirting, while the volleyball courts stood empty, their nets fluttering lazily in the breeze.

They chose a spot just beyond the high tide line, close enough to catch the ocean's rhythm but safely out of reach of rogue splashes and flying beach balls.

With a dramatic flourish, Chanice dropped her oversized tote and spread her towel.

"This is it, prime real estate," she declared, planting her water bottle like a flag.

Dani shook out her own towel beside her and knelt to dig through her bag for sunscreen.

Chanice plopped down, sunglasses already on, and tilted her head toward Dani. "Okay, enough mystery. I want to see this fabled swimsuit in its full glory. Off with the cover-up, let the beach worship commence."

Dani rolled her eyes, but a grin tugged at her mouth. She stood, untied the waist of her gold wrap, and let it slide away, revealing the sleek black suit beneath.

"Oooooh, damn," Chanice said, sitting up straighter.

"That neckline? That gold trim? Ma'am, this is an event."

Dani laughed, shading her eyes with one hand.

"Well, you look magnificent yourself."

Chanice looked like she'd stepped out of a Delia's catalog, bold, Black, and nearly six feet tall. A strappy bikini glinted beneath her lime-green wrap, oversized gold hoops flashed in the sun, and her coral lipstick matched her polished toes.

"That's us," Chanice declared, pulling a bag of grapes from her tote. "Two magnificent divas soaking in the sun. Now sit your radiant self down, and let's talk about anything but work, or being interviewed by the police."

Dani lowered herself onto her towel, the sun warming her shoulders, the sea stretching out before them like an open page. For the first time in days, she could breathe.

She'd first met Chanice when the woman had called the school looking for a tutor for her daughter, Tamira. A single mother working full-time at the bank, Chanice hadn't had time for nonsense and made that clear to both Dani and Tamira. She'd hired Dani without hesitation, her sharp eyes all business.

Now Tamira was a nurse in Charlotte, still calling Dani Ms. J like she was that stubborn seventh grader, arms crossed, silence her only defense.

"Can you believe we've been friends almost ten years?" Dani murmured, mostly to herself.

"You're stuck with me," Chanice said, bumping her shoulder. "I knew it that first day. Tamira had an attitude, so I stayed to protect you, but you wrapped her around your finger and taught her how to write an essay."

Dani laughed. "I remember you brought your own coffee and said you didn't trust a white woman to make it strong enough."

"I still don't," Chanice said with a grin. "When Tamira passed that final, we celebrated with those sad little wine coolers from 7-Eleven and watched Living Single reruns on your busted TV."

The memory bloomed warm in Dani's chest as they kicked off their sandals, the ocean ahead of them wide and glittering. "You wore that denim vest you thought was the height of fashion," Dani teased.

"That vest was stylish," Chanice shot back. "But you had that haircut, what was it? A shag? A bird's nest?"

"It was layered," Dani said, mock-offended, shaking out her towel with a snap. "Everyone had that cut in '87. It was very Meg Ryan."

Chanice flopped onto her towel, pushing her sunglasses to the top of her head. "Girl, Meg Ryan wouldn't have been caught dead with that helmet. You looked like a backup singer in a Christian rock band."

Dani snorted. "You're lucky I like you."

"You're lucky I put up with your skinny white ass," Chanice retorted, laughing as she snatched the sunscreen from Dani's hand. "You burn like printer paper."

Dani sighed. "The second a UV ray sees me, my skin starts writing a will."

"Well, pass that arm over," Chanice said, snapping the bottle open. "I didn't come all the way to the beach to watch you get skin cancer."

Dani held out her arm. "You're such a mom."

"Damn right," Chanice said, rubbing in the sunscreen in practiced circles across Dani's arms and back with the confident efficiency of someone who'd done it a thousand times before.

She paused mid-stroke, eyes narrowing to the right. "Well, hello."

Dani followed her gaze. Two men jogged onto the sand near the volleyball nets, sun-drenched, all muscle and swagger, the kind who knew they looked good and didn't care who noticed. One had tousled dark blond hair and a grin straight out of a soda commercial. The other was leaner, with honey-brown skin, sharp cheekbones, and a smile that could stop traffic.

Both stripped off their shirts in one smooth motion, revealing skin bronzed and cut, shoulders sculpted by hours in the surf, abs that looked carved rather than earned. Conversations nearby actually paused as they crossed the sand.

The blond tossed a ball into the air and leapt to smash it over the net, wiry strength moving through long limbs with effortless grace. His sun-kissed hair curled slightly at the ends, dark sunglasses hiding his eyes. Mid-thirties, Dani guessed, thirty-nine at most.

She realized she was staring.

Chanice let out a low whistle, still holding the sunscreen. "It's hot on the beach today," she murmured, sliding her sunglasses down her nose for a better look.

Dani arched a brow. "You gonna finish my back or go join the team?"

"Multitasking, babe. I'm nothing if not efficient." Chanice grinned, resuming her circles absently, slower this time, her gaze locked on the Latino with the killer smile.

"Okay, I see why you're impressed," Dani admitted. "Look at those shoulders. I bet he spends half his life in the gym."

Chanice nodded. "And that clean fade? Jawline like a knife? He's got the mature heartthrob thing down cold."

"Moves like he owns the place," Dani added, watching him swagger back to the line and serve.

He tossed the ball, swung hard, and sent it sailing long, straight into the sand behind the court.

"Whew," Chanice whispered. "I'd give up carbs to get inside those black trunks."

Dani's mouth curved despite herself. "You love carbs."

"I do," Chanice sighed, fanning herself. "But I also love that man's triceps. That's all I'm saying."

The blond scooped up the ball with a laugh. "Nice serve, Diego! You aiming for the ocean or what?"

Diego shook his head, grinning. "Just warming up. Watch this." He bounced the volleyball once, shifted his weight, then launched forward, arm snapping high as he blasted the ball over the net with a wicked spin.

Chanice dropped back on her towel, eyes closed, moaning. "I think I just came on the beach."

Dani smirked. "Careful, Chanice, don't cause a tidal wave out here."

Chanice cracked one eye open, grinning.

"What about the blond one? You checking him out?"

Dani rolled her eyes but couldn't hide the smile tugging at her lips. "Who, me? I don't ogle men on the oceanfront."

"I know that's a lie," Chanice said, eyes sparkling.

The men began playing in earnest, their bare feet kicking up sprays of hot sand as they moved into position. The blond jumped to serve, the ball arcing high before slamming down across the net with a satisfying thwap. Diego dove, muscles coiling as he rolled, sending the ball sailing back with a practiced bump.

"Damn, Diego," the blond called, grinning as he reset. "Didn't know you still had that in you."

Diego brushed sand from his arm, laughing.

"Don't get too impressed. I'm just saving my best moves for the second set."

Dani's gaze lingered on the blond. "Does he sound… familiar to you?"

"Good familiar or bad familiar?" Chanice asked, eyes never leaving the court.

"I swear I've heard his voice before." Dani frowned, trying to place it.

Down the beach, the rally picked up speed, sand spraying, bodies leaping and twisting, their shouts carrying over the waves. A few kids with dripping ice cream cones stopped to watch, and a cluster of tourists leaned in, drawn by the rhythm of the game.

Diego slid sideways, eyes locked on the ball. "You can't get this one past me."

The blond cocked his arm and smashed the ball over the net with a wicked twist.

"Too slow, Diego," he teased.

Diego laughed, calling back, "Yeah, yeah. Just wait. You might have the highlight reel, but I've got the comeback."

And then it hit her.

"Oh my God, it's him!" Dani fanned herself with her hand, staring like she'd spotted a celebrity in the wild.

"Who?" Chanice asked, shading her eyes.

"Gavin Larkhurst. From WKNS." Dani's voice dropped to an urgent whisper.

Chanice blinked. "*Gavin Larkhurst*?"

Dani nodded so hard her sunglasses nearly slid off. Her pulse quickened, a small thrill running through her chest. "Yes! I listen to him every weekday morning, that's Gavin Larkhurst."

"I always pictured him as a Black man," Chanice said with a shrug.

"I knew he'd be handsome, but not like that." Dani gestured toward the game.

Chanice grinned. "Mmhmm. Guess the news is a little more interesting in person, huh?"

Dani snorted. "I'm going to put my feet in the water. Wanna race?"

"Please," Chanice said, already standing. "I'm not pulling a hamstring for your ego."

They made it ankle-deep before the cold shocked up their legs. The May water still carried winter's bite.

Dani hissed through her teeth, arms stretched like balance beams. "Why is it always colder than you think?"

"Because nature is rude," Chanice said, wading beside her. A wave rolled higher, foam swirling around their calves and tugging at the sand beneath their feet. Both women gasped, then burst into laughter.

For a moment, they just stood there, breathing in salt and sun, watching the horizon shimmer and roll. Gulls wheeled overhead, their cries blending with the slap of the waves.

Dani glanced sideways. "We could keep going. Brave it."

Chanice shook her head firmly. "You're not dragging me in there till June."

"Coward," Dani teased.

"Absolutely," Chanice said without shame.

When the next wave hit a little higher, they both yelped and turned, trudging back toward their towels.

Dani sat cross-legged, letting the sun warm her shoulders while sand clung stubbornly to her damp legs.

The guys were still playing, skin gleaming with sweat. Gavin leapt to spike the ball, and it landed with a thud in the sand.

Chanice plopped down beside her, brushing stray grains from her thighs. She slid her sunglasses to the tip of her nose and peered over the rims, eyes narrowing before a slow smirk tugged at her mouth.

"My granny would say those guys are a tall, cold drink of water."

Dani followed her gaze despite herself. "Your granny's right."

Chanice hummed in agreement. "Who knew radio had abs?"

Dani grinned, eyes still tracking Gavin as he high-fived his teammate. "You ever been with someone like that?"

"You mean confident? Older, still has all his hair and teeth, probably knows how to pronounce Merlot?" Chanice asked, settling back on her elbows.

"Something like that." Dani laughed.

Chanice's gaze lingered on the court, her expression softening. "Once. Long time ago. Didn't last. He moved to Atlanta for a job when Tamira started fifth grade. Timing was all wrong. But I still think about him sometimes."

Dani glanced over, surprised by the wistfulness in her friend's voice.

Chanice shrugged and smiled faintly. "Maybe you should go say hello."

Dani arched a brow. "And say what? 'Hi, I've been stalking your voice since 1992, and now I see you've got a six-pack to go with it'?"

Chanice burst out laughing, head tipping back. "Please. You're smoother than that."

"He's probably married." Dani dismissed the idea with a wave.

"Then he'll say so. And if not?" Chanice nudged her arm. "You'll think of something smart."

A flicker of awareness sparked in Dani's chest—low and unexpected. She glanced back at the court. Gavin was jogging for a stray ball, sunglasses hiding his eyes, yet his focus felt locked on her. He scooped it up in one smooth motion, and the unmistakable weight of his gaze sent a warm flush up her neck before she could look away.

Her pulse quickened, a flutter rising in her stomach as if he'd reached across the sand and touched her. She forced herself to breathe, but the feeling lingered, subtle, undeniable.

"Girl, I've got goosebumps from the current you two just threw off," Chanice said, fanning herself. "If it gets any hotter, I'm gonna need a cold drink and a chaperone."

Dani snorted, rolling onto her stomach and flipping open a magazine. "Please. He was just getting his ball back."

"Yeah, and he took the scenic route." Chanice arched a brow.

The volleyball game broke up not long after, sweaty, sandy, full of easy laughter. Gavin and his friend high-fived, slung towels over their shoulders, and headed toward the water. Dani and Chanice tried not to stare, but subtlety had never been Chanice's strength.

"He's not married," Chanice muttered. "No ring. And he's giving bachelor energy."

"Would you stop?" Dani tried not to smile as she stood and reached for her water.

"I will not. You've been single since Clinton was inaugurated. The universe just dropped a man in front of you. It's a sign."

Before Dani could reply, a rogue gust of wind caught her towel, sending her magazine skittering across the sand like a crab.

"Damn it," she muttered, scrambling around Chanice to chase after it.

She was about to lunge when a shadow fell across her hand.

A long, tanned arm reached down, plucked it up, and held it out with a grin that could've melted asphalt in February.

"You dropped this."

His voice was deep, velvety, low timbres curling around words like smoke. The kind of voice made for late-night radio... or a dangerous pirate.

And somehow, it sounded exactly the same as it did on the air.

Dani blinked, startled by the surreal moment of hearing that voice directed at her.

Gavin Larkhurst stood in front of her, holding out the rescued pages, eyes glinting with quiet amusement.

He was damp from the ocean, saltwater sheening his skin. A bead of water slid from his collarbone down the slope of his shoulder, threading through the sun-kissed hair on his chest before disappearing into the waistband of his swim shorts.

Dani's mouth went dry. She wasn't trying to stare, but she couldn't look away from the water's slow, tantalizing path across his torso, all the way to where the fabric clung low on his hips.

Smack.

Chanice's hand landed sharply on her calf.

Dani jolted, heat flaring in her cheeks as she snapped her gaze back to his face.

Gavin's smile twitched, subtle but unmistakably amused.

Chanice muffled her laugh behind her towel; Dani didn't dare look at her.

She took the magazine carefully, avoiding his fingers. Her eyes flicked to the cover.

Seductive Secrets: Unlock Your Inner Temptress.

Heat rushed to her cheeks.

"Thanks," she managed, her voice shaky.

Gavin's lips curved, a playful sparkle in his eyes. He chuckled. "Any time, Siren."

Dani blinked, caught off guard by the nickname. A flush crept up her neck, though she tried to play it cool. "Siren?" she echoed, a small smile tugging at her mouth.

His grin deepened. "Yeah. Fits on a lot of levels."

He leaned closer, and she caught a whiff of salt, sunshine, and man, subtle but potent. The kind of natural cologne no bottle could mimic: an aphrodisiac wrapped in saltwater and sunburned charm.

Flustered, she fumbled the magazine, then blindly tossed it at Chanice.

Gavin brushed sand off his hand, still smiling. "You two looked like you were enjoying the game."

Right, the game, Dani thought. Not your chest. Definitely the game.

"Uh, yeah. Hard not to watch," she said, standing too quickly and wobbling in the sand. Gavin reached out to steady her.

"You were, you know, playing like it was the Olympics or something, just with more abs."

Chanice's shriek of laughter made her wince.

"I mean energy. Olympic-level energy."

Gavin grinned. "I'll take either one."

Diego jogged over, sand kicking up behind him. Wiping seawater from his face, he smirked. "Hey, man, you holding court over here after that epic volleyball fail?"

He shot a playful look at Chanice.

Chanice laughed, shaking her head.

"Oh please, Diego, keep dreaming," Gavin protested.

"Sounds like he won," Dani said, smiling at their easy banter.

Gavin grimaced. "He always wins, even when he doesn't."

Dani laughed, a flutter sparking in her belly.

"I'm Gavin," he said, offering his hand. "Nice to meet you."

"Dani." She shook it, his grip firm and warm. "This is my friend, Chanice."

Chanice gave a little wave from the towel, eyes twinkling behind her shades. "Big fan of your voice," she called.

Gavin chuckled. "That's one I don't hear every day."

"Don't let her start quoting news reports," Dani teased.

He grinned, clearly enjoying himself. "Well, now I'm flattered. I'll try not to ruin the image with sand and sweat."

Diego smirked at Chanice. "It's sad, really. His voice is his only redeeming trait."

She arched a brow, lips curving. "Hush. Jealousy makes your forehead wrinkle."

Gavin laughed at his friend's dramatics. "You guys here for the day?"

"Celebrating the first good beach day of the year," Dani said, tucking a strand of hair behind her ear as the breeze whipped it loose again.

"Excellent." Gavin's grin widened. "Can I buy you an ice cream? Call it a thank-you for the moral support."

Chanice perked up. "Only if it comes with sprinkles and a legally binding agreement that you're paying for mine too."

"I'd be honored, mi carita," he said, smooth as honey, clearly catching the sparkle in her eyes.

Chanice tilted her head, amused. "Is that your sweet-talk voice? Because it's working."

Dani's cheeks warmed. "You two did all the work and put on the show. We should probably buy you a cone."

Gavin leaned closer, smiling. "Consider it positive reinforcement so you'll go out with me again."

Her laugh caught in her throat, heart fluttering more than she expected. "Well, since I'm a teacher, I do love a good reward system. What do you say, Chanice?"

Chanice stood, brushing sand from her legs. "I'd love an ice cream, thank you," she said with a grin.

Dani pulled on her cover-up and adjusted her sunglasses.

"Can you believe this is happening?" she whispered.

Chanice nudged her with an elbow, grinning. "Believe it? Girl, I manifested this."

Diego nudged Gavin. "Is it just me, or did the temperature go up ten degrees?"

Gavin didn't bother pretending to look away from Dani. "Nope. Definitely hotter."

Dani shot them both a sideways glance. "If your brains are overheating, there's a whole ocean you can dunk yourselves in."

Chanice smirked. "Or better yet, summon two cones and a cabana boy with a fan."

Gavin held up his hands. "Alright, message received, less ogling, more ice cream."

The four of them burst out laughing as the waves rolled in, the sun blazing overhead, and for now, everything was exactly as it should be.

Chapter Seven

The ice cream stand near 15th Street bustled with lazy summer energy.

Children darted between sun-bleached picnic tables like fireflies, squealing with joy, while parents leaned back in plastic chairs, half-laughing, half-wrangling sticky hands. Somewhere nearby, music crackled from a tinny speaker, old pop blurred by distance.

Dani stood beside Gavin, her shoulder brushing his arm, the closeness sparking heat low in her chest. He was tall, easily six foot something, and she felt every inch of the difference when she tilted her head to meet his eyes.

His sun-faded navy tank clung just enough to suggest lean strength, and his board shorts looked worn by a hundred waves.

When he spoke, the low rumble of his voice came almost too close, igniting a crush she wasn't ready to admit.

Which was ridiculous. She had to be older by a few years, and she definitely didn't carry that easy, athletic looseness he did.

Where he was all angles and sun-browned muscle, she was soft in places she tried not to think about,

a little lumpy here, a little squishy there.

She shifted her weight, suddenly conscious of every inch of her swimsuit beneath her cover-up, every curl frizzing in the humidity.

Standing next to him felt like standing beside a glossy surf ad, and she was not the one people paused to look at.

"Tell me you're at least getting a double scoop," Gavin said, nodding toward the stand. "Single scoops are for quitters."

Dani arched a brow. "Bold words from someone who looks like he survives on air and protein powder."

He laughed, warm and easy. "Hey, I eat real food. I just metabolize like a golden retriever."

She smirked. "Must be nice."

His eyes swept over her, not in a gross, sizing-up way, but like he was genuinely curious. "I don't see a thing wrong with your metabolism."

Dani rolled her eyes, though her mouth twitched. "Careful. I might actually believe you if you keep talking like that."

"I live for danger," he said with a wink. "Besides, you strike me as someone who orders the good stuff, none of that sad, fat-free strawberry nonsense."

She laughed despite herself. "Mint chip. With rainbow sprinkles. Judge me if you dare."

He grinned. "Trouble. I knew it."

A few yards away, Chanice and Diego perched on the wooden railing at the edge of the dunes, sipping cherry slushies. Chanice swatted Diego's arm, playful but firm, and he grinned like he'd just scored.

A pair of kids darted past the stand, laughter trailing behind them as a napkin and popsicle wrapper fluttered to the ground. Gavin stepped forward without hesitation, scooped up the trash, and dropped it into the nearest bin.

"It's wild how much of this stuff ends up in the water," he said, frowning.

"I know. It's really bad in the summer," Dani agreed.

He shot her a sideways grin. "Want to spend your Saturday picking up beer cans and fishing line with me? WKNS is recruiting for Clean the Bay Day."

She lifted a brow as they reached the counter. "Wow, you really know how to sweep a girl off her flip-flops."

Gavin chuckled low, his grin crooked. "What can I say? Trash talk turns me on."

They were still snickering when the family in front of them got their cones, and Dani and Gavin stepped up.

"What'll it be?" The teenager behind the counter gave them a bored look, then blinked, doing a double-take. "Wait… Ms. Jones?"

Dani smiled in surprise. "Hi… Tyler, right?"

"Yeah!" His face lit up. "You were my favorite teacher. I still have that short story you gave me feedback on, even though I was just trying to impress you with all that metaphorical deer stuff." He chuckled, then nodded toward Gavin.

"What can I get you?"

"Mint chip with rainbow sprinkles," Gavin said. "And double chocolate."

While they waited, he nudged Dani gently with his elbow.

"So, what do you think? Saturday? Gloves, trash bags, stinky garbage, what more could a woman want?"

She smirked. "You really do have a persuasive gift."

"I'm not saying it's sexy," he said, taking his cone and handing hers over with a mock flourish, "but there's something kind of great about doing a little good while getting muddy."

"Thanks, Tyler," Dani said as she took her cone. "See you around this summer."

"Sure thing, Ms. J." He grinned before turning to the next customer.

Dani took a thoughtful bite as she and Gavin settled on a nearby bench.

"So, this is your idea of a date?"

"Not officially." He licked his cone. "This is me offering you a glimpse into my glamorous weekend life."

She snorted. "If I swoon any harder, I might pull a muscle."

"How about this, you show up, and you get my eternal gratitude. Plus, tacos after."

"Tacos?" she repeated, feigning shock. "Why didn't you lead with that?"

"I was saving it for the close." He wiped a smudge of chocolate from his lip. "So... you in?"

"Actually", Dani tilted her head, pretending to think, "I'd already planned to go. But if it makes you feel better, your pitch was excellent."

The breeze shifted, cool against her skin, carrying brine and something colder. Movement caught her eye.

She blinked.

A man walked the shoreline toward them, broad-shouldered, tall, maybe in his sixties. A white linen shirt hung open, flapping over frayed cutoffs. He moved with a lumbering ease, careless, as if sand didn't belong on his boots.

Boots.

Her breath caught.

Heavy leather boots, scuffed and salt-stained. On the beach.

Something about it felt wrong.

"Dani?"

She startled. Gavin was holding out their cones, his grin fading into concern.

"Sorry," she said quickly. "What were you saying?"

"I was saying", he chuckled, though his eyes followed hers to the beach, narrowing, "that I had a whole speech prepared, but maybe I should've led with dessert."

She smiled automatically, but the breeze shifted again, brine, cold, ancient.

The stranger had stopped, staring out at the water less than fifty feet away. His long, greasy hair was pulled back, strands whipping loose in the wind. His beard, wild and uneven, looked hacked at with a pocketknife. No sunglasses. No smile.

Just that familiar indifference that made her skin crawl.

She froze.

Carl Rendell.

The sun pressed hot against Dani's skin, yet a sudden chill knifed up her spine. She couldn't tear her gaze from the man. With slow, deliberate ease, he lifted a hand and waved, not at them, but out toward the sea, where nothing waited. No boat. No one. The gesture was fluid, practiced, like muscle memory. Then he dropped his arm and kept walking, boots chewing up the sand.

He hadn't seen her.

Or had he?

Doubt coiled in her chest, clamping her breath short, as though a hand pressed hard against her ribs.

Dani glanced toward the boardwalk, where Chanice and Diego laughed, his hand resting casually on her knee. Then back to Gavin, who was watching her, brow furrowed.

She searched for words but found only fear raw, unshaped, impossible to name.

"Hey," Gavin asked gently, "you okay?"

"I'm not sure," Dani said, her voice tight. Then, louder: "Chanice!"

Chanice looked up mid-laugh, her smile faltering. "What's up?"

"That guy." Dani pointed to the retreating figure. "Do you see him?"

Chanice and Diego moved closer, curiosity tugging at their faces. Chanice lifted a hand against the glare, squinting down the beach.

"Yeah, I saw him," she said, nose wrinkling. "Looked like some old bass player who never got the memo his band broke up. Why?"

The knot in Dani's stomach tightened.

What unsettled her more, the man himself, or the possibility that he'd seen Chanice too?

"I think… it might've been Rendell."

Chanice turned fully, her expression dropping. "Wait. Are you serious?"

Before Dani could answer, Gavin's head snapped up. "Rendell?" His brow furrowed. "As in Carl Rendell?" He didn't wait for a reply; he shoved his melting cones into the hands of a bewildered family in line, his attention gone from dessert entirely.

"I'm not sure," Dani said quickly. "It probably wasn't him. That guy just looked like him."

Gavin's voice dropped, firm and edged. "He's wanted for questioning about that church fire. It was the lead story Friday."

Diego let out a low whistle. "How do you even know that guy, Dani?"

Her breath hitched. She turned toward the spot where Rendell had vanished between two hotels. "It's complicated," she whispered.

Chanice's hand found her shoulder, grounding her. Gavin stood taller beside her, his gaze sharpening, protective.

"Do you think he saw you?" Chanice asked quietly.

Dani didn't answer. She didn't need to.

The breeze rose, tugging her hair, stirring the sand.

Behind them, a seagull cried and children laughed, sounds too bright, too far away.

"I need to go," Dani said abruptly, already turning.

"Wait." Gavin stepped forward, pulling a business card from his wallet. He flipped it over, scanning the back for space. "Can I give you my number?"

She paused, wary. "For a news story or a date?"

His grin faded into something steadier. "Maybe both," he said. "But I'll let you decide."

After a beat, Dani gave a small nod.

Gavin jogged back to the stand, borrowed a pen from Tyler, and scribbled his number on the back of the card before handing it to her. Then, with a hopeful glance, he snagged a napkin from the counter and held out the pen. "And can I have yours?"

Dani hesitated, then wrote her number on the napkin and passed it to him. Gavin folded it carefully and slid it into his wallet, the faintest smile tugging at his lips.

Chanice and Dani gathered their things, shaking sand from towels and brushing grit off their legs. Around them, the beach pulsed with careless life, kids shrieking, radios blaring, gulls wheeling overhead. A vendor's voice cut through it all, hawking hot dogs and lemon ice.

Dani scanned the crowd again. Her gaze snagged on a tall man in mirrored sunglasses. Her heart lurched, then eased when she realized he was just a teenager demolishing a funnel cake. Still, her body didn't get the memo; her shoulders stayed tight, her breath shallow.

She tried to match Chanice's easy pace, but every footstep behind them made her flinch, every shout from the boardwalk scraping her nerves raw.

Every stranger's face seemed too sharp, too lingering, as though it might peel back and reveal him if she stared too long.

"It's gonna be okay," Chanice murmured, looping their arms together with practiced calm. "He didn't see you."

Probably.

But doubt gnawed at her, chewing holes in her certainty.

It had teeth. If he'd seen her, if it really had been Rendell, not just a stranger with the same gait, the same build, what the hell was she supposed to do now?

Tate had told her to call a detective. She still had the card at home. But what could she say? I might have seen Carl Rendell? I'm not sure, it could've been a trick of the light?

They'd think she was imagining things.

Or worse, they'd believe her.

And Dani wasn't sure which terrified her more.

Chapter Eight

"I'm going to go home and take a shower," Chanice said, hovering in the doorway as if she didn't want to leave Dani alone. "But I'll be back with pizza and a movie from Blockbuster."

Her voice was light, aiming for casual, but her eyes lingered.

They drifted around the room as if memorizing it: Dani's flip-flops kicked off by the couch, the half-finished glass of ginger ale on the coffee table, the hoodie draped over the armrest. Finally, with a breath too close to a sigh, she stepped into the heavy afternoon humidity.

The screen door creaked and slapped shut. A moment later came the hum of her car, fading down the street. Silence crept in behind it, curling into the corners like fog.

Dani stood still, grateful for Chanice's steadiness and relieved for the solitude. The house felt too quiet, but at least the quiet was hers. She showered quickly, hoping the hot water would rinse away the weight in her chest, the sting behind her eyes. It didn't.

Afterward, she pulled on faded cutoffs and her softest Cranberries T-shirt, the collar stretched from years of wear. It was the only thing that felt normal.

Exhaling shakily, she knelt by the bag she'd dropped Friday night and pulled out the card Officer Tate had given her at the dance.

Detective Marcus Gates
Virginia Beach Police Department
2nd Precinct

The phone number was written in neat block print. Dani stared at the name until it settled heavy in her stomach. This was the man they wanted her to call if Rendell resurfaced.

Such a small card. Plain. Unassuming. Yet it felt like a door cracked open to something much bigger, darker, something she wasn't sure she wanted to step into.

She sat on the edge of the couch, the card in one hand, the cordless phone in the other. The refrigerator hummed in the kitchen. Outside, the city moved on in its indifferent rhythm: cars gliding past, voices carrying from the boardwalk, a dog barking once before cutting off.

Shakespeare leapt onto the back of the couch, tail flicking against her shoulder. Rosalind curled tighter on the blanket beside her, one paw twitching in dream.

It had been Rendell. She could still see the posture, the greasy hair, the boots, who wore boots on a beach? It hadn't just been resemblance. Recognition had sunk claws into her and held fast.

At the time, she'd been sure. But now doubt leaked in, slow and steady. What if she'd imagined it? What if her brain had conjured what her fear wanted to see? The memory replayed in her mind like static-filled film: grainy, unreliable.

Then the phone rang, sharp and sudden, slicing through the quiet.

She flinched, heart jolting as the sound ricocheted off the walls, far too loud in the still apartment. The cordless buzzed in her hand, steady, insistent.

Roz blinked, flicking her tail in mild offense, as if scolding her for the disruption.

Dani stared at the phone for half a beat before pressing **TALK**. "Hello?"

"Hey, Dani?" Gavin Larkhurst's voice came low and tentative, like he wasn't sure he should've called.

She blinked, pulling the phone back to check the screen as if she hadn't heard right. "Gavin?"

"Yeah." A pause, a breath. "Sorry to bother you. I just... wanted to say I really enjoyed meeting you today."

Her fingers curled around the couch cushion, suddenly alert. "Oh. Thanks. I... me too."

"And," he added softly, "I figured I'd check in. Make sure you're okay. I keep thinking about the beach... when you froze up. That looked rough."

Her throat tightened. She gripped the detective's card like a reflex. "I thought it was Rendell," she whispered. "I think it was."

A silence stretched, not awkward so much as heavy. Gavin exhaled slowly. "I'm worried for you, Dani. Rendell's a wanted man. You don't know what he's capable of."

"I know." Her voice was small. "I have Detective Marcus Gates' number right here. I was just... trying to work up the nerve to call."

Gavin gave a short, almost nervous laugh, lighter now. "I know Marcus, we're friends. Play ball sometimes. I even roped him into Clean the Bay Day once."

Her gaze dropped to the card.

Detective Marcus Gates.

She traced the raised lettering with her thumb, slow, uncertain.

Shakespeare nudged her leg. Rosalind stared, taut as wire.

"I'll call," Dani murmured, mostly to herself. "I promise."

"Good." Gavin hesitated, then let a little warmth creep into his tone. "And hey, I'm glad I'll see you next Saturday."

"I'm looking forward to the tacos," she said, aiming for light, though the weight in her chest refused to lift. "Talk soon, Gavin."

They hung up. For a moment, she just stared at the phone. Then, with a breath, she dialed the number beneath Marcus' name.

Her pulse ticked at her throat as the line rang.

"Virginia Beach Police Department, Precinct Two. How may I direct your call?"

"Detective Marcus Gates, please. I was given this number."

"One moment."

Hold music filled her ear, bland piano, vaguely familiar.

After a few beats, another voice came on, brisk but not unfriendly. "Detective Gates' desk."

"This is Danica Jones," she said, shifting her grip on the phone. "I have information about Carl Rendell."

A pause. "Please hold."

The line clicked. Silence.

Her fingers clenched around the phone. Shakespeare climbed into her lap, stepping clumsily over Roz before curling up. Dani barely noticed.

Then a calm, steady voice came through. "Marcus Gates."

"Hi. This is Danica Jones. Officer Tate gave me your number, he said to call if I saw Carl Rendell."

"Yes, Ms. Jones. Thanks for reaching out. I was actually planning to contact your school Monday to set up a time to talk." His tone sharpened. "Rendell's gone missing."

Dani hesitated. "I, think I saw him today. Just for a second, but I'm almost sure it was him."

Silence stretched on the line.

She shifted in her seat, her free hand resting on Shakespeare's warm fur. Her heart thudded, heavy and insistent.

"Where?" Gates asked, his tone suddenly sharp.

"On the beach. Fifteenth Street. He walked right past me."

The image rose again, his gait, casual and unhurried, as if he belonged there.

That wave. Her stomach twisted.

"I'm not a hundred percent sure it was Rendell," she admitted, softer now. "I just saw him, and everything in me froze."

"Could my partner and I meet you there?" Gates asked.

"At the beach?" Her voice cracked, dry.

"Yes. I'd like to get a look at the scene."

Dani glanced at the window. The sky outside was already darkening, clouds rolling in. Her throat tightened.

"Okay," she said at last. "Fifteen minutes."

The sky had gone from dull gray to gunmetal by the time Dani saw the unmarked sedan ease to the curb near the Fifteenth Street boardwalk.

A cold breeze curled in off the ocean, tugging at her hair as she stood near the ice cream stand where she'd first spotted Rendell.

77

A man stepped out of the car, tall and broad-shouldered, his charcoal suit cutting a clean line against the wind. He buttoned his coat with the smooth, practiced ease of habit, then paused, scanning the scene.

His skin was deep brown, warm against the harsh light; his jaw strong, his cheekbones sharp, touched with a few threads of silver at the temples.

A neatly trimmed beard framed a mouth set in a firm line.

He moved toward her with the stillness of someone who noticed everything and revealed nothing.

"Danica Jones?"

Dani nodded, brushing windblown strands from her face. "Yes."

"Marcus Gates," he said, flashing a badge as another man joined him. "This is my partner, Detective Pete Doran."

Doran was wiry, pale-faced, with thinning blond hair whipped by the breeze. He already had a notepad open, his pen scratching in clipped strokes.

"Ms. Jones," Gates said with a nod, his voice steady, his eyes intent. "Tell us what you saw."

She pointed toward the sand. "He was right there. Twenty, maybe thirty feet from the boardwalk."

They followed her down the steps. Footprints crisscrossed in all directions, blurred by wind and tide. The ocean crept in, hissing over the beach.

"He stopped about here, looking at the water. Then he lifted his arm and waved before walking south, toward the hotels. He didn't run. He didn't look around, either."

Doran lifted his head. "Did you see who he was waving to?"

"No. I didn't see any boats or anyone who seemed to notice him."

"What time was this?" Gates asked.

"Early afternoon. Maybe one-thirty. I was here with my friend Chanice and with Gavin Larkhurst."

Gates kept his eyes on the sand. "What was Rendell wearing?"

"Cut-off jeans, an open white shirt, and brown boots."

Doran muttered as he wrote, "Boots on the beach in May. Odd choice."

Gates looked at her. "And you're certain it was Rendell?"

"I can't say a hundred percent. I only met him once at school."

Dani crossed her arms, steadying herself against the wind. The memory flickered: Rendell, angry, dismissive.

Not threatening, not then. But still.

Doran paused mid-scribble. "Tate mentioned you'd met him. Can you tell us about that?"

She shifted her weight, gaze drawn south, to where Rendell had vanished. "He came to see me. About his nephew."

The wind picked up, tossing sand across her shoes. Storm coming.

"He said Brian was staying with him while his parents were out of town. Claimed I was feeding him religious propaganda. He wanted me to give Brian an alternate assignment. Said The Pardoner's Tale was trash, sending the wrong message to teenagers. I told him Chaucer was part of the curriculum, and Brian was fine. He didn't like that. Rendell wanted to opt him out, but he wasn't Brian's legal guardian. He said he'd get a note from the parents."

79

Gates exchanged a look with Doran. "Did he give you a number?"

"No. And when I asked Brian later, he had no idea what I was talking about. Said it had been weeks since he'd seen his uncle."

Gates glanced down the beach toward the hotels, thoughtful. "Tate also said you were talking to another woman about Rendell at the school dance. Why?"

"That was Dorothy Swan. She taught him in seventh grade. Said he was disruptive, hard to control."

A drop of rain splashed her cheek. Dani tilted her face up as more followed, first scattered, then steady. The sky had gone bruised gray, clouds twisting like something alive. The air shifted: salt, wet asphalt, the metallic bite of a storm.

She brushed at the moisture, but her unease deepened. The beach, open a minute ago, now felt stripped bare.

Rendell was still out there. Somewhere.

Doran snapped his notebook shut and glanced at Gates. "Can we give you a ride?"

Dani blinked. "I'm fine to walk."

"We'd prefer you didn't," Gates said. His tone left no room for argument.

Her apartment wasn't far, a second-floor walk-up in a weathered 1950s beach cottage. The white siding peeled in places, wisteria vines climbing wild across the sagging porch. A narrow staircase clung to the side, leading up to her door. Above it, a porch light buzzed, flickering against the heavy dusk.

Dani climbed out of the sedan and glanced back at the detectives. "Thank you for the ride."

Gates gave a single nod. "Call us if you see or hear from Rendell again."

She gave a tight nod in return, then climbed the stairs. The lock clicked beneath her key, and she slipped inside.

Light filled the small apartment as she flipped the switch. Her keys landed on the coffee table with a soft clatter.

Shakespeare padded ahead, tail twitching, nails clicking faintly against the floorboards.

Dani stopped.

A prickle stirred low at the base of her neck.

Slowly, she turned toward the window.

Across the street, something shifted, a faint ripple in the shadows beneath the trees, where the porch light couldn't quite reach.

Her body went still. Breath shallow. Eyes locked on the dark.

"It's nothing," she whispered.

"Just the light. Just the wind."

But her pulse wouldn't settle. Because some part of her, the same part that had frozen at the beach, knew better.

Chapter Nine

The week flew by, and before she knew it, the weekend had arrived. With only three weeks until summer break, Dani kept her students busy with a steady stream of assignments. Work kept the days moving and chaos at bay.

The kids tried every trick to wear her down: whining, bargaining for movies, pleading for parties. Dani only smiled, unshaken, and pressed on with quick drills and activities that kept the lessons rolling.

By Saturday morning, she woke to the soft hum of her radio alarm. Golden light filtered through the curtains, warm and forgiving after the frantic pace of the school week.

Her alarm clicked, and Gavin's familiar voice spilled into the room: "*Good morning, Virginia Beach! We're coming to you live from Great Neck City Park for Clean the Bay Day! It's a warm, humid start, but don't worry, a refreshing breeze should keep us steady in the low eighties. Come join me and the WKNS crew as we roll up our sleeves and make a difference together!*"

In the kitchen, the scent of fresh coffee filled the air. Shakespeare and Rosalind twined around her ankles, meowing impatiently until she filled their bowls. She smiled, setting her mug on the counter as they dove in.

A flutter stirred in her chest, catching her off guard and sending a thrill down her spine. Her pulse quickened at the thought of seeing him, and a quiet buzz of nervous excitement spread through her limb.

For a moment, she let herself imagine Gavin standing in her sunlit kitchen, leaning against the counter, an easy smile tugging at the corners of his mouth. The way his eyes caught the light, deliberate and hungry, flushed her skin.

That quiet confidence, the kind that didn't demand attention but owned it anyway, was intoxicating. A low, steady burn lit in her belly.

She caught herself with a sigh before the daydream wandered further. She'd only met him once.

And yet the quickened pulse, the sudden shyness, the reckless spark in her chest, those signs were unmistakable. Something new. Something thrilling. Could it be real?

She didn't know. But the thought lingered, curling at the edges of her mind, tugging a smile to her lips.

After finishing her coffee, Dani showered quickly and pulled on her oldest shorts and a worn T-shirt. Not much to impress, but perfect for wading into the muddy banks of the Lynnhaven River.

She double-checked her supplies, work gloves, trowel, a few threadbare towels retired from bathroom duty, before heading out to her gold 1991 Renault.

Guiding the car down Great Neck Road, she passed Cox High School, its parking lot silent and empty.

A few minutes later, she turned into Great Neck City Park. Sunlight glanced off the hood as the trees swayed above her, welcoming her into the green.

The park, nestled among some of Virginia Beach's elegant homes, was a quiet, often overlooked pocket of wilderness, where the Eastern Branch of the Lynnhaven River spilled into the Chesapeake Bay. Taking the path into the woods, Dani felt the air shift.

Cooler here, under the canopy of pines and oaks, where golden light filtered through branches and a soft mist clung to the underbrush.

The scent of damp earth and salt lingered in the breeze, an invitation, and a warning.

Damp earth mingled with the briny tang of the river. Beneath her boots, the ground was soft, scattered with pine needles and moss glowing green-gold in the dappled light. Birds flitted overhead, their calls bright and busy, while the breeze stirred the leaves in a gentle rustle.

As she neared the end of the path, the muffled quiet gave way to the thump of music and the buzz of voices.

Moments later, Dani stepped into the clearing and reached the pavilion by the water just as Gavin wrapped up a quick rundown with a group of volunteers.

The WKNS crew handed out neon-orange trash bags and thick rubber gloves, their chatter filling the air with an easy energy.

She hung back at the supply table, listening. "Okay, folks," Gavin said, his voice warm and animated, "this isn't just about picking up trash; it's about showing the bay a little love. Every bottle, every scrap of plastic we haul out today keeps our water cleaner, our wildlife safer, and our beaches more beautiful."

A ripple of agreement moved through the crowd.

"So spread out, stay hydrated, and if you find anything weird, flag me or someone from the crew. Trust me, the bay coughs up some wild stuff." His grin drew a few laughs.

Dani couldn't help smiling. He held their attention so easily, confident without being overbearing, serious about the cause but still approachable. That magnetic ease she'd noticed the first time they met was on full display, tugging at something warm and reckless inside her all over again.

And he was definitely easy on the eyes.

Clipboard in hand, sunglasses pushed up into his tousled sandy hair, his faded Keep the Bay Clean '96 T-shirt hugged broad shoulders and chest. Worn gym shorts and beat-up sneakers clung to a frame built for movement.

He looked up and caught her staring. A slow grin tugged at his mouth as he held out a pair of gloves. "There're my reinforcements," he said. "You ready to fight the good fight, Dani?"

"Aye, aye, Captain." She accepted the gloves with a wry smile.

Sliding them on, she glanced at the riverbank. "So, what do you think we'll find? Treasure? Lost beach toys? Somebody's sunken beer cooler?"

"No guarantees," he said, falling into step beside her as they led a group toward the shoreline. "Last year we pulled out a shopping cart, a couple of bikes, and somebody's lawn chair."

"Sounds like a classic Saturday in Virginia Beach." Dani wrinkled her nose, then smirked sideways. "You can't impress me with the lure of exotic garbage."

Gavin clutched his chest, mock-wounded. "Ouch. I'll have you know my garbage is top-tier."

"Good to know you're bringing your A-game."

"I haven't even started." He winked, giving her shoulder a playful nudge as they stepped onto the riverbank.

People spread out along the shoreline. Dani drifted toward a quiet bend where reeds grew tall along the muddy edge. The water shimmered under the mid-morning sun, herons gliding low with slow, graceful wings. In the distance, someone shouted after spotting a rusted scooter lodged in the marsh grass.

Dani waded carefully, the mud sucking at her boots. The breeze tugged her hair loose from its braid as she bent to pick up a battered soda can and drop it into her bag. Laughter and conversation floated through the air, easy and familiar among the locals.

Beside her, Gavin crouched to snag a plastic bag caught in the reeds. "You know," he said, tossing it into his sack, "this is a lot more fun with company."

"I'd agree if it weren't for the smell," Dani teased, nudging a half-buried beer bottle with her boot before scooping it into her bag.

Gavin grinned. "That's my cologne. Eau de Low Tide. Very exclusive."

She laughed. "Mmm, earthy, with a hint of decay. You wear it well."

"Comes with a side of mystery muck and maybe a tetanus shot," he said, fishing a rusted can from the mud.

"Romantic," she shot back, smiling as they moved down the bank. "You really know how to show a girl a good time."

"Wait 'til you see what's wedged under that dock." He winked. "Stuff of legends."

Up the bank, an older woman held up a sodden bikini top like a trophy. "How scandalous!"

Her friend called back, "I just found the six-pack that goes with it!"

Laughter rippled through the volunteers.

Gavin tilted his head toward Dani, eyebrows raised. "Should we be concerned?"

"If we find shoes and a wallet, maybe," she said, chuckling.

They rounded a bend where the shoreline dipped into a muddy inlet, and Gavin stopped.

"Well," he said, cocking his head, "would you look at that sad little sea beast."

Dani squinted at the half-submerged shape tangled in reeds. "Is that a giant pink flamingo raft?"

Gavin smirked. "Looks like someone's good time went a little saggy."

She nudged it with her boot. "More like a bad time. Definitely not the kind of float you want drifting down the river."

Grabbing a corner of the raft, she heaved, water sloshing noisily as it resisted. "Ugh, it's heavier than it looks."

"Careful," Gavin said, stepping closer. "This might turn into a two-person extraction."

"You saying I need backup?" Dani arched a brow.

"I'm saying that raft's got more fight than it should." He leaned in beside her, gripping the plastic wing.

"Ready?"

"One, two, pull!"

The raft slurped free with a soggy squelch, jerking Dani backward straight into Gavin's chest. His arms left the raft, catching her.

For a moment, neither moved.

The deflated flamingo bumped lazily against their legs.

His breath brushed her ear, warm and startling.

"You okay?" His low murmur grazed her skin. A pause, heavy, then softer, rougher: "Because from where I'm standing, you feel like trouble."

Trouble, indeed. His body heat, the faint tang of sweat and sunshine, wrapped around her like a current. Every nerve tingled, hyper-aware of how close his hand was to hers, how near his mouth was if she only turned her head. She didn't breathe, afraid the moment would break.

"Nice save," she whispered, her voice unsteady. She felt her own smile tug, unbidden, but she didn't dare look at him, because if she did, she wasn't sure she'd stop herself from closing the space.

"Teamwork," he murmured, the word sliding over her like a touch.

Her heartbeat kicked. Slowly, she turned to meet his gaze.

His eyes locked on hers, intense, amused, a teasing smile at the edges. "You've got mud on your nose," he said, voice lower now, almost private.

She swiped at her sleeve, suddenly too aware of the inches between them.

"Thanks for the heads-up." Her tone came out husky, betraying her.

His gaze flicked to her lips, just for a beat. Then he stepped closer, tugged the hem of his shirt, and brushed the smudge away himself. "I'm always willing to get dirty."

She rolled her eyes but didn't move back.

"You might regret that. There's plenty of mud out here."

Shouts from other volunteers cut through the spell, tugging reality back.

Gavin ducked under a low branch, heading toward a half-submerged scooter in the reeds. Dani followed, boots squelching. When the mud shifted beneath her, she slipped, balance faltering.

"I wouldn't mind mud wrestling with you," Gavin said, flashing a crooked grin as he caught her hand. This time, he didn't let go right away.

Her laugh came out breathless, pulse racing. She steadied herself, hand braced against his chest for a heartbeat, heat flaring sharp and undeniable before she pulled away.

"Maybe next time," she managed, cheeks burning.

The banter. The sparks. The way her body lit up just from being near him. It was more than play, more than harmless fun. Something restless stirred inside her, dangerous and thrilling all at once.

She barely knew him. But with Gavin, everything felt different, both safe and thrilling. A flicker of hope stirred beneath the surface, mingling with the warmth still lingering where their hands had touched.

She drew a steadying breath, reminding herself to take it slow. But the truth was, part of her was already leaning into whatever this was and whatever it might become.

89

"Well, I hope you don't expect me to stuff that poor flamingo into my garbage bag," she said, nodding toward the pink raft.

"Are you kidding? I'm giving it a Viking funeral." He hauled the limp raft up the bank.

"A proper send-off for a true survivor."

"Too bad we don't have a name for her."

"She looks like a Charlene."

"Charlene it is." Dani gave the float a solemn nod. "Rest in peace, you beautiful mess."

As she and Gavin wrestled the soggy raft up the bank, a few volunteers wandered over, curious about their prize.

A man in a faded fishing hat chuckled. "That thing's seen better days."

"The bay's kind of like this old raft," Gavin said with an easy grin. "She's taken a beating, but she's still floating."

Dani glanced out at the glittering water before turning back. "People forget how much the bay carries, fishing, tourism, whole towns built around it."

A young woman wiped sweat from her brow. "Yeah. My dad's boat shop would fold if the water went bad again."

Gavin nodded, still catching his breath. "It's been worse. Back in the '80s, nobody wanted to swim here. Too polluted. Clean the Bay Day started because regular folks got tired of watching it die."

That earned a few quiet smiles and nods. Someone murmured, "Glad we came," and another volunteer raised her trash bag in salute. "Let's make this count."

"One soggy raft at a time," Gavin added, grinning sideways at Dani.

She laughed, the tension between them shifting but not gone, humming under her skin, warm, insistent.

Her gaze drifted back over the water, sunlight scattering across its surface. The work ahead was heavy, the bay still fragile. But beneath it all, a flicker of hope held fast. Like the people gathered here, the bay wasn't broken. Not yet.

Chapter Ten

The morning haze had burned off by early afternoon, leaving the sun heavy with humidity. Dani and Gavin had fallen into a rhythm: work until exhaustion set in, rest in the shade, then push back out again.

Some of the early volunteers packed up at lunchtime, but fresh faces trickled in to replace them, neon-orange trash bags bright against the shoreline.

Dragging her tenth bag of garbage to the drop-off, Dani wiped the sweat from her brow and trudged up the path. She collapsed onto a bench inside the gazebo overlooking the bay, grateful for the shade. Her legs and back ached, but in that satisfying way that came from doing something that mattered.

Country music drifted from the WKNS speakers, Reba McEntire's voice carrying on the breeze. Dani hummed along, letting her eyes drift shut.

She felt Gavin before she saw him, a subtle tug in the space beside her. He dropped onto the bench, soaked through and grinning, his shirt plastered to him, the bridge of his nose pink from sunburn.

"If I collapse next to you, will you promise not to think less of me?" he asked, easing back with a tired grin.

She turned toward him, smirking. "Only if you promise not to mention how dirty I am."

He leaned in just enough for her pulse to quicken, his voice low and teasing. "Dirty?" His lips curved. "I was trying to be polite. But if you want to talk about how dirty you are…"

The sentence trailed, suggestive and warm. Her brows lifted, amusement sparking despite the heat in her chest.

"I'm literally covered in grime and sweat," she shot back.

"Good look on you," he said with a lazy shrug. His gaze softened as it met hers. "Real. Strong."

The words landed with more weight than she expected, heat blooming under the grit and sweat. Dani's heart stumbled, her smirk fading into something almost shy.

She glanced away, shaking her head. "Careful, radio man. Flattery like that might get you roped into hanging out with me more."

He opened his mouth to reply.

"If you two slackers are done flirting," a voice cut in, "I brought backup."

Dani blinked, half-grateful, half-disappointed at the interruption.

Detective Gates strode up the gazebo steps, a grin tugging at his mouth.

The last time she'd seen him, he'd been rumpled in a suit and tie, worn down by the job. Today, in black jeans and a crisp white button-down stretched over broad shoulders, he looked startlingly relaxed.

The badge might not have been clipped to his belt, but the cop's energy clung to him all the same.

Trailing him was a woman navigating the damp grass in sky-high wedges, a halter dress as white and pristine as her oversized sunglasses.

She looked like she'd taken a wrong turn on her way to a garden party, her gaze flicking longingly back toward the parking lot.

"Hey, look who's still standing," Marcus said, clapping Gavin on the back before turning to Dani. "Good to see you, Ms. Jones."

"Dani, please," she said, scooting over on the bench and brushing damp curls off her face.

"This is Carla," Marcus added, gesturing as the woman slipped neatly into place beside him. "Carla, this is Dani, and that mess next to her is Gavin Larkhurst."

Carla's smile was polished, camera-ready. "Hi. I've heard you on the radio, Gavin. Your voice is even better in person." Her tone was smooth, practiced, the kind of compliment that landed like a feather and stuck like glue.

"Thanks for listening," Gavin said, returning the smile, though his was more polite than warm.

"Nice to meet you too," Dani added with a friendly nod. She took in Carla's immaculate hair, dewy skin, and perfect dress and wondered how she could look so untouched by the heat, mud, and general chaos of the day.

"I'd shake your hand," Dani said with a wry smile, "but I'm clearly too gross."

Carla laughed lightly, flicking a glance at Dani's boots. "You're rocking the rugged look. Very field chic."

"You here to work?" Gavin asked, one brow arched.

Marcus sank onto the bench with theatrical exhaustion. "You look like you've got it covered. I'd only slow down the operation."

Gavin stretched out his sore legs, grinning. "Says the guy who showed up in black jeans. To a shoreline cleanup."

"Jeans are timeless," Marcus replied, deadpan. "Unlike that swamp couture you're rocking.

Is that a fern on your sock?"

Dani snorted, unable to help herself. "You know it's bad when the guy who smells like cologne and sarcasm is judging your outfit."

Carla gave Dani a once-over, not unkind, just curious. "It's impressive, really. You're actually out here doing the work."

"Somebody's got to," Dani said lightly, brushing a fleck of mud from her arm. "Turns out the bay doesn't clean itself."

Carla hummed, amused, but already glancing at her watch. Her car keys twirled idly around one manicured finger.

"We passed a smoothie bar on the way in," she said, already stepping back. "I'm going to grab us something cold, Marcus. Be back soon."

She didn't wait for an answer before striding toward the lot.

Gavin watched her go, then shot Marcus a sidelong smile. "You've got a keeper. She hasn't run screaming yet."

Dani leaned back, muttering under her breath, "She already is. Just politely."

Marcus sighed, his smirk slipping into something quieter. "I have a way of scaring women off.".

"Or maybe I just pick the ones already halfway out the door."

Dani glanced at him, caught off guard by the raw honesty. Gavin looked like he was about to quip, then hesitated, something unreadable flickering across his face.

Before anyone could speak, a shout cracked the air. "Hey! I need a little help down here!"

All three turned.

The lazy rhythm of the afternoon snapped taut. Even the birds seemed to hush, their chatter tapering off into uneasy silence.

Dani and Gavin rose, the sudden shift prickling along Dani's skin.

Overhead, a lone cloud slid across the sun, dimming the light. A restless breeze stirred the trees, carrying the damp, heavy scent of mud and decay.

Marcus fell into step with them, his easy grin gone, his shoulders tightening into a cop's alertness.

They followed the path toward the riverbank. Shadows stretched long across the cattails, the air heavy, close. Gulls wheeled above with sharp, startled cries.

Dani slowed, her breath catching. Ahead, Gavin paused too, glancing back even as Marcus pushed forward to the water's edge.

A volunteer stood waist-deep in the river, about a dozen yards out. His arm waved, frantic. His eyes were wide.

Whatever he'd found wasn't just big.

It was wrong.

On the shoreline, voices dropped to uneasy murmurs.

Clouds drifted across the sun, washing everything in muted shadow.

The volunteer wrestled with a shape half-hidden in the reeds, its bulk resisting as though the river didn't want to give it up.

"Stay here," Gavin said, his voice low and firm, eyes locking on Dani's. Then he waded in without hesitation.

Marcus followed, jeans dragging heavy in the silt as he pushed through the undergrowth.

Dani bristled at the command. She wasn't someone who stood back, not when her gut buzzed like this. Not when every instinct whispered that this mattered. She lingered only a moment before stepping in after them. Her boots sank into the spongy bank, water seeping in cold around her soles.

Each heave brought the shape closer. Reeds slipped free like reluctant fingers. Behind them, the river smeared a dark, viscous trail. Branches slapped against her arms as she pushed through.

Her breath caught when she saw the outline clearer.

Gavin glanced back, frowning. "Dani"

"I'm fine." Her voice was quiet, steady. "Let me help."

Then the smell hit, rank and sweet, a rot that clawed at the back of her throat.

The shape resolved into an enormous sack, bloated and streaked with algae. The canvas sagged under the weight of whatever it carried.

Had it drifted from deeper in the bay? Or been placed here, hidden until the tide betrayed it?

Dani reached for it.

Her fingers sank into something slick, rubbery, unnatural. Not fabric. Not anything she knew. Cool to the touch, as though it resisted the sun.

The texture slid under her grip before catching, silky, stubborn. Sunlight glanced off its surface, revealing faint geometric patterns in the weave.

"What the hell is this?" she murmured.

Together, they dragged it ashore.

It hit the sand with a wet, sloshing thud. A fresh wave of stench rolled out, sweet, sour, stomach-turning.

"Whatever's in here," Gavin muttered, pinching his nose, "it's ripe."

Flies buzzed in, landing quick and eager.

Dani stepped back, arms prickling, as the sack shifted and another puff of rot escaped.

"Does anyone have a knife?" Marcus rasped, eyes fixed on the bundle.

"In my Acura," Gavin added, tossing Dani the keys. "Glove compartment."

Grateful for the escape, she jogged up the path, shoes squelching in the grass.

The blue Acura waited under the pines. She yanked open the door, rifling through papers and gum wrappers until her fingers closed on the folding knife.

As she hurried back, her stomach still knotted from the stench, she spotted Carla. Perched neatly on a bench, she plucked at her wedge sandals with delicate precision. Two sweating smoothies sat beside her, beads of condensation dripping down the plastic cups. Carla grimaced faintly, flicking a stubborn blade of grass from her strap, as if the mess of the shoreline were the only real nuisance here.

Without looking up, Carla called out, "Tell Marcus to come find me when he's done with his... swamp thing." She wrinkled her nose, sipping delicately from the pink straw. "And remind him his smoothie is melting."

Dani didn't bother replying.

Down by the water, a small knot of volunteers clustered at the shoreline, their voices pressed into whispers.

Marcus accepted the knife from her with a brief nod before crouching down, the blade poised over the waterlogged sack, his jaw set.

For a moment, he didn't move.

Then, with one swift stroke, he cut.

The fabric gave way with a wet, tearing sound.

Something heavy slid free: an arm, bloated and discolored, tumbling onto the sand with a sickening flop. Gray skin sagged over swollen muscle.

The fingers splayed wide, stiff yet reaching, as if the last motion had never stopped.

The air snapped with gasps.

Someone gagged and turned away.

Flies swarmed in a sudden frenzy, their buzz sharp against the silence that followed.

Dani's lungs seized.

Gavin's hand twitched toward her, then stilled mid-gesture, as though caught between instinct and restraint.

The hesitation was so small, so quick, but it cracked something open in her chest, an awareness, sharp and unsteady, that the ground beneath her was shifting.

99

And in that instant, with the dead weight of truth sprawled across the sand, Dani knew: nothing about today could be undone. Whatever came next, there was no going back.

Chapter Eleven

A steady echo of splashes bounced off the tiled walls of the Mayflower Apartments' indoor pool, mingling with the low thrum of an old-school R&B mixtape from a battered boombox. The air was thick with chlorine and humidity, clinging like a second skin.

Above, rain streaked the skylights in slow tears, dulling the daylight into a silvery haze.

Chanice and Dani lounged near the shallow end, chairs tipped back in lazy comfort. Chanice's curls were wrapped in a lemon-yellow scarf that matched her flowy cover-up, her bronze skin glowing under the overhead lights. She smirked faintly, eyes half-lidded as she surveyed the room.

Beside her, Dani fidgeted. One foot tapped against the table leg, nudging their half-melted tumblers of tea and rustling the spread of the Sunday Virginian-Pilot. Her oversized WKNS 1997 Bay Cleanup T-shirt clung damply to her frame, the stretched neckline slipping low enough to reveal the strap of a black one-piece swimsuit.

Her curls were twisted into a messy topknot, still wet from the pool.

Chanice nudged the paper with her toe. "If you steal the comics again, I swear I'm writing a letter to the editor."

Dani didn't look up. "Please. You still haven't finished last week's Dear Abby."

"That woman had layers," Chanice said, patting her scarf like a crown. "You can't rush emotional depth."

"Emotional depth? It was about her boyfriend hogging the remote."

"Exactly. Betrayal like that takes time."

They both snorted.

Dani reached for her glass. "Just admit you love the drama."

Chanice raised her hand in mock solemnity. "I live for drama. But only the kind that doesn't require me to leave this chair." She smoothed the newspaper flat over her knees. "Hey, listen to this:"

"Volunteers at Saturday's Clean the Bay Day discovered something rather gruesome in the Lynnhaven River. Virginia Beach residents Dani Jones and Gavin Larkhurst, along with Roy Santorino and Detective Marcus Gates, found the concealed body."

The laughter and splashes around them drained into static.

Dani's stomach cinched tight, her mouth going dry despite the humidity. She sat up, pulse quickening.

"What?" Her voice cracked sharp. "How did they get our names? Nobody even talked to me!"

"I heard Gavin on WKNS yesterday," Chanice said carefully. "Figured you were with him."

"I was at first. But when they pulled it out, when I saw him" Her throat closed. "I knew him, Chan. And Gavin told me to leave. Said I shouldn't stay, that it was... too much. He promised he'd handle it."

She swallowed hard. "What else does it say?"

Chanice scanned the article. "The body has been identified as Carl Rendell of Virginia Beach. Rendell had been missing since May

10. He was wanted for questioning in connection with the fire at the Eastern Church of God."

She drew a slow breath and read on. "According to authorities, the victim had been tightly wrapped in a canvas tarp before being submerged in the river. Dr. Gilbert Lawrence, the medical examiner assigned to the case, stated Rendell had been murdered, wrapped like trash and dumped in the bay."

It didn't feel real.

He'd seemed like the kind of man who'd outlive everyone else on sheer noise and force-of-will swagger made flesh. Impossible to picture him silent.

And yet she'd seen him. Bloated. Lifeless.

The reek of rot clinging to the reeds.

The way the canvas stuck to his skin.

Her stomach lurched.

And Gavin...

No call. No text. Nothing. She'd trusted him, let him glimpse past the guard she usually kept welded shut. And now, silence. Coiled and waiting, like something ready to strike.

Her name in the paper. His voice on the radio. Right there beneath the headline, paired together.

No heads-up. No warning. Just exposed.

A pulse pounded behind her eyes. The sounds of that day came crashing back, wet sloshes through cattails, gulls crying overhead. Then the body breaking through reeds, heavy and slick, water rippling with each drag. The sour reek. The metallic taste rising in her throat.

"Dani?" Chanice's voice cut through like a blade.

Dani flinched, breath snagging.

"You okay?" Chanice lowered her magazine, brow furrowing.

Dani blinked, realizing her hands were clenched tight, nails digging into her palms, her foot jittering against the tile. She forced her fingers to uncurl one by one.

"I'm fine," she rasped. "Just thinking."

Chanice gave her a look. "Thinking doesn't usually look like a panic attack."

Dani exhaled slowly, chest still tight, nerves buzzing like frayed wires.

"There's more," Chanice said, tapping the newspaper. "Want to hear it?"

Dani's eyes stayed fixed past the diving board. "Sure. Read away."

Chanice adjusted her sunglasses, clearing her throat with mock drama. "Brace yourself. The Virginian-Pilot does not hold back"

"Rendell, a prominent member of the Eastern Church of God, played a key role in the congregation's campaign to reintroduce prayer in public schools. He served as both deacon and treasurer, overseeing spiritual and financial matters. Known for his steady presence and deep involvement, he was regarded as a guiding voice in matters of faith and policy. Detective Marcus Gates declined to comment but urged anyone with information to contact authorities."

Dani's jaw tightened. The official silence only made the questions multiply. What were they keeping back?

The pool's security door creaked open, then clacked shut with a hollow echo. Dot Swan stepped onto the tile walkway with the same steady stride she used in the school hallways.

Her gray hair was combed back neatly, and her belly pressed against the faded denim cover-up that hung loose over her thin legs.

In her hands, a plastic container sat swaddled in a red dish towel, corners tucked tight as if it held something precious, or still warm.

"I saw the news this morning," Dot's voice echoed across the water. She set the container on the little plastic table between their loungers. "So, I made you banana bread."

Dani blinked. "How'd you know we were down here?"

Dot shrugged, slipping out of her Birkenstocks. Her toes were painted a pretty blue. "Please. It's Sunday. You're either here or at the beach by noon, depending on the weather."

Chanice laughed softly. "You should work for the FBI."

"Only if they pay in lottery tickets and decaf." Dot smirked, lowering herself into the third lounger with the grace of someone who refused to let age steal her comfort.

She glanced at Dani. "You okay?"

Dani hesitated. The answer pressed heavily on her tongue. "Not really." Her eyes fixed on a ten-year-old cannonballing into the deep end, water erupting in a spray of noise and light that felt a world away from what clawed at her chest.

"I went from curious to horrified in seconds," she said, her voice quiet, flat. "One minute we were laughing, pulling garbage from the reeds."

105

She swallowed hard. Her fingers gripped the chair until her knuckles whitened.

"I couldn't stop seeing it. The way the canvas had stuck to his arm. Every time I closed my eyes last night, I was back there. I keep flashing back to the beach where he'd waved with that same arm to someone. And the smell. I can't scrub the scent out of my nose. It just lingers, like it followed me home."

Dot gave a slow nod, the kind that said she recognized real grief. "You don't have to be okay. Not today. And banana bread helps."

Chanice smiled faintly and peeled back the dish towel with mock reverence. "Dot's banana bread is the best kind of medicine."

"And you're lucky I like you both enough to make it," Dot said dryly, then turned back to Dani. "They shouldn't have used your name."

The shift hit like a split seam tearing open. Dani's chest burned, shock sparking into something sharper.

"Yeah," she said, voice low and clipped. "I didn't even know until Chanice read it in the paper, then told me Gavin used it on air."

Her words trembled at the edges, not with weakness but with the strain of keeping herself reined in. Her pulse hammered at her temples.

Chanice's sidelong glance was quiet, alert.

"I heard it first on WKNS," Dot muttered.

"I know he's a reporter, but come on," Dani said, her words tumbling faster now. "I'm a teacher, for God's sake. The parents are going to lose it. Mr. Herring's already paranoid about the school's image. What if this blows up?"

"You're a person, not just a teacher. It's not like you killed him, right?" Dot raised an eyebrow, daring Dani to disagree. "And as for Gavin, are you saying he used your name to juice up his exclusive?"

"I don't know," Dani snapped, then winced at her tone. She drew in a breath, trying to steady herself, but her fingers still dug into the lounge chair. "I thought we had something. I don't even know what. But now it feels like he used me."

Chanice reached over, brushing Dani's arm. "Girl, he messed up. Like Toss-Out-His-Number messed up."

Dot nodded knowingly over the rim of her tea. "Classic man move. Asks for your help, then does what he wants."

Dani let out a shaky breath. Her voice softened, but her eyes still burned. "I keep replaying it. The way he looked at me before I left, like he cared. He even stepped in front of me when they uncovered the body, like he was trying to shield me. Told me I didn't have to stay."

Chanice tilted her head. "That doesn't sound like a guy using you. More like a guy trying to keep you from breaking."

But then, nothing.

Dani's jaw tightened.

No call. No text. Not even a "Hey, you good after discovering a dead body together?"

Dot set her cup down, frowning. "He should've checked in. No excuse. But some men go quiet when they care. Doesn't mean it feels any better."

"Guess I'm only worth something when I'm part of the story."

Chanice snorted. "If he can't see you're the headline, then he needs new glasses."

Dot cut a slice of banana bread, the steam curling up like comfort itself.

She slid it toward Dani. "Eat," she ordered. "Then if you still want to torch his résumé, I'll loan you Arthur's propane torch."

The bread didn't fix anything, but it helped.

Dani managed a faint smile. "You mean your husband? The man who won't even let you touch his grill tongs?"

"Mm-hm." Dot nodded solemnly. "That's the one."

"Wow." Dani arched an eyebrow. "You're really offering me top-shelf vengeance."

"Only for crimes of the heart." Dot's smirk could have sliced butter.

Chanice snorted. "Arthur would notice that torch was gone before dinner."

"He'd live," Dot shrugged. "We've been married thirty years. The man's survived worse."

That cracked a smile from Dani. "Damn. Remind me never to cross you."

Dot's look was playful but edged with knowing. "Honey, the secret is patience... and a sharp memory."

Dani sighed. "Why is it that whenever things finally start going well, poof. Dead air. Like tuning into a busted radio station."

"Because men are the emotional equivalent of the internet." Chanice smirked. "Takes forever to connect, and the line always drops right when it gets good."

Dot let out a low chuckle. "Don't forget the loading screen of excuses"

Dani's smile flickered, thin and tired. "Yeah, well, Gavin crashed like bad tech. Remind me again why we bother?"

Chanice only shrugged. "Hormones. And fairy tales."

With a sly grin, Dot added, "Oh, men have their uses. Built-in toys."

Their laughter carried bright across the pool.

But Dani's chest still soured with the truth. "Gavin and I didn't get that far."

Leaning in, Dot's voice went dry. "He probably couldn't find your front door if you lit it up with sparklers and handed him a map."

"Please." Chanice snorted. "Gavin's got that voice and those arms, but I bet he's packing a floppy disk"

The laughter faded, leaving silence in its wake. Dani's foot stilled. Chanice's smile softened. Even Dot's gaze drifted, distant.

The pool's surface shimmered. Someone had died. And whatever came next, they all felt it was going to change everything.

"It's in the obits," Dot said. "The family must've submitted it right after the ID went public. Maybe they'd already written it and were just waiting for confirmation."

Chanice nodded slowly. "Guess that makes sense. If he'd been missing for weeks."

Flipping through the paper, Dani found the obituaries. Near the bottom of the page, two brief sentences:

"Carl M. Rendell, 57, died May 11, 1996. A graveside service will be held at 1 p.m. on Wednesday in the Princess Anne Memorial Park.".

Chanice whistled. "How did they make arrangements so quickly?"

"I'm surprised the police released the body," Dot drawled.

"Strange," Dani murmured, more to herself than the others.

A splash cracked through the humid air, sending ripples across the pool. Ice clinked in Dot's thermos as she lifted it to her lips.

Dani stared at the obituary, her gaze unfocused. Questions spun restlessly, circling like a fly behind glass.

Who was Carl Rendell, really?

Why had he stormed into the school?

Had he chosen her deliberately?

And who killed him, then dumped his body in the bay?

Her chest tightened. Relaxation was impossible; every breath just sharpened the questions. All those years of Murder, She Wrote reruns hadn't prepared her for this. Real life was raw, frightening, full of loose ends.

Still, she pictured Angela Lansbury's calm, steady gaze.

What would Jessica do?

She wouldn't sit by the pool eating banana bread while the clues piled up. Jessica would be out there visiting scenes, asking questions, noticing what no one else did.

Dani's fingers twisted the armrest.

Her throat felt dry, like she'd swallowed pool water the wrong way.

She looked at Chanice and Dot, flipping magazines and sipping iced tea like it was just another lazy Sunday.

But it wasn't. Not for her.

Rendell had come to her for a reason. She didn't know why, but she wasn't going to ignore it. She'd helped recover his body. Now she had to help uncover the truth.

Dani licked her lips. "So," her voice came out louder than she expected, "I think I'm gonna go to the funeral."

Chanice lowered her paper an inch, one brow arching. "You trying to catch a killer," she asked, "or audition for Dateline?"

Dani smirked, but it fizzled almost immediately. "Neither. I just…" She glanced back at the obituary. "Maybe if I go, I'll see something. Someone acting strange."

Dot and Chanice exchanged a look before Dot snorted and tapped the side of her thermos with a lacquered nail. "Please tell me you're not gonna show up in all black, hiding behind the shrubs with binoculars."

"I'm not being dramatic," Dani muttered, though even she wasn't sure that was true. "It's just, Rendell came to the school. He asked for me by name. And now he turns up dead on Clean the Bay Day"

Chanice straightened, folding her newspaper aside. "You're serious?"

Dani nodded, hesitant at first, then firmer. "Yeah. I didn't think much of it then, but now…" Her voice faltered. "Now it doesn't feel random. What if I was the last person to see him alive?"

Silence pressed in. Even the kids at the far end of the pool seemed quieter, their laughter muffled by tile and by the weight of Dani's words.

"Maybe Brian's parents will be there," she added softly, almost to herself. "I still haven't reached them."

Chanice arched a brow. "So, you're planning to, what? Ambush grieving relatives at the funeral?"

Dani's jaw tightened. "I just want to see who shows up. No one will think it's strange. I did help recover the body."

Dot leaned back in her lounger, crossing her arms. "I'll go with you."

Dani blinked. "Really?"

Dot nodded. "I taught Rendell back in the day. And Brian's mother, too. So, if anyone asks, I've got a built-in excuse. Plus," she gave Dani a look, "I can keep you out of trouble."

A half-smile tugged at Dani's mouth. She didn't know what she expected to find at the funeral: closure, answers, maybe just a flicker in someone's eyes that confirmed her instincts.

All she knew was she had to go. Pretending it hadn't happened wasn't an option.

Chanice sighed, shaking her head. "Lord helps the killer with the two of you at that gravesite."

Dani didn't laugh. She couldn't. She had to see this through.

Because Rendell had come to her.

Because someone had silenced him.

And because the dead still deserved to be heard, even if she had to be the one to listen.

Chapter Twelve

Yesterday's storm passed, leaving everything outside washed out and gray. Late-afternoon light crept through the windows and settled over the apartment like dust. Shadows stretched across the hardwood, and the air still carried the faint metallic tang of rain.

She'd spent Memorial Day catching up on shopping and laundry, though neither chore had lifted the heaviness in her chest. Sleep had been fitful, broken by haunting dreams. Each time she woke, the memory of finding the body clung to her.

Two days had passed since Clean the Bay Day, and she still felt the ache in her arms from hauling that soggy raft. Her muscles protested with every stretch and shift, a constant reminder that Carl wasn't done with her yet.

Now she sat cross-legged on the living room floor, encircled by legal pads, manila folders, highlighters, and a battered copy of The Canterbury Tales, bristling with sticky notes. A blue pen clung, forgotten, behind her ear.

To anyone watching, she looked like a teacher prepping for the week ahead. But Dani wasn't building a syllabus. She was building a timeline.

Trying to stitch order out of chaos,

Shakespeare sprawled across her most crucial folder, Rendell, chin perched imperiously as if guarding state secrets.

Every attempt to move him earned only a lazy stretch and a blink. Roz, meanwhile, swatted highlighters under the couch, uninterested in their importance.

The pages around her were a sprawl of crossed-out timelines, names underlined to oblivion, arrows looping between dates like a conspiracy web.

Still, the story refused to snap into place. The harder she pressed, the more jagged the pieces became.

Her fingers tapped a restless rhythm against her notebook.

Every time she blinked, the images returned: reeds tugging at her legs, the sour rot of canvas, waterlogged skin against her hands.

She told herself she was organizing facts, but really, she was just trying to quiet the buzzing in her chest. To prove that something, anything, still made sense.

Mid-sentence, halfway through rewriting a note she'd already scrawled twice before, the knock came.

Three firm raps.

Like punctuation.

Her pen froze.

She hadn't checked her answering machine all day. She hadn't needed to. If Gavin had called, she would have felt it.

The knock came again.

Same rhythm. Familiar.

Tightening something low in her chest.

Her mind urged her to stay still, let the silence win. But her instincts whispered otherwise.

It was Gavin.

Still, she sat motionless, pulse ticking upward, anger and curiosity tangling in her ribs. She didn't want to see him, not after the radio stunt, not after days of silence.

And yet, she wanted answers.

She stared at the mess on the floor for a beat.

Then moved fast.

The papers went first, shuffled into a manila folder and crammed beneath a cushion. Chaucer followed, buried in a tote bag and slid out of sight behind the couch. Highlighters, sticky notes, all swept into the end table drawer, the snap of wood sharper than she meant.

She didn't stop to question it.

Maybe she didn't want him to see how deep she'd gone.

Maybe she just didn't trust him.

She pushed to her feet, wiping damp palms on her shorts. Her bun had collapsed hours ago, stray pins poking at her scalp. A neon sticky note clung to her ankle like a brand.

She left it and crossed the room, heart in her throat, and opened the door.

Chapter Thirteen

Gavin stood just beyond the screen, hands stuffed awkwardly into the back pockets of worn jeans slung low on his hips.

His gray Georgetown T-shirt stretched across his chest, the collar frayed. Damp hair curled at the edges, like he'd run wet hands through it instead of using a towel.

He looked up. "Hey. Before you throw me down the stairs."

She arched a brow.

"I brought peace offerings." He lifted a bakery box like a white flag. "Sugar and cinnamon. Plaza Bakery."

The crease between his brows, the way his eyes searched hers, tightened something low in her belly. She wanted to slam the door, then open it just to kiss him.

Her arms stayed crossed.

"You think cinnamon rolls make up for blasting my name to half the city and linking me to a homicide?"

His jaw ticked. "You're right. I shouldn't have said it. It was not only inconsiderate, it was dangerous."

She stared at him, waiting.

"I should've asked. Or at least warned you." He exhaled.

"Is that an apology?"

He steadied the box against his side, like it mattered too. "It's a start. I can do better if you'll let me."

"Good. Because I'm a teacher. I grade these things."

A faint smile curved his mouth. "What am I working with, a C-minus?"

"D territory," she said flatly. "But you brought carbs, so I'll consider extra credit."

"Should I write an essay?"

"That depends." She stepped back a fraction. "Do they have cream cheese frosting, or are you wasting my time?"

He let out a breath, half laugh, half relief. "God bless the curve."

She didn't smile, not quite. But she opened the door wider. "Come in. If they're stale, you're getting an F."

He brushed her arm as he passed. "Noted. Though I should warn you, I still don't get semicolons."

"Then it's a good thing I'm not writing your obituary."

He sank onto the couch, bakery box balanced on his knees. She hovered by the counter, arms folded, foot hooked behind her like she was pinning herself in place. An ache pressed behind her eyes; she hadn't slept, and food was the last thing she wanted.

Roz cracked one eye from her nest by the folders, yawned, and went back under. Shakespeare sprawled across her notes like a furry landmine.

As Gavin leaned forward, hand extended in cautious truce, the cat narrowed his eyes and hissed.

Gavin jerked back. "Okay. Message received."

Dani didn't blink. "He hisses at phonies."

"Look, Dani, I wasn't going to use your name, but my station manager wouldn't air the story without all the volunteers' names. I meant to call, but then things went crazy."

"Crazy," she echoed, flatly. "How convenient."

Gavin exhaled but didn't look away. "My brother's wife went into labor weeks early. The baby's fine now, but they needed help with the older kids. I drove to Richmond and stayed until things stabilized."

"I'm glad the baby's okay. But tell me, do they not have phones in Richmond?" She leaned against the counter, arms tight across her chest.

"I called. You didn't pick up."

"I have an answering machine."

"I know." His hand raked the back of his neck. "I didn't know what to say."

"How about, 'Sorry for using your name on the air like an idiot. And also for vanishing after flirting with you all day.'"

"Right." He gave a short, humorless laugh, then straightened. "I'm sorry for using your name on the air like an idiot. And also for vanishing after flirting with you all day."

Her eyes narrowed. "You don't get credit for parroting me."

He lifted the white box like a shield. "I brought pastry."

"You brought guilt carbs. Not the same."

A faint smile tugged at his mouth, but it didn't reach his eyes.

"You're still mad," he said finally.

She nodded once. "And your time's up."

He looked down, fingers worrying the hem of his T-shirt. "Okay." He shifted to stand, shoulders tight, jaw set, not angry, just resigned.

And somehow, that was worse.

It would've been easier if he'd gotten defensive, if he'd smirked and spun it in that reporter's voice. Then she could've snapped back, slammed the door, felt righteous. But he didn't. He just accepted it.

And that made her falter.

Her arms dropped. "I felt like you used me," she said, the words rough, smaller now, but no less true. She didn't add that she'd replayed every moment, waiting for the phone to ring.

His gaze lifted, eyes locking on hers with a heat that stopped her breath.

"I'm sorry," he said again, voice low. "I should've looked out for you. I wasn't thinking about your safety, and that's on me. I never meant to make you feel used, but I know intent doesn't erase the damage."

And there it was, that flutter behind her ribs, the one that made forgiveness too easy.

She exhaled and stepped forward. Bare feet silent against the wood, she flipped open the pastry box. The smell of cinnamon and sugar spilled out, warm as a bribe.

"Apology accepted," she said, tearing into a roll. "But don't get smug. I can handle myself. The cinnamon just makes forgiveness taste sweeter. You're still on probation."

Gavin leaned back against the couch with a sigh, like he'd been holding it since he knocked. "Small victories."

Dani didn't look at him right away. She bit into the roll, chewed, and let the silence stretch long enough to remind him he was lucky she hadn't slammed the door in his face.

"Dinner? As part of my ongoing groveling tour?"

Her brow lifted. "A whole dinner? This your idea of buying a retrial?"

"Bribing the judge with seafood and charm."

She licked cinnamon sugar from her thumb.

"Tempting. But I picked up oysters from Bonny and Sons and planned to cook them tonight."

That surprised him.

"Oysters?"

"I had a craving. Salty, unpredictable, and a total train wreck if you mishandle them." She tilted her head.

"Ring a bell?" Gavin leaned forward, elbows on his knees.

"Are you inviting me to your messy dinner?"

She hesitated just long enough to make him sweat. "Yeah. But you're shucking."

His grin broke wide. "Deal."

From the floor, Shakespeare let out a dramatic meow and stretched like he'd just woken from centuries of slumber.

With deliberate disdain, he padded to the couch, paused at Gavin's feet, and after a long, silent standoff, leapt onto his lap like a king bestowing favor.

Gavin froze. "Is this... acceptance?"

"They're probably just hungry," Dani said with a raised brow.

Rosalind, quieter and softer, curled around Gavin's ankles, butted his shin with quiet authority.

"You're being evaluated," Dani warned, already heading for the kitchen. "They don't let just anyone stay for dinner."

"I figured." Gavin studied Shakespeare. "What's the protocol? Tribute? Felt mouse? Catnip?"

"You wish. They've bitten my exes before."

Shakespeare hopped to the arm of the couch, fixed Gavin with an unblinking stare, and sneezed.

Gavin blinked. "That feels like a warning."

Dani snorted, pulling oysters from the fridge. She set out a cutting board, a lemon, and a knife.

Gavin gently relocated Shakespeare to the floor and wandered over.

They moved around each other like awkward dance partners, clumsy at first, then finding a rhythm. She handed him an oyster knife, watching as he cracked the shells with a mix of determination and vengeance.

"They offend you personally?" she asked, slicing tomatoes, her knife tapping in a steady rhythm.

"Just making sure they know who's boss." He winced as brine splashed his shirt.

Rosalind circled their ankles like a tiny kitchen supervisor, while Shakespeare claimed a chair to observe, tail flicking lazily.

Dani jerked her chin toward the waiting food bowls. "Feeding duty's yours."

Gavin grinned, scooping them up. "I'll try not to get hissed at this time."

Crouching, he offered Rosalind the first bowl. She accepted with dainty enthusiasm, like a polite dinner guest.

Then came Shakespeare, who stared at him with open suspicion.

"All right, judge," Gavin murmured, holding out a few treats from his palm.

The cat sniffed, paused, then, with the air of someone doing a favor they'd later deny, flicked his tail and licked the treat before settling in to eat.

Gavin straightened with a smug grin. "Boom. Cat diplomacy achieved."

At the stove, Dani sautéed garlic in olive oil, the scent warming the apartment with that sharp, savory bite.

She splashed in white wine, let it hiss, then added butter and parsley.

Barefoot, hair twisted into a messy knot, she moved with practiced ease, wooden spoon in one hand, tasting spoon in the other.

Together, they plated the oysters, Gavin shucking and passing them down while Dani spooned on the bubbling sauce. She added lemon wedges with a final flourish.

"Can you open the wine in the fridge?" she asked, smiling despite herself.

They ate on the small deck, knees brushing under the table, conversation softening into an easy rhythm, radio drama, school gossip, and why his brother thought Sage was a better baby name than Oregano. By the last empty shell, the weight pressing on her chest had eased.

Afterward, they drifted back to the couch.

Dani nudged aside a few legal pads with her socked foot and sank down first.

Gavin slid in beside her, knees brushing again. Shakespeare perched like a sentry on the armrest, tail flicking.

"Thanks for letting me stay," Gavin said quietly.

She gave him a teasing smile. "You're on probation."

"Yeah, but before it was knives. Now it's sarcasm with training wheels."

"I warned you not to get comfortable."

"Never," he murmured, and his hand brushed hers on the cushion as he leaned closer.

Her breath caught, just the whisper of contact, but it jolted through her chest. She glanced down at their fingers, then back up.

His gaze was steady, patient, asking without pushing.

Dani bit her lip. Every reason to pull away crowded her mind, and yet, underneath the noise, was an undeniable pull.

She closed the distance. The kiss was cautious at first, testing, but the moment his mouth responded, warm and insistent, everything inside her unraveled. His hand slid to the back of her neck, tangling in loose strands of hair. The press of his body drew a sharp breath from her lips.

For a heartbeat, the world narrowed to the warmth of him, the taste of him, the steady pull that had been impossible to ignore. Then Dani pulled back slightly, just enough to rest her forehead against his, her chest heaving. Silence wrapped around them, heavy, intimate, broken only by the faint rush of air through the apartment.

"I..." she started, but the words tangled in her throat.

Gavin's thumb brushed her jaw in a slow, grounding motion. "I'll wait," he said softly, as if reading her hesitation and daring her to breathe.

Dani swallowed, heart still racing, and gave the smallest nod. Somewhere outside, a siren wailed, a reminder that the world was still turning, messy and dangerous. But in this small bubble, everything else could wait.

For now.

Chapter Fourteen

Dani slipped out of her third-period class at exactly 11:30 on Wednesday, leaving her students absorbed in a quiet writing assignment.

A lively substitute, more sprite than adult, floated through the room, offering help and encouragement with gentle patience.

Closing the door softly behind her, Dani stepped into the still hallway. She adjusted the strap of her bag and started toward the office, her footsteps echoing faintly.

Ready or not, she was on her way to the funeral.

Dot was already at the front desk, leaning against the tall counter as she scrawled her name on the sign-out sheet. The lobby smelled faintly of copier toner and the lemon cleaner the janitor had used an hour earlier. Overhead, the fluorescent lights hummed in their usual off-key chorus, throwing a flat, white glow over the stack of outdated magazines on the waiting chairs.

Dani paused by her mailbox on the way out, catching sight of two pink message slips tucked neatly inside. She skimmed the first with a smile.

"Chanice can't make lunch. Her mentor's dragging her to a loan committee meeting and walking her through monthly reports. Bank management training, apparently."

Dot gave an approving nod. "She's climbing fast."

"I'm proud of her," Dani said, still smiling.

Then she unfolded the second slip, and her smile faded. "Ugh. Mrs. Fens finally called me back after a week, and I missed it. Now I get to play the thrilling game of phone tag."

Dot winced. "Classic."

Dani held up the slip between two fingers, as if more detail might appear in better light. It was frustratingly vague.

Mrs. Fens phoned.

No number. No message.

No promise to call back.

She turned toward the front desk, where the school's gatekeeper sat behind a fortress of sticky notes and intercom wires.

"Mrs. Haley?" Dani asked, holding up the pink slip.

The older woman looked up, glasses low on her nose, silver curls tucked neatly into a helmet-like style. Her lavender cardigan, soft and slightly pilled at the cuffs, gave her an air of warmth and immovability.

A strand of faux pearls caught the light at her collar. "Yes, dear?"

"Did Mrs. Fens say why she was calling?"

Mrs. Haley sighed softly. "Well, dear, I'm not as sharp as I used to be. I don't recall the details, but I did ask if she wanted me to page you. She said no, just left her name, and hung up before I could say goodbye."

"Thanks," Dani said gently, though frustration edged her tone.

"Try catching her at the funeral," Dot murmured. "They'll be there. Carl was her brother, after all."

Dani frowned as they pushed through the heavy glass doors at the front of the school. The late-afternoon air met them with a warm gust, tugging at her jacket. She adjusted her bag higher on her shoulder, pumps clicking against the concrete steps.

"You taught her too, right? What do you know about her?"

Dot gave a small smile, part sympathy, part resolve, as she fell into step beside her. She pulled her scarf tighter around her neck, eyes on the parking lot where the last few cars were pulling out.

"Detective Dani, let's save it for lunch."

They stopped at the Surf Rider, sliding into a vinyl booth by the window, the savory scent of fried seafood already making their mouths water.

A local favorite, the restaurant was cheerfully nautical, wooden beams draped with fishing netting, taxidermized fish, and walls crowded with photos of proud fishermen.

Tall glasses of iced tea sweated on the table as they shared a plate of crab cakes, golden, crisp-edged, and dusted with a hit of Old Bay.

At first, their conversation stayed light: school gossip, students, the latest staff meeting, but the funeral lingered between them.

They traded gossip, tricky students, a colleague's baffling new haircut. But gradually, like the tide easing back from shore, the talk slipped into deeper waters.

"I didn't realize Amanda Fens was Carl's sister right away," Dot said, dabbing delicately at the corner of her mouth with a napkin.

"She married and changed her name, so it took a second to connect the dots. She was two years behind Carl in school."

"Understandable," Dani said with a slow nod, sipping her tea.

Dot leaned back, eyes narrowing in thought. "Honestly, I don't remember much about her. Quiet girl, kept to herself. Never made an ounce of trouble."

She gave a dry chuckle. "I do remember feeling relieved. After teaching Carl, I'd braced for another Rendell drama, attitude, mountains of referral paperwork. But Amanda was different. A little scatterbrained, maybe, but harmless."

"Did you ever meet their parents?" Dani asked, swirling the ice in her glass.

"You know, I don't think I did." Dot chuckled. "But now that I'm thinking about it, I did teach his cousin Denny. He was probably ten years younger, but the resemblance to Carl was uncanny."

After lunch, they headed west along Laskin Road to Virginia Beach Boulevard, leaving behind the oceanfront clamor, the tourists, beach shops, and boardwalk chatter fading in the rearview mirror.

Turning north onto Great Neck Road, they passed quiet neighborhoods shaded by pines and maples, then low bridges over marshland where reeds swayed in the breeze and herons stood like statues in the shallows.

The entrance to Princess Anne Memorial Park was marked by a modest sign and a stretch of freshly trimmed lawn.

New, as cemeteries go, the grounds were orderly to the point of sterility. No towering angels or ivy-cloaked mausoleums, just rows of flat grave markers sunk into the earth, each bearing little more than a name and two dates.

Dani stepped out of the car, chilled not just by the breeze lingering after the morning's rain but by the blank uniformity around her.

"I want at least a Dearly Beloved Wife on an upright stone," Dot muttered as they started up the gravel path, her heels crunching with indignation.

Dani snorted, walking a step ahead. "Flat markers are easier to mow around. Very practical. Death by landscaping efficiency."

At the crest of a low hill, a dark green funeral tent stood like a silent sentinel. Beneath its scalloped edges, rows of folding chairs were half-filled with mourners, faces etched with uncertainty, voices hushed as if caught between duty and curiosity. Black dresses, gray scarves, and the occasional ill-fitting suit formed a muted sea of grief.

Near the front, a small family huddled close.

Brian stood stiff in a baggy gray suit that hung awkwardly on his frame. Beside him, his father, a man with fiery red hair, was impossible to miss even beneath the old black ball cap he wore. Broad-shouldered and tense, his face was drawn and unreadable as he scanned the crowd.

Next to Brian stood a petite woman with sharp, brittle features, Amanda Fens, Dani guessed, her eyes flicking nervously from face to face, never settling. She clutched Brian's hand so tightly she seemed to sway with the breeze like a kite straining against its string, as if he were the only thing keeping her anchored.

Dot veered off to greet familiar faces, her voice low and warm amid the quiet murmurs. Dani stayed behind, her gaze narrowing on a custodian methodically trimming a nearby plot with a weed whacker.

The mechanical hum sliced through the stillness, a jarring reminder that life went on beyond this somber bubble.

She edged closer to the tent, eyes scanning the neatly arranged chairs, the faces beneath the green canvas. Her mind raced, cataloging every detail: a stiff posture, a furtive glance, a whisper carried on the breeze.

Anything could matter.

Her fingers itched to take notes, but she kept them still at her sides, alert, waiting. Somewhere in this carefully controlled moment was a secret, a thread she could follow.

Her gaze caught a flicker of movement. A man in a dark jacket stood apart from the others, tall and lean, with sallow skin stretched tight over sharp cheekbones. His posture was too rigid, as though he were holding himself unnaturally still. A shadow of stubble framed a mouth set in a hard, unsmiling line. His eyes, cold and calculating, were locked on Brian's dad.

Without a word, he slipped into a seat near the back, deliberately concealing himself behind other mourners. The faint scent of cheap cologne trailed after him, a sharp, synthetic citrus tangled with the heavy bite of cloves, leaving a strange, unsettling edge in the air.

She was still studying him when she felt a familiar presence at her back. Before she could turn, a hand touched her shoulder.

She startled, glancing over to find Gavin close. His blond hair was tousled by the breeze, his black dress shirt open at the collar. A quiet weariness lingered in his eyes, as if he'd been carrying a weight all day.

"Hey," he said softly, his voice rough.

Her pulse jumped. "Hi. I'm glad you came."

Their eyes held. Dani's mind slipped, uninvited, back to Sunday, to the kiss that had begun slow and tentative, a cautious question that became an answer. It had deepened into heated touches and whispered promises, the kind that left fingerprints on her thoughts. Even now, the memory sent warmth curling low in her belly.

He'd pulled away eventually, breathless, murmuring with regret, "I have to be up early. It's a school night."

She'd nodded, understanding, though a selfish part of her had wanted to pull him back.

Later, he'd called just to say goodnight. Somehow, one goodnight stretched into another, and they found themselves laughing over small confessions, favorite songs, and childhood embarrassments. His voice dipped lower when he teased her, and she caught herself smiling in the dark, twirling the phone cord around her finger. By the time they realized it was past midnight, she felt she knew him in ways that surprised her.

Now Gavin gave her a small, knowing nod, and she returned it with a quiet smile, a silent acknowledgment of what still simmered beneath the surface.

A woman in a black minister's robe stepped forward, her presence quiet but commanding. Her salt-and-pepper curls were pulled into a low twist, and fine lines framed her steady eyes. She carried a worn, leather-bound Bible, its edges softened by years of use.

When she spoke, her voice was calm and even, lifted by the faint breeze stirring the tent canopy.

"Dearly beloved," she began, "we are gathered here today not just to lay Carl Michael Rendell to rest, but to remember him as a neighbor, a brother, a friend, a servant of the church."

Dani stood at the back with Gavin beside her, close, but not crowding. His hand hovered just behind hers, not touching but near enough for her to feel its warmth. His presence was steady, more comforting than she wanted to admit.

"I knew Carl from his years of service to this church," the minister continued. "He was a good listener, deeply committed, never afraid to speak the truth as he saw it. He led us through difficult times, especially during the push to bring prayer back into public schools."

A breeze lifted the hem of Dani's black dress. Gavin leaned slightly closer, his body angled toward hers.

"He was also our treasurer, and he carried out that responsibility with care," the minister said, her voice warm but firm, carrying easily to the edges of the tent. "Every number added up. Every record was in order."

A quiet rustle passed through the mourners. Dani caught a flicker of disbelief in Amanda Fenz's posture.

Her brows drew together, lips parting as if she might speak. She glanced at the man beside her, her husband, who gave the slightest shake of his head. Amanda swallowed whatever protest had risen and dropped her gaze, fingers tightening on Brian's shoulder.

At the front, the minister folded her hands. "At this time, I'd like to invite anyone who wishes to share a memory of Carl. I know Samuel Watson wanted to say a few words."

A man in a tailored charcoal suit stepped forward. In his mid-sixties, with a neatly trimmed salt-and-pepper beard, he carried himself with quiet dignity. Taking a breath, he addressed the mourners.

"Carl was a quiet guy," Samuel began, his voice steady but tinged with something personal. "But he had this way of being exactly where you needed him, right when you needed him. I worked with him at the middle school on Lynnhaven Road. And he wasn't just the night custodian, he was the one who stayed behind to tighten a desk leg or mop up a spill no one else admitted to. He didn't make a show of it; he just got it done. No complaints, no fuss. That was Carl."

Dani blinked at the mention of the school.

That was new. She hadn't known Carl had worked for the district.

For someone so deeply tied to the church, she wouldn't have expected him to take a custodial job in a public school. Was this before or during the campaign to bring prayer back?

It didn't quite line up, unless the campaign started after he left the school. Or maybe because of it.

Samuel's voice cracked, but he pressed on. "He gave what most of us hold back, his time. I never asked where he got the money; none of us did. But somehow, Carl always managed to donate, to the church fund, the youth program, the food pantry. He never wanted recognition or big announcements, just folded bills slipped into envelopes, groceries left on porches, gas tanks mysteriously filled."

He paused, swallowing hard. "And it wasn't just money. If someone's car wouldn't start, Carl showed up with jumper cables. If a kid needed a ride home from basketball practice, he was already there. He was always there."

Samuel blinked a few times, then gave a weary smile. "I'll miss his laugh, loud and sudden, like it surprised even him. And I'll miss seeing him on the back steps of the church before sunrise, cradling that old metal thermos, steam rising as he watched the sky shift from black to blue."

He gave a final nod. "Rest well, Carl."

Something shifted in Dani's chest, something she hadn't expected. She'd only known Carl Rendell through a narrow lens. But here, in Samuel's words, Carl became someone else entirely. A man who gave his time without asking for thanks. A man who saw what needed to be done and simply did it.

How many versions of a person could exist at once?

The thought unsettled her, made her want to dig deeper, past what was on paper, past what people were willing to say aloud.

As Samuel returned to his seat, the minister stepped forward again. "We ask for justice and for peace. May Carl's memory guide us, and may his loss not pass unacknowledged. Someone took him from this world, but his spirit remains among us."

The ceremony continued.

Ashes to ashes. Dust to dust.

The family stepped forward in silence.

Amanda, pale and trembling, laid a white lily on the casket, her hand lingering a moment too long. Brian hovered close, protective but uncertain, his gaze darting between his mother and the crowd.

Beside them, Brian's father moved stiffly. He bent to place a single red rose on the casket, his jaw tight, eyes dry. Straightening, he brushed at the sleeve of his dark jacket, an unnecessary gesture, then stepped back without a word, expression hidden beneath the brim of his ball cap.

When the final prayer ended, mourners drifted quietly toward their cars. Chairs scraped against the grass, low murmurs rose, and the breeze rustled the edges of the tent.

"Gavin," Dani whispered. "Look."

Off to the side, Brian stood with his parents. His father's jaw was tight as he spoke, voice low. Whatever he said made Amanda's shoulders tense and Brian stiffen, as if scolded.

"Do you know who he is?" Gavin asked.

Dani nodded slightly, her gaze never leaving the trio. "I think that's Carl's brother-in-law."

"I don't like how he's talking to them," Gavin muttered.

Amanda gave a quick nod at whatever was said, then caught Brian's arm. Together, they moved off in haste, heads bowed, avoiding eye contact as they made for a weathered brown sedan parked beneath a live oak.

"That was fast," Gavin murmured, leaning closer. "Like they were told to clear out."

"Maybe," Dani said. "Oh, look, he's not done."

"Who's that?" Gavin asked, eyes narrowing.

The man in the dark jacket was striding toward Brian's dad, his steps quick and sharp. His gestures were agitated, jabbing the air, while the other man's face stayed flat, unreadable. For a moment, they stood nearly nose to nose, their exchange terse and low.

"I don't know," Dani said, her tone careful. "But I'd bet money he's not here just to pay respects."

Both men turned away and climbed into a beige pickup parked a short distance off. As it rolled down the gravel drive, Dani caught a glimpse of the faded logo on the door

Crandall Packing Company – Virginia Beach.

"That name mean anything to you?" Gavin asked.

"No," Dani said, her voice tight.

Silence settled between them as they watched the last of the mourners drift away. The tent flapped softly in the breeze, its green canopy sagging now that the weight of the ceremony was gone.

After a moment, Gavin shifted beside her, uncertain. "I've got to get back to work. Can I call you later?"

"I'd like that," Dani replied, her gaze still tracing the thinning crowd.

Before leaving, Gavin stepped closer. His eyes met hers, steady, grounding, something warm cutting through the chill that had settled over her. He leaned in and brushed a brief kiss against her temple.

"Take care," he murmured.

"You too."

And then he was gone.

Dot appeared a few moments later, brushing her palms down the legs of her slacks.

"Sorry I wandered off," Dot said as she rejoined her. "I saw a couple of ladies I hadn't seen since my mother's funeral. Turns out they knew Carl's parents back then."

She lowered her voice, leaning in. "They said the Rendells were the perfect couple on the surface, but there were always whispers about trouble behind closed doors. Money problems. And something about a scandal involving Carl's father that never made the papers."

Dani's brow arched. "What kind of scandal?"

"I'm not sure yet," Dot said, straightening her scarf. "But I'll put some feelers out and see what turns up."

She hesitated, glancing toward the road where the last cars were pulling away. "Oh, and one of them asked about Denny. Apparently no one's seen him in weeks."

Dani slowed, her hand brushing the edge of the car door. Dot caught the hesitation instantly, following her gaze.

Amanda stood a few yards away, her face pale beneath the shifting shade of the oak. The wind teased strands of hair loose from her bun, and she clutched her purse with both hands, knuckles white against the strap.

"Mrs. Fenz?" Dani asked carefully.

Amanda blinked, as if startled by the sound of her name. "You, you're Dani Willis, right? From the middle school?"

"Yes."

Amanda took another step closer, glancing around as though making sure they were alone. Her voice trembled. "I shouldn't be here. I just, there's something I need to tell you. About Carl."

Dot exchanged a quick look with Dani, the kind that spoke volumes: tread lightly.

"What about him?" Dani asked.

Amanda's gaze flicked toward the tent, now empty but for the caretakers dismantling chairs. "Not here," she whispered. "Someone's watching."

She turned back toward the sedan, eyes wide with fear, and before Dani could respond, she was already retreating, heels crunching on gravel, dress whipping in the wind, until the car door shut and the engine roared to life.

The sedan pulled away, taillights flaring red against the pale gray afternoon.

Dot exhaled. "Well," she said softly, "that didn't feel like a social call.".

"Thank you for coming. I'm sorry I didn't speak earlier," she said, her voice thin and uncertain. "Brian just told me who you were. I'm Amanda Fenz. You've been trying to reach me?"

She didn't ask why. The question hung unspoken.

Dani stepped forward, afraid the woman might bolt.

Amanda's unease was palpable. "Yes. I assume you know your brother came to see me at school."

Amanda cut in. "What? No. Why?" Her voice faltered as her gaze darted back toward Brian and the safety of the car. Her fingers twisted together, as if she were unraveling herself.

"Well," Dani said gently, "he wanted me to give Brian an alternative assignment, so he wouldn't have to read a section of The Canterbury Tales."

Amanda blinked, visibly confused. "That doesn't sound like Carl. He was offended by it?" She stared past Dani toward the fresh grave, as if the answers might still be buried there.

Dani softened. "I didn't mean to bring this up at his funeral. Maybe we should talk later."

But Amanda shook her head quickly, eyes fixed on the burial site.

When she spoke again, her voice was firmer, though her gaze never lifted to Dani's. "That won't be necessary, Ms. Jones. I have no problem with what Brian is reading in class. He doesn't need alternate assignments."

She turned abruptly and walked back to the brown sedan, her steps uneven on the gravel. Sliding into the driver's seat, she pulled the door shut. A beat passed. Then the engine roared to life, and the car spat gravel as it sped down the narrow road.

Dani and Dot stood watching, the silence between them thick with unspoken questions.

Dani exhaled as she slid behind the wheel. "Well, that solves that."

"Did she seem scared to you?" Dot asked, settling into her seat with a soft sigh.

"She's probably shaken," Dani said, though her voice lacked conviction. "Her brother was murdered."

Dot didn't answer right away. Her gaze lingered on the grave, where the crew had begun lowering the casket and filling the earth.

139

"I'm not so sure," she said finally.

"Did you see her looking at the grave? Like she expected Carl to jump out of it?"

"Maybe she's still hoping it's a bad dream." Even as Dani spoke, the words tasted hollow.

"Maybe." Dot's tone was flat, edged with something unsettled.

That's when it struck Dani, maybe Amanda's fear didn't come from shock or grief, but from something older. Deeper.

Skeletons in the family closet, hidden behind Sunday-best smiles.

She thought back to Amanda and Brian at the service, Amanda's hand clamped on her son's shoulder. Not comforting him, but holding them together. As if she were afraid to let him go.

And Dani wanted to know why.

Chapter Fifteen

The Saturday after the funeral, Gavin took Dani to a hole-in-the-wall Chinese restaurant. The tables were greasy, the menus sticky, but the dumplings more than made up for it.

Afterward, they wandered through the Marine Science Museum, drifting past glowing fish tanks and the hushed stillness of the salt-marsh exhibit.

By the time he pulled into his driveway, the sun was low, casting a soft gold over everything. His brick ranch sat tucked beneath two sprawling oaks, their branches creaking gently in the wind.

"This is it," Gavin said, nudging the screen door open with his foot as Dani stepped onto the porch. Wind chimes tinkled overhead, and the wicker bench groaned, as if to greet her.

He gave a sheepish smile. "My very own slice of 1960s suburbia. Try not to be too dazzled."

Dani arched a brow. "So, mid-century architecture. Do you have shag carpeting?"

"Show some respect for the era," he teased, leading her through the narrow living room. "Hardwood's original. The kitchen's barely been updated since the Cold War. And yes, the bathroom is exactly as beige as you're imagining."

"God, I knew you were hiding a secret beige life."

He shot her a sideways glance. "Just wait."

They moved to the back of the house, Dani's tennis shoes whisper-quiet on the worn floorboards. Gavin slid open the glass door, ushering her into a sun-drenched room where wide windows opened to the warm spring air.

"Okay," Dani said as she stepped inside, the breeze catching the hem of her tank dress and teasing it against her bare legs.

A fitted T-shirt clung beneath, soft against her arms.

She turned in a slow circle, taking it all in.

"This is nice. I take back what I said."

"See? This is where the magic happens," Gavin said, flopping into a glider and propping his feet on a mismatched ottoman.

The sunroom stretched wide across the back of the house, glowing with the golden light of early evening. Its paneled ceiling bore water stains from storms past, but a ceiling fan spun lazily overhead.

Potted plants crowded the windowsills and corners: spindly spider plants, a half-dead fern, and a terracotta pot that seemed to hold nothing but dry dirt. The concrete floor was softened here and there by woven rugs tossed down like afterthoughts.

"I sit here, ignore deadlines, drink too much coffee, and pretend I know how to grow basil," he added, waving at the barren pot.

"That's basil?" she asked.

"I own a pot with seeds. The basil part is still theoretical."

She laughed low and warm, then eased into the wicker chair across from him, its frame groaning in protest.

Above them, a squirrel scurried across the roof, claws scratching at the shingles before it paused to peer down through the screen, like a nosy neighbor.

Just beyond the porch, birds splashed in the birdbath, scattering droplets into the air like confetti.

In the distance, a lawn mower sputtered, coughed, then died, leaving behind a hush that wrapped around the sunroom.

Gavin watched her settle in, then patted the cushion beside him. "That chair's rude. Always groans when someone sits in it. Come over here; mine's much more accommodating."

Dani smirked. "I doubt it will hold both of us."

"Please," he said, grinning.

She arched an eyebrow but stood, sauntering over with theatrical reluctance.

"Fine. But if this chair gives out, I'm blaming you and filing a claim with whatever insurance company covers smartass reporters."

"That's fair," Gavin said, still grinning.

She tried to perch on the wide armrest, but he shifted at the last second, pulling her off balance. She landed squarely in his lap with a startled squeak.

"Gavin!" she half-laughed, half-scolded, her hands braced against his chest.

He looked up at her, feigning innocence. "Sorry. Clumsy chair. Must've shifted."

"Uh-huh." She smirked but didn't move.

His hands had already found the curve of her waist, fingers flexing gently. The playful glint in his eyes met the flicker in hers. Her breath caught when his thumb traced lightly along the hem of her shirt.

"Are you always this grabby with your houseguests?" she murmured.

"Only the ones who steal all the good egg rolls and hoard the fortune cookies," he said, voice low.

She tilted her head, her mouth hovering inches from his. "I left you one fortune."

"Yeah," he said. "It told me: Eat another cookie."

"Sorry," she whispered, then kissed him.

At first, it was soft and tentative, both of them testing the waters. But it deepened quickly as heat surged between them. His hand slid up her back, fingers splayed between her shoulder blades as she leaned in, her body pressing close.

Her own hand curled around the back of his neck, fingertips threading into his hair, holding him there. He made a quiet sound, half-sigh, half-growl, and kissed her harder. His mouth moved with growing urgency, and she answered with a hunger that startled her. Tilting her head to draw him deeper, her other hand skimmed the line of his jaw, then down his chest.

The sunroom seemed to dissolve around them, lost in a blur of golden light and shadow. The faint peep of frogs outside was barely audible over the rush of blood in her ears. The scent of warm earth and jasmine curled through the air as his hands roamed lower, anchoring her closer.

When they finally broke apart, breathing hard, she leaned her forehead against his.

"So," she said, voice slightly husky, her fingers idly tracing the collar of his shirt, "this is where you do your best thinking?"

"Right now, I'm thinking about spreading you out on the rug and having my way with you," Gavin murmured, brushing a strand of hair from her cheek.

Dani's breath hitched, a slow smile curling at the edge of her lips. "Is that a promise or a threat?"

Gavin's eyes darkened, a playful grin tugging at his mouth. "Depends. Are you ready to find out?"

Her heartbeat quickened as she tilted her head, eyes sparkling. "You sure you're prepared for that?"

"Absolutely. And I'm counting on you to make it unforgettable."

She smirked, leaning in just enough for him to feel her breath. "Then I guess I better keep kissing you."

His laugh was low in his throat, but his eyes didn't leave hers. "Oh, definitely," he said.

She kissed him again, this time slower, more deliberate. Her fingers curled into the fabric of his shirt as she deepened the kiss, and he responded in kind, his hand sliding up the curve of her spine to pull her closer, until there was no space left between them.

The glider creaked beneath their shifting weight, but neither of them noticed. Gavin's other hand settled at her hip as her lips traced a slow path along the edge of his mouth, then down to his jaw.

He let out a shaky breath. She answered with a smile pressed against his skin.

Her fingers slipped beneath his shirt, grazing the warmth of muscle, then drifting lower.

He caught her wrist gently.

"Dani..." Her name lingered, a tether between restraint and longing.

She drew back just enough to catch his eyes. "You're not backing out on me now, are you?"

His gaze held hers, steady and unflinching, a heat building in the silence. "Not backing out. Just... reminding you where this could lead."

Her fingers curled into the hair on his chest, urging him closer, daring him. "I know exactly where it's going."

For a half-second, he hesitated, the moment teetering on an edge. Then came the exhale, low and surrendering. "Then I'm right there with you."

And then his mouth was on hers, hard and urgent, like he'd been holding back too long. His first tangled in her shirt, hauling her closer until no space remained between them. Her gasp melted into his kiss as the heat surged higher.

She shifted on his lap, sliding to straddle him fully. The hem of her dress rode up her thighs.

The old chair groaned beneath them, one sharp creak, then the crack of a protesting armrest. Neither of them paused.

His hands moved over her like he was memorizing her, every stroke of his fingertips winding the tension tighter, hotter, until it felt ready to snap.

Another loud pop from the wood.

He broke away with a breathless laugh, forehead resting against hers. "This chair's gonna collapse and ruin everything."

"You mentioned something about the floor," she whispered, kissing him again.

"Noted," he murmured, already losing himself in her again.

The feel of him, the urgency, swept her away until a faint noise interrupted, an echo at the edge of awareness, easy to dismiss. Gavin's teeth captured her earlobe, his warm breath light on her throat before he took her mouth again. But it came again, threading into the silence between their breaths, persistent enough to make her falter and pull them both back.

A knock at the front of the house, followed by the rattle of the screen door. Then the doorbell rang, loud, impatient, unmistakable.

"Hey, Gavin, you outside?"

The sudden voice froze them both.

Gavin let his head fall back against the chair with a thud. "You've gotta be kidding me."

Dani bit back a laugh, still half-wrapped around him. "Expecting someone?"

"Not unless you count the universe testing my patience." He eased her off his lap and onto her feet.

Tugging his shirt straight, one hand automatically covered the bulge in his jeans as he shot a glare toward the door.

"Go away!" he shouted.

The sunroom door creaked open, and Marcus strolled in like he owned the place. "I'm gonna get a complex if you keep yelling at me like that," he teased, dropping into the nearest chair.

His detective's uniform was as rumpled as ever, tie loose, collar undone, fatigue etched in the lines of his face. The fading light glinted against his dark skin, but his smile stayed easy.

"Hi, Detective Gates," Dani said, tentative but polite.

"I'm off duty. Call me Marcus." He tipped her a nod. "So, you two got dinner plans?"

Gavin straightened, still flushed from the kiss Marcus had just interrupted. "Plans? Yeah, we had plans. Private ones. You ever heard of knocking?" His voice carried more bite than usual, though the look he shot Dani softened at the edges.

Marcus just smirked, unbothered.

"Seriously," Gavin pressed, "you can't just walk in here like it's your place. Some of us were in the middle of something. Uninvited guests buy the pizza," he muttered finally, though his crooked smile gave him away.

"Fair enough. Pepperoni and supreme?" Marcus disappeared inside to use the phone.

Dani leaned closer to Gavin, lowering her voice. "Is this normal?"

Gavin shook his head. "Marcus doesn't show up in a suit just to hang out."

"So, something's up," Dani murmured.

"Yeah." His mouth curved wryly. "Give it time. He'll spill as soon as the first slice hits his plate."

Chapter Sixteen

The doorbell rang just as the sun slipped below the horizon, painting the sky in watercolor shades of orange and pink. Heat still clung to the porch, and somewhere in the distance, a dog barked.

A minute later, Marcus reappeared from the front door with his spoils: two greasy Domino's boxes stacked in one hand, corners sagging with oil, and a two-liter bottle of Coke Classic tucked under his arm like a football.

He strode into the sunroom wearing the smug grin of a man who believed he'd just made a crucial contribution to civilization.

"Pizza's here," he announced, dropping the boxes onto the glass-top table with theatrical flair. "All the major food groups: bread, cheese, and fat."

Dani smirked as she flipped open a lid. "Ah yes, a balanced meal, just like the food pyramid taught us in school."

"If the FDA had any integrity," Marcus said, slumping into a chair, "pizza would be its own category."

They each grabbed a slice, steam curling off the cheese, and settled into the worn patio chairs. For a few minutes, the sunroom filled with the simple sounds of chewing, soda fizzing, and cardboard rustling. Outside, a lawn mower buzzed in the distance, and someone's radio drifted faintly with Third Eye Blind.

"This crust tastes like it was made during the Cold War," Gavin said, licking sauce from his thumb.

Marcus took a long swig straight from the bottle. "It was. Domino's has been stockpiling these since '85."

"Which makes it authentic," Gavin deadpanned, reaching for another slice. "Like eating your way through a Nirvana B-side."

Dani laughed. "Grungy, undercooked, and somehow still better than half the menu."

Marcus leaned back with a weary sigh, resting the soda bottle on his chest. "Mock all you want; this is peak Friday night cuisine."

Gavin snorted. "All it's missing is Blockbuster and a VHS so worn the tracking lines are permanent."

Marcus grinned. "Careful, I've got Speed and Men in Black in my backpack."

Dani arched a brow, wiping her fingers on a napkin. "Okay, but serious question, did you actually come over for pizza and Keanu Reeves, or is this a drive-by hangout with a hidden agenda?"

Marcus tilted his head, feigning thought. "Maybe I just missed you guys."

Gavin shot him a look. "Carla dump you?"

Marcus lifted his slice in salute. "Yes. But that's not why I'm here." His voice shifted, humor thinning. "Rendell's case is going nowhere. Three weeks in, and every lead's a dead end. His background's spotless, no priors, no flagged accounts, no angry exes, no shady ties. It's like the guy lived in a bubble."

The words cut through the easy hum of conversation.

Gavin froze mid-bite. Dani stilled, her napkin half-folded in her hand.

Casually, she said, "Marcus, did you know Carl Rendell worked nights as a school custodian?"

Marcus narrowed his eyes. "Yeah. Part-time at the church too, until two years ago, when he quit to focus full-time on that prayer-in-school case."

"So…" Dani's tone was measured now, deliberate. "Where'd all the money come from?"

Marcus blinked. "What money? His accounts are practically empty. The church barely paid him minimum wage."

Dani shook her head. "His friend at the funeral said he always had money to help people. Rendell was the guy who always had cash to lend."

Marcus frowned.

Gavin leaned forward, interest sparking. "That doesn't track, unless he had another income or hidden accounts."

"Right," Dani said quickly. "What if he stole the money? Or ran some kind of scam? Think about it: quiet church worker by day, secret swindler by night."

"Whoa, slow down," Marcus cut in, his voice slipping into that calm, detective register. "You can't just throw out accusations. You got any facts to back this up?"

Dani blinked, her brain catching up to her mouth. Heat rushed to her cheeks. "No. Not really. Just a hunch. I've probably read too much Chaucer."

Marcus gave her a long look, equal parts curiosity and caution. "Chaucer?"

"Yeah." Dani shrugged, self-conscious but pressing on. "The Pardoner's Tale. Guy preaches virtue by day, scams people for relic money by night. Hypocrisy wrapped in holiness. Greed rotting everything underneath."

Marcus's brow furrowed, not dismissive, but intent, like he was filing it away.

"I don't know," she said, her voice softer now. "Carl reminded me of the Pardoner. Everyone talks like he was a saint, but sometimes the ones who look most put together are just the best at hiding the cracks."

She hesitated. "And he really had a reaction to that story. It hit a nerve. And honestly, that feels like the thread where Rendell's whole story starts to unravel."

Her voice dropped slightly. "And… you remember those two church fires last year?"

Gavin's eyes narrowed. "Yeah. Both burned to the ground, both conveniently when no one was around."

Dani nodded. "Exactly. And then Carl's church burns too? Maybe it's a coincidence, but it feels like a common thread."

Marcus leaned back, expression easing but thoughtful. "Okay, I see where you're going, but Doran and I checked all this out, and it's a dead end. Besides, I'm off the clock. You got any beer, Gav?"

Gavin snorted. "You know where it is."

Marcus chuckled through a mouthful of pizza, then stood with a grunt, brushing crumbs from his pants. "Don't eat the last slice while I'm gone."

He disappeared into the kitchen, his footsteps fading down the hall.

Gavin leaned back, wiping his hands with a napkin, but his gaze stayed locked on Dani. "You've really been carrying this, haven't you?"

"I can't let it go," she said, her voice tight. "He came to see me at school, and then we pulled his body out of the water. That means something. And those fires… it's like pieces of the same puzzle."

Gavin's jaw tightened. "Dani, I don't want you caught in the middle of this."

"No," she shot back. "He didn't just wander onto my campus by accident. That wasn't random, Gavin. That was unfinished."

"Unfinished?" His voice sharpened, frustration breaking through. "You're talking about putting yourself in danger. This isn't some Scooby-Doo mystery, it's real. It's dangerous. And you're treating it like fate."

Before Dani could answer, Marcus returned with a beer in one hand and another slice in the other. He froze, eyes flicking between them.

"Everything okay?"

Neither spoke.

Marcus eased into his chair and popped the cap, the fizz filling the silence. "Look, I know Rendell's death is eating at you, Dani. I get it. But I told my captain the same thing I'll tell you: we've got nothing. No leads. No motive. Just a dead man."

Dani looked away, her jaw tight. "So that's it? Just call it hopeless? Someone murdered him, Marcus. That doesn't happen without a reason."

Marcus sighed, leaning back as the ceiling fan ticked overhead like a slow metronome. "I'm not giving up," he said, steady. "But you need to let me do my job. Leave the sleuthing to the professionals, Dani. You've already been through enough."

Dani's eyes snapped up, sharp as a blade. "Enough? Enough for who, Marcus? You think because I'm not in uniform I'm powerless? I can handle myself, and I will handle this. Don't tell me to step back."

Silence fell heavy between them, the weight of everything unsaid pressing into the room. Outside, frogs had claimed the night, their chorus rising steady and relentless, like a heartbeat under the dark.

Some stories don't stay buried.

And Dani wasn't finished.

Chapter Seventeen

It wasn't much more instinct than strategy, stitched together with restless energy and too many unanswered questions. As much as Gavin and Marcus wanted her to back off, she couldn't ignore the unease that had been gnawing at her since Carl Rendell's funeral. And, truth be told, part of her fire came from them, the way they'd tried to sideline her, as if she couldn't handle the truth.

That only made her more determined to find it.

The fire. The money. Carl's body, pulled from the Lynnhaven, like something the river had finally decided to give back.

Everyone else seemed ready to move on, to chalk it up as a tragedy and let it fade. But Dani couldn't. Something was wrong, and until she understood what, her grief wouldn't settle.

Students poured out of the school, their voices rising into the afternoon air. Backpacks bounced, sneakers slapped against the sidewalk, and the warm June light gilded everything in gold. Only a few weeks left in the year, and everyone was counting the days until vacation.

She slid her gradebook, lesson plans, and a stack of essays into her tote, slung it over her shoulder, and grabbed her purse.

Dot leaned out of her classroom, a pencil tucked behind her ear. "Heading out early today?" she asked, peering over her glasses.

"Barely," Dani said with a tired smile. "Just trying to escape before someone ropes me into chaperoning something."

Dot grinned. "Smart girl. Got any hot plans with Gavin?"

"Nope. Just me, a stack of essays, and the quiet sob of my red pen."

"Mmhmm," Dot said, unconvinced. "Don't lie to me."

Dani rolled her eyes but didn't deny it. "I thought I'd stop by the Eastern Church of God before heading home."

"Hmm. You sure that's a good idea?"

"Probably not." Dani adjusted the strap on her tote. "But I'm doing it anyway."

Dot tilted her head. "You think someone there's gonna give you what you're looking for?"

Dani gave a humorless smile. "I'm not even sure what I'm looking for."

"Well," Dot said, folding her arms, "sometimes digging too deep turns up things you can't put back."

"Sounds like a fortune cookie."

"Maybe. But sometimes those are right. Just… be careful, honey."

"I'm always careful."

Dot snorted. "No, you're not. That's why I like you."

The humid Virginia air hit her like a damp blanket the moment she stepped outside, thick with honeysuckle and hot asphalt. Cicadas buzzed from the trees, their steady drone a warning that summer was already here. She tossed her things into the back seat of her aging Renault, the upholstery warm to the touch, then climbed in and cranked the A/C.

Traffic on Pacific Avenue was light. Tourists drifted along the sidewalks with ice cream cones and sunburned shoulders, dragging beach towels like banners behind them.

Heading south, Dani passed worn motels and surf shops, then crested the Rudee Inlet Bridge, the sharp smell of fish and diesel flooding in as boats winked in the late sun. Beyond the bridge, General Booth Boulevard stretched out, wide and sun-faded, lined with pines and waterlogged ditches from the last rain.

She drove past the curved white walls of the Marine Science Museum, glowing in the afternoon light.

Just yesterday, she and Gavin had walked this same stretch, wandering past the salt marsh exhibits before ending up back at his house. She could still feel the ghost of his hand at her back, the way his voice dropped when they got close, the way he looked at her, like he already knew how she tasted.

One touch, and she was tangled in his lap like breathing didn't matter.

Intense.

Unexpected.

Very nearly something more, until Marcus barged in. Pizza in hand, full of warnings, killing the mood without even realizing it.

Textbook cockblock. Dani had seriously considered weaponizing a spring roll.

Still, she couldn't stop thinking about Gavin, how he'd looked at her like he wasn't afraid of the fire burning inside her.

Yeah. She wanted to see him again.

And next time, she wasn't stopping at the couch.

She shook her head, dragging her focus back to the road as Hugh Mongous loomed into view, the towering fiberglass gorilla at the Ocean Breeze Waterpark gates, arms stretched in his eternal, cartoonish welcome.

Back in '85, the original statue had burned, a strange local tragedy. No one was hurt, but the whole city mourned. For weeks, flowers piled at the gates like it was a real grave. It was just a mascot, but the fire unsettled people, like something sacred had been lost.

That was the thing about fires: sometimes it wasn't what they destroyed, but what they stirred up.

But the church fire felt different. It left behind not just ash, but unease, and questions didn't burn away easily.

Soon, Dani made the left turn toward Sandbridge, and the city fell behind as the trees closed in. Thickets of pine and wax myrtle framed the two-lane road, sunlight breaking through in restless patterns of gold and shadow.

Her tires hummed against the pavement, a low drone that matched the unease in her chest.

Marcus had told her to let it go.

Gavin said she was chasing shadows.

But Rendell was tied to her now, whether she liked it or not. Instinct whispered louder than reason.

Beyond a leaning fence line, the Eastern Church of God came into view. Just a few weeks ago, it had stood proud in this quiet corner of Virginia Beach, white clapboard siding, a modest steeple, tidy rows of pews. Sunday school classrooms. A nave full of hymns. A narthex that smelled of coffee and donuts.

Now it was a hollowed-out skeleton. The roof had collapsed in a tangle of blackened rafters. The steeple lay shattered across the entryway, its iron bell cracked and half-buried in debris. The sanctuary windows gaped empty, jagged teeth of melted glass clinging to the frames. The faint smell of smoke still lingered, baked into the bricks.

Silence pressed close, broken only by the chirp of cicadas in the nearby trees. Along the foundation, a few wildflowers had sprouted, delicate pink blooms pushing through the cracks.

Dani pulled her car to the edge of the lot and stepped out. Gravel crunched under her sandals as the late-afternoon sun pressed heavy on her shoulders. She squared herself toward the ruins, as if the answers she needed were waiting inside the ashes.

She didn't know how yet, but this place mattered.

A tall, silver-haired man in a short-sleeved shirt and jeans was picking through the wreckage. His face was worn and lined, sweat darkening the fabric across his back. He straightened when he noticed her, shading his eyes against the sun.

"Can I help you, ma'am?"

"I was at the funeral for Carl Rendell and thought…" Dani hesitated, glancing toward the collapsed steeple.

"Not much left here," the man said quietly. "I'm Deacon Frank. Were you close to Carl? I've met a number of his friends, but I don't remember you."

"I'm Danica Jones," she said, brushing a damp strand of hair from her face. "I only met Carl once, but I was there when his body was recovered from the Lynnhaven River. I'm very sorry for your loss."

"Welcome, Ms. Jones."

The voice came from behind her.

Dani turned to see Reverend Wilkins standing near the crumbling sidewalk, framed by the scorched outline of what had once been the church entrance. Tall, with a dignified posture that carried the weight of her flock, she wore a simple, flowered dress that fluttered in the faint breeze. Her silver-streaked hair was pulled into a neat bun, and the deep lines at the corners of her eyes and mouth spoke of both kindness and long endurance.

"Ah, yes. I read about you in the paper, and I remember seeing you at the service," Reverend Wilkins said with a faint, weary smile. "I make a habit of memorizing faces, it helps in my line of work."

Dani returned the smile, then let her gaze drift back to the burned-out shell of the church. "I wanted to see what had happened here."

"It's a hard sight," Deacon Frank said, his voice low, his eyes on the rubble. His mouth pulled downward, as if he were mourning not only Carl, but the very soul of the building itself.

Dani glanced again at the wreckage, her heart tightening. She felt compelled to ease the rawness in the man's voice.

"Will you begin rebuilding soon?"

"There's no money for that," Reverend Wilkins said quietly, her tone steady but edged with finality as she looked over the ruins.

Dani tilted her head. "But Carl was the treasurer. Wouldn't the church's funds be in the bank?"

Deacon Frank's eyes flicked to the minister, then back to Dani. "They were, but Carl kept all the records: ledgers, donation logs, even the insurance paperwork."

Dani turned toward the charred frame of what must have been the office. "So there's no way to verify anything?"

Wilkins exhaled and rubbed the back of her neck. "Not anymore."

Dani looked between them. "Then where does that leave the money?"

Frank answered first. "Carl didn't always tell us everything as it happened."

Wilkins smoothed the front of her dress, her voice measured. "He mentioned setting aside funds for a restoration project, fixing the roof, updating fire alarms. Said he was working on estimates."

A thought snapped into place. "You mean he was holding the cash here? In the church?"

Reverend Wilkins hesitated, her fingers tightening briefly around the edge of her sleeve before she nodded once. "He preferred to keep things close, said it was easier that way. The money might have been here, yes, in cash or checks, waiting to be deposited."

Dani's gaze swept the ruins, the heat pressing down on her shoulders. "So if the records and funds were here, the fire destroyed both."

"Exactly." Wilkins shifted her weight, clasping her hands a little too neatly before her. The pause stretched, heavy and deliberate. Then, almost reluctantly: "Carl's death... there are questions. About the money. About why someone might have wanted him gone."

A faint breeze stirred the ash across the pavement, gritty and restless. Dani's eyes lingered on the wreckage, her mind ticking over the details, unease curling low in her chest.

"It doesn't add up," Dani said slowly. "A treasurer keeping cash and records inside the church?"

Frank shook his head. "Carl was cautious. Some would say secretive."

Wilkins's expression tightened. "That kind of secrecy can protect you, or make you a target."

Dani's jaw hardened. "So someone might've killed him for the money."

Wilkins nodded, grim. "And the fire made sure we may never know."

Silence fell. Somewhere in the charred skeleton, a beam shifted with a low creak. Dani didn't speak. Her gaze stayed on the ruins, but her mind spun, fast and relentless, her instincts prickling.

Reverend Wilkins seemed to sense it. "I know what you're thinking," she said softly, though a fine line had formed between her brows. "But Carl was a good man. He cared for this church. He just held on too tightly."

Dani gave a polite nod. "I should let you get back to your work. Thank you for your time."

Wilkins inclined her head, though a shadow crossed her expression. "Be careful, Ms. Jones. Dig too deep, and you may find yourself in danger."

Dani's smile was tight, almost reflexive. She turned back to her car, but the words stuck. Coming from anyone else, she might have brushed them off as bluster or deflection. But from a minister? The unease hit deeper.

She slid into the driver's seat, her hand pausing on the ignition. Was Reverend Wilkins warning her that someone was watching? Maybe Dani was already closer to the truth than she realized.

The burned skeleton of the church loomed against the sunlight, shadows stretching across its broken frame. Whatever had happened here, it hadn't ended with the fire. A shiver ran through her as she left the ruins.

Winding back toward General Booth Boulevard, the traffic thickened, but Dani's thoughts stayed tangled in the ashes, the fire, the missing money, Carl's death.

Halfway to the beach, Dani swung into a weathered 7-Eleven. A group of teenagers lounged by the ice machine, laughing and shoving each other.

She pulled into a side spot and cut the engine, her eyes catching on the battered phone booth tucked beside a dented ice chest. Inside, a heavy directory hung from a chain, its cover curling with age.

Stepping into the booth, Dani scanned the scratched plexiglass walls, the names, numbers, and declarations of love, most of them misspelled. She sighed, flipped through the dog-eared pages, and found it.:

Rendell, C. M.

Her brows rose.

Only one listing. Apparently, Rendell wasn't a common name in Virginia Beach.

She jotted down the address: 501B 17th Street.

Just as she let the book fall closed, her eye caught on the line above it.

Rendelf, C. 1925B Pacific Avenue.

Rendelf. Odd. Maybe a typo. Maybe not. She copied it, too, before sliding the directory back into place.

Back in the car, she steered toward Seventeenth Street, winding through the narrow grid behind the hotels and boardwalk shops. Old bungalows with wide porches leaned against mini-golf courses and corner pubs.

Five blocks up, she found it. The clapboard siding was cracked and curling, weeds splitting the sidewalk. A rusted bicycle frame slumped against the porch rail, swallowed by ivy. In the yard, a lopsided sign advertised a one-bedroom apartment for rent.

Dani sat there for a moment, her fingers tightening on the wheel. What exactly was she doing? She wasn't a detective. She was a teacher with a tote bag of ungraded essays in the back seat.

And yet, her gaze slid to the crooked rental sign swaying in the breeze.

Maybe it was instinct. Maybe it was stubbornness. Either way, Dani wasn't done yet.

Chapter Eighteen

Dani slid out of the car, steadying her nerves as she slipped on a mask of confidence. The sun sagged low, casting long shadows across the cracked sidewalk. The crooked rental sign creaked in the humid breeze, as if warning her to turn back.

1 BR Apt Available Quiet Tenants Only.

She hesitated for a moment before knocking.

What was she even hoping to find here? A clue left in plain sight? Someone who remembered Carl Rendell as more than a headline?

The door creaked open. A petite woman stood there, cheeks thick with powder, hair curled into a yellow-blond helmet that owed more to dye than genetics. Her smile was polite, even welcoming, but the warmth stopped short of her eyes.

Dani felt it instantly: a faint tension beneath the surface, like a wire pulled too tight. The woman's hand lingered on the doorknob, as if debating whether to let go, her shoulders angled just slightly toward the inside of the house. A trace of perfume clung to the air, sharp and floral, but beneath it, Dani caught a whiff of stale smoke. She didn't need years of detective work to sense it, the woman was guarding something.

"Here to see the apartment?" the woman asked brightly. "It's small, but perfect for you."

"I... um." Dani reeled, caught off guard by the cheery tone. Her brain scrambled for a cover story, something harmless, forgettable. "I, yes. My husband and I are... looking."

The word husband left her mouth before she could stop it. She didn't even have a boyfriend, exactly the kind of panicked lie you regret the second it lands. Gavin would've raised an eyebrow at that one.

Then again, Gavin raised an eyebrow at most of her choices lately.

She braced for suspicion, but none came.

"Oh, it'd make a sweet little love nest," the woman said, unfazed. "I'm Courtney Skylar. I live downstairs with my Ronnie. We like to keep things quiet around here."

Her smile didn't falter. "The last tenant was a nice, quiet fella," she added. "Didn't make a peep, really."

A prickle traced the back of Dani's neck. Quiet could mean respectful, it could also mean invisible and easy to overlook.

Courtney paused just long enough for Dani to notice, then added lightly, "He passed not too long ago. Hope that doesn't bother you."

Dani's stomach tightened. The word passed was wrapped in sweetness, but it crawled across her skin. She hadn't expected the reality to hit so hard. It was one thing to chase a trail of questions; another to stand in the space where the answers had lived.

She forced her voice to stay steady. "He didn't die in the apartment, did he?"

"Oh no, nothing like that." Courtney waved a powdered hand, airy, dismissive. "Come on up. I haven't finished clearing out his things yet, but his family's coming tomorrow. I could have it ready for you by Sunday."

As Dani followed her up the narrow, creaking stairs, she studied the woman's movements. From behind, Courtney walked with careful, deliberate steps, as if the floorboards might betray her balance.

Her fingers, tipped in chipped coral polish, gripped the banister. Her teased blond bun was stiff with spray, towering like a relic from the 1960s. Fragile from behind, Dani guessed she was well into her seventies.

"There are three units in the house. Ronnie and I take the first floor. This apartment has its own entrance," Mrs. Skylar said, pointing to a door at the end of the hall. "We'll go out that way. Now, don't mind the mess, just imagine it cleaned up."

She opened the door with a little flourish, and Dani stepped inside.

Small was an understatement. Two chairs huddled beneath the window, and the bed practically touched the kitchenette, a mini-fridge and a shallow sink squeezed into the corner. The lone window was half-choked by an aging A/C unit that wheezed like an old man catching his breath, pushing out lukewarm air.

A dusty ray of light fell across the room, leading to a narrow door.

"That's the bathroom," Mrs. Skylar said. "Shower, toilet, sink. Door sticks in the humidity."

Dani pictured Carl Rendell's tall frame trying to wedge himself into this space. The thought almost made her laugh—until she noticed the belongings.

A carton half-filled with clothes. A pile of books stacked carelessly beside it.

A few socks and a crumpled T-shirt lay on the carpet, where a dust bunny clung to a chair leg as if the room itself had exhaled and settled into neglect.

Mrs. Skylar caught her glance. Her voice dropped, soft as a confession: "It's a shame about Carl."

Dani's breath snagged. A chill prickled her skin despite the humid air.

"Who?" she asked, the false curiosity scraping her throat on its way out.

"The man who lived here," Mrs. Skylar said, folding her hands neatly in front of her. "Polite. Paid rent on time. Did odd jobs for us, put in those back stairs himself." She nodded toward the hall. "Big man, but gentle. I don't know why someone would've killed him."

Dani kept her face smooth, her tone light. "He was murdered?"

The word hung there, thick as the air in the little room.

"Oh, honey, don't be scared." Mrs. Skylar let out a laugh, though it wavered. "It happened far from here. And with Ronnie and me downstairs, you'll be as safe as can be."

Unease flickered through Dani; her heart thudded once, hard, against her ribs.

"I didn't mean to frighten you," the woman added quickly, twisting a ring around her finger. "Carl was a sweet soul. He prayed with us sometimes."

Something in her voice tugged at Dani, like she was smoothing a blanket over something jagged. Had she seen more than she wanted to admit?

Dani studied her, the faint lines bracketing her mouth, the way her eyes slid just off Dani's gaze. Maybe she was simply being kind. Or maybe she knew more than she let on.

"Do you go to church?" Mrs. Skylar asked suddenly.

Dani blinked at the shift. "Not really."

"Oh." Courtney's smile returned, faint and fixed. She gestured toward the pile near the box. "Carl was very spiritual. Kept his Bible and books right there, always close at hand."

Dani followed the gesture, her gaze catching on the frayed spine of a book perched at the top.

The Canterbury Tales.

Recognition flared like a spark. The battered copy jutted out, its cracked spine unmistakable. Weeks ago, Carl had shoved it in her face, his cheeks blotched red as he ranted about filth and moral decay.

Of course, it made sense. This was his home, his book. But seeing it here, under these circumstances, made her stomach twist.

The memory jolted through her, Carl's voice, low and coiled, each word edged with something brittle and dangerous; his eyes pinning her in place like a specimen. He hadn't just disagreed with the text, he'd taken it as a personal offense, and she'd felt the heat of his anger clinging to her skin long after he left.

Now the book was here.

And Carl was dead.

Her fingers twitched at her sides, wanting to touch it where it sat in plain sight, bold as a dare. She shifted her weight from one foot to the other, edging closer to the shelf under the pretense of glancing around the room. The book seemed to wait for her, its spine catching the thin light.

She drifted nearer, drawn as if it might hold answers.

"Anyway," Courtney sighed, moving toward the window. "The family'll be here tomorrow." She fiddled with the curtain cord, not noticing Dani's inattention.

Dani shifted her purse higher on her shoulder, fingers brushing the strap as if to steady herself. Her weight tilted forward, one foot sliding subtly toward the box before she caught herself. She cleared her throat and pulled back, her eyes darting anywhere but the book. "How much is the rent?" she asked quickly, forcing her gaze away.

"Hundred fifty a week, five fifty a month. Water and electric included; the rest are on you"

Dani fumbled in her purse, the rustle covering the faint scuff of her shoes as she angled a step closer to the shelf. "I wish I had a pen to jot that down."

"I'll fetch you one." Mrs. Skylar smiled brightly, already turning toward the hallway. "Be right back."

The moment her footsteps echoed down the stairs, Dani lunged for the stack. She scanned the titles: The Bible. The Christian's Guide to Healthy Living. Dianetics. The Lion, the Witch and the Wardrobe. The Pilgrim's Progress.

An odd mix, devotion, fantasy, self-improvement.

Her hand hovered, then closed around the Chaucer. The cover was worn smooth, the pages slightly warped. Well read? Well loved? Or just handled too often by a man obsessed with what belonged in a school curriculum?

She rifled quickly through the box: clothes, pots, a cracked mug, a frayed towel. Nothing more. Rising, she realized she was still clutching the book.

The stairs creaked.

Her breath hitched. Without thinking, she slipped the Chaucer into her purse. The spine scraped the zipper; its weight settled at her hip like a secret.

By the time Courtney reappeared with the pen, Dani was scribbling rent figures on the back of a receipt, muttering about discussing it with her husband.

"Please let me know," Mrs. Skylar said cheerfully. "You seem real sweet."

Dani forced a smile, waved, and made a swift retreat down the back stairs. She didn't breathe until she was behind the wheel, one hand gripping the steering wheel, the other pressed to the purse with the stolen book inside.

She waved once more, then drove off, her pulse still thudding.

Chapter Nineteen

Later that evening, Dani crouched at the coffee table, her hair twisted into a messy knot. She wore gray sweatpants and a faded Women of Shakespeare T-shirt, the fabric stretched thin with age. A purple dry-erase marker was tucked behind one ear, and a half-eaten granola bar teetered on the edge of her notebook.

Shakespeare lounged on the back of the sofa, one paw draped lazily over a cushion, while Rosalind perched below him like royalty, watching Dani with regal indifference.

"You know," Dani muttered, taping a notecard labeled **CARL RENDELL MURDERED?** to the top of the oversized graphic organizer she'd smuggled home from school, "if either of you had opposable thumbs, I could really use a research assistant."

Roz blinked.

Shakespeare sneezed.

She sighed and rocked back on her heels, surveying the chaos. A haphazard web of notecards and color-coded Post-its sprawled across the laminated board. Names. Dates. Fragments that didn't quite fit.

One sticky note was sprawled across the center: **Bible, Dianetics, and Chaucer, why together?**

Beside the board, a cluttered stack of books leaned precariously against a table leg. The Canterbury Tales sat at the top, its worn cover catching the lamplight, glaring up at her like an accusation.

"You'll vouch for me, right?" she asked the cats. "I'm not a thief. I'm... an unofficial archivist."

Shakespeare yawned.

Roz licked her paw.

Dani almost believed herself. Almost.

She exhaled slowly, telling herself she had a handle on things, that the pieces were falling into place. For half a heartbeat, she almost felt safe.

Then two brisk raps, followed by a hesitant tap, splintered the fragile calm. Her heart jolted. She sprang up, brushing cat hair from her knees, already knowing who it was before she even checked the peephole.

Gavin.

Rain speckled his jacket, darkening the fabric. Damp hair clung to his forehead, droplets sliding along the sharp line of his jaw. His calm, steady eyes met hers through the glass.

Dani's breath caught. Heat curled low in her chest, disorienting, dangerous. For a split second, she felt herself slipping.

But she didn't look away.

Behind her, the mess waited, the notes, the timelines, the book she shouldn't have taken. For once, she didn't sweep it away. She wanted him to see.

Because if he was going to tell her to stop, if he was going to push her back from the edge again, she needed to hear it now.

Not so she could change his mind, but so she could decide whether to keep going without him.

So she could stop wasting her time. He could either meet her where she was, or she'd move forward without him.

173

She opened the door and let the mess behind her speak for itself.

"I didn't call," he said, tapping the folder in his hand, "because I wasn't sure I should even bring this to you."

Dani stepped back, nerves tightening around her ribs. "What is it?"

"Information Marcus passed to me," Gavin said, entering, his gaze sliding over the room, taking in the scatter of notes, the taped-up timelines, the photos layered across the floor. His eyes caught on The Canterbury Tales, then on her, not judgmental, just alert.

He shut the door and lingered a moment over the graphic organizer pinned to the wall. His mouth tightened. "You've been busy."

"Everyone needs a hobby," Dani said, too dry, too fast. The knot in her chest cinched tighter.

Gavin dragged a hand through his damp hair. "Dani, this isn't a hobby. The police should be handling it. You need to step back before you get hurt."

She held his gaze. Steady. Unflinching. "And if they miss something? If no one's asking the right questions?"

His jaw ticked. "Then you give them what you've got. I'm not telling you to stop collecting information. I'm saying don't go poking in places that will put you in real danger. Read it, digest it, and let the right people act."

Dani tilted her head, folding her arms around herself. "So I get the facts... but I stay on the sidelines?"

Gavin nodded. "Exactly. The puzzle pieces are yours to see. But you don't try to assemble the whole thing alone."

Her silence was an answer.

He studied her for a beat longer, then let out a sharp breath through his nose.

With brisk, resigned movements, he crossed to the couch and dropped onto it. The folder landed on his lap. "Alright," he muttered. "Then you need to see this."

He flipped the file open, fanning out clippings and police reports over her already-crowded coffee table. Rosalind cast him a regal glare but held her ground. Shakespeare, delighted by the new chaos, hopped down to investigate.

"He had a second identity," Gavin said flatly, tapping one report. "Carl Rendell wasn't his only name."

Dani stilled.

"Marcus traced the money to accounts, a driver's license out of Ohio, even a birth certificate, all under Caleb Raines. Different parents. Different birthday. Same face."

The words landed like a stone in her chest.

"And the kicker?" Gavin's voice darkened.

"Caleb Raines is tied to an open case in Allegheny County: missing church funds. Guess who signed the building permit back in 1986?"

Her mouth went dry. "Caleb?"

"Bingo."

Dani sat back hard, the room tilting. She thought of Carl Rendell: quiet neighbor, punctual worker, the man who'd slammed Chaucer in her face like it was poison.

But none of it had been real. Carl Rendell was a mask. Behind it was Caleb Raines, thief, liar, maybe worse. A past too jagged to stay buried.

Her stomach turned. Carl Rendell had been a ghost hiding in plain sight, playing a part.

But Caleb Raines?

That was deliberate. Calculated. Criminal.

Dani blinked, forcing herself back to the present.

Gavin watched her, his head tilting. "What are you thinking?"

She reached for the graphic organizer. "That I've been asking the wrong questions."

His brow lifted, but he let her continue.

"I've been focused on who Carl was and why he sought me out. But maybe the real question is: what was he after?" She tapped the board. "Why embed himself in two different churches? That's a long game. There are easier cons."

"You think he was looking for something specific?" Gavin asked, his voice measured.

"Maybe," Dani murmured. "And maybe someone found out."

Silence stretched, heavy.

Finally, Gavin asked, "Do you think it's still at the church site?"

She didn't answer right away. Her gaze slid over her notes… then to the battered book still sitting among them.

Eventually, she shook her head. "I went to the Eastern Church of God today. It's gutted. Whatever Carl or Caleb was chasing, it's long gone."

His brow furrowed, but before he could press, she added, "I also went to Rendell's apartment today. Pretended I was looking to rent."

He froze. "Jesus, Dani."

"I was careful," she said, too lightly.

"That's not the point. If he was killed over this, you think walking into his apartment is smart?" His voice dropped, sharp and low.

"I wasn't poking around." Her chin lifted. "I was following a lead. You said it yourself, this is bigger than a fake name and a burned church."

His hand raked through damp hair, the motion tight with frustration. "You could've called me."

"And said what? 'Want to tour a dead man's apartment with me?'"

The pause that followed was taut, bristling.

Then Gavin's shoulders eased, just slightly. "What did you find?"

Dani hesitated. Her fingertips brushed the cracked spine of The Canterbury Tales, its presence stark among her messy notes.

Gavin's eyes tracked the movement. He frowned.

"The Canterbury Tales?"

She nodded. "It was in a box with other books. I couldn't leave it."

He picked it up carefully, thumbing the fragile pages. "You think it means something?"

"I don't know," she admitted. "But Carl shoved it in my face and told me to stop teaching it. Whatever it meant to him, it mattered."

177

"You stole a dead man's book."

"I borrowed it," she corrected.

His mouth quirked, half-exasperated, half-admiring. "You're impossible."

Dani's crooked smile deepened. "That's what makes me useful."

Taking a steadying breath, Gavin said, "I know I'm repeating myself, but you do realize Rendell was murdered? Someone killed him. I don't want you anywhere near that kind of trouble."

"Well, it's not like I stumbled across a bloody knife or a signed confession," she shot back coolly.

She picked up the battered book and dropped it onto the table.

It landed with a dull thunk, then cracked open on its spine.

A thick clump of pages spilled free, scattering like a shuffled deck.

"Damn it," she muttered, reaching for the yellowed pages. "I was going to mail it back to the Fenz family, but now" She froze.

Most of the fallen pages were brittle. But a few stood out: newer, stiffer, unnervingly white. She plucked one free.

Not Chaucer.

A bank slip.

Her pulse jumped.

She sifted faster, pulling out more deposit and withdrawal forms, all stamped First National Bank. Each one tucked deep among the medieval text like someone's private filing cabinet.

She held a withdrawal slip up to the light.

Ten thousand dollars.

Her breath caught.

Carl Rendell hadn't just been hiding. He'd been sitting on money. Serious money.

Gavin crouched, lifting a handful of papers from the floor. His brows knit. "These aren't book pages."

Dani leaned closer, watching his eyes flick over the ink.

"They're bank records," he said, voice low. "Deposits, withdrawals, thousands at a time. And these two?" He held them up. "Each for ten grand."

Dani's stomach knotted. "People don't just shove this kind of paper trail in a Chaucer anthology."

Gavin's gaze met hers, grim and sharp. "No. They hide it when they know someone's coming for them."

Chapter Twenty

Rockefeller's outdoor deck buzzed with the early evening crowd.

Boats bobbed lazily in the marina beyond the railing, their hulls slapping gently against the pilings. Gulls wheeled overhead, squawking over scraps as the scent of shrimp, butter, and Old Bay seasoning drifted on the salty breeze.

Dani slid into a booth with a chilled glass of Sauvignon Blanc, the condensation cool against her fingers. She was early, but she didn't mind.

People-watching was a quiet pleasure. Dani let her gaze drift across the restaurant.

A server navigated the tables with too many plates, a couple leaned in close, laughing, and a man at the bar checked his watch.

Outside, a group of sunburned tourists spilled off a dolphin-watching tour, clutching souvenir tote bags. Beyond them, a fishing charter idled while the captain shouted directions to a dozen passengers unloading coolers and gear, their wide grins suggesting at least a few decent catches. A deckhand hosed down the deck as someone snapped photos by the bait stand. June tourist season was in full swing.

Chanice arrived moments later, her laugh as bold as her Rocking Red lipstick. "Girl, you look like you've been listening to oral presentations all day."

"Ha. Hard no," Dani said, swiping a menu. "But thanks for the vote of confidence."

Dot trailed behind, giving Dani a quick side-hug before taking the seat across from them. "So, is this a girls' night, or are we pretending we just came for the hushpuppies?"

"Can't it be both?" Dani grinned.

They ordered happy hour specials: steamed shrimp, hushpuppies with honey, crab dip, and two-for-one cocktails. As the sun crept lower, the conversation turned to family updates, a mutual friend's questionable dating choices, and inevitably to Dani's dating life.

"Girl, you're red in the face, and we haven't even gotten refills yet," Chanice laughed.

"I'm not blushing," Dani protested.

"Oh, please," Dot said, sliding into the seat next to her. "You're the color of steamed crab legs. And we haven't even said his name yet."

"Whose name?" Chanice asked, tilting her head with exaggerated innocence. "Gaaaavin?"

Her eyes sparkled with mischief behind thick lashes, and the corners of her glossed lips twitched, barely hiding a grin.

She leaned forward, elbows on the table, the picture of faux sweetness.

Dani groaned. "You guys are relentless."

"We're invested," Dot said. "There's a difference."

"Exactly," Chanice chimed in. "We care deeply about your well-being. And also, this slow-burn love story is killing us. Spill. Have you gone all the way, or what?"

Dani took a sip of her wine to stall. "No."

"No?" both women chorused.

"Why not?" Dot demanded. Her gray hair was swept back off her forehead, and her wire glasses slid down her nose. The leopard-print leggings clashed gloriously with her oversized T-shirt that read I'm not arguing, I'm just explaining why I'm right.

"You said making out was good. Like, fireworks-on-the-beach good."

"It was," Dani admitted. "But there's a lot going on."

Chanice leaned across the table. "Okay, but seriously. What does he kiss like? Soft? Confident? One of those 'I know what I'm doing, but I'm gonna let you lead' situations?"

Dani tried not to smile. "You sound like you've been reading those books with Fabio on them again."

Chanice snorted, flipping a hand like she was dismissing a bad wig.

"Please. Fabio could never. I'm strictly Black romance. Give me a man with a fade, a plan, and emotional availability. But don't change the subject."

Dani gave a helpless little shrug, a guilty smile tugging at her lips. "Fine. Gavin's a really good kisser. The kind that makes you forget where you are, your name, your plans, everything." She paused, letting the words hang in the air as she lifted her glass. Chanice and Dot leaned in, eyes wide.

"And his hands..." Dani trailed off, taking a slow sip of wine before continuing, her voice lower now. "They're rough in all the right ways. Strong, steady, warm. The kind of hands that make you think, 'Okay, what else can those do?"

Both women squealed like teenagers.

Chanice fanned herself with a napkin. "And yet, somehow, you haven't sealed the deal?"

"I barely know him!" Dani protested. "Either a body shows up or one of his friends does. The timing's never been right."

Dot narrowed her eyes. "Girl, please. You trusted him with murder-adjacent secrets. That's practically co-signing a mortgage and arguing over a kitchen remodel."

Chanice leaned in, a wicked smile tugging at her lips. "Alright, spill. Are we talking shirts off, hands wandering below the belt? Just give us the rating."

Dani groaned and buried her face in her hands. "I am not having this conversation in a restaurant, in public, during happy hour."

"Oh, yes, you are," Dot said, grinning like she'd just won a prize.

"We need answers," Chanice chimed in, wiggling her eyebrows. "For educational purposes, of course."

Dani laughed, shaking her head as she lifted her glass. "Trust me, that's all I've got to tell."

Dot dropped her voice to a dramatic whisper. "So, what's the hold-up? If he's that good... why not just go for it?" She flashed Dani a sly smile.

"Sounds like he's worth the trouble." Chanice nodded solemnly. "Seriously. Is he old-fashioned, or is he a murder suspect?"

Dani took a breath, swirling the wine in her glass as she searched for the right words. "Honestly? It's not that I don't want to."

She glanced out at the water, the soft glow of the sun catching the edge of her glass. "It's just I'm not twenty-five anymore. Back then, it was easy to dive in and figure it out later."

She paused, her voice quieter now.

"But these days, the stakes feel higher. The minute it goes there, there's no going back. And right now, everything's a little messy. If I let myself fall into him, I'm not sure I'd come back up with my head on straight."

Dot made a soft noise of understanding. "You're afraid it'll cloud your judgment."

"Exactly," Dani said quickly.

But even as the word left her mouth, she wasn't sure it was the whole truth. Gavin made her feel unsteady in a way that was equal parts thrilling and dangerous. He was kind, attentive, and disarming without even trying. And when he looked at her, it was like he saw past the polished version of herself she showed the world to the part she didn't let anyone see, and that frightened her a little.

"That's valid." Chanice took a slow sip of her drink. "But sometimes, your heart knows before your head does."

Dani smiled, but it was tinged with distant memories. "And sometimes your heart walks you straight into a dumpster fire. With a smile on your face and your hands full of gasoline."

Dot let out a bark of laughter, while Chanice raised her glass in mock salute.

"I'm just saying," Dani continued, swirling her wine, "sex is great until you catch feelings, and then you find yourself sitting outside Waffle House, crying in your car and listening to sad mixtapes you made for yourself."

Chanice laughed. "Okay, but at least make it a Denny's. You've got standards."

They clinked glasses, laughter spilling between them like sunlight off the water.

"Now, if y'all are done," Dani said, setting her glass down with a soft clink, "I need your help."

Chanice leaned back in her chair, one eyebrow arched, the playful sparkle still dancing in her eyes. "Oh? This sounds serious."

Dani reached into her bag, the zipper rasping open, and pulled out a folded envelope. She slid it across the table with two fingers, like it might burn her if she held on too long. "I found this at Carl Rendell's apartment. He'd hidden these bank slips inside a book."

Chanice's brow shot up. She half-stood, palms braced on the edge of the table. "Hold on! His apartment? When were you in his apartment?"

Dani lifted a shoulder, unapologetic. "Yesterday. It's up for rent, so I thought I'd check it out."

Dot's chair scraped against the floor as she leaned forward, eyes wide. "You're like a cat testing all his nine lives. Are you sure that was a good idea?"

Dani smirked, resting her elbows on the table, unbothered. "I wouldn't have found this otherwise."

Chanice dropped back into her chair with a groan. "One of these days, you're gonna drag us all into an early grave."

"Will you please take a look at it, Chanice?"

Her friend sighed but was already tugging the slips free, curiosity winning over protest. She separated them into two neat piles of deposits and withdrawals, her brows knitting tighter with each slip. Then her eyes widened. "Okay, he was putting in two grand every other week… and taking out ten thousand at the end of each month."

"Ten thousand?" Dot sputtered, nearly dropping her drink.

"That's not rent money, that's drug-dealer-level money."

Dani nodded slowly. "That's more than I make in two months. And this guy was a church treasurer?"

Chanice shuffled the slips again. "It doesn't make sense. Unless he had a really good side hustle no one knew about."

Dot leaned in, voice low. "And hiding the records in a book? He had to know that was risky. Maybe he was laundering money, extorting someone, or just plain stealing it."

Dani glanced around, then lowered her voice. "Gavin told me the police have linked Carl Rendell to another identity: Caleb Raines. And it turns out Raines was connected to a church in Allegheny County that shut down after fifty grand was stolen from them. No charges were filed, and Raines just… vanished."

Chanice blinked, processing. "So, you think Raines changed his name to Rendell, and stole from the church here, too? And someone found out and killed him?"

"Whoa." Dot gave a low whistle and sat back, her expression sharpening. "That's calculated."

Chanice reached for the stack of slips on the table, her playful energy gone. She flipped through them with practiced focus, the clink of her bracelets the only sound for a moment.

"I'll dig," she said, tapping the pile. "These dates and amounts, it's a pattern. There may be dummy accounts. If he was laundering money, the bank's data might already have red flags buried in it."

Dani glanced at the older woman. "And, Dot, you've got connections. I need you to find out everything you can about Brian's family, their background."

Dot smiled knowingly. "Consider it done. If there's a whisper in this town, it'll find its way to me."

Dani took a deep breath, feeling the weight of the case but bolstered by the support at the table. "Thanks, both of you. I couldn't do this without you."

Chanice clinked her glass against Dani's. "Team mystery, right?"

Dot grinned. "With romance on the side."

Dani rolled her eyes, but the smile tugging at her lips betrayed her.

Chanice leaned in with a smirk. "Maybe you and Gavin could run a little reenactment tonight."

"You know, suspect and detective. He cuffs you, asks the hard questions."

Dot gasped, delighted. "You have the right to remain sexy. Anything you say can and will be used to drive him wild."

Chanice burst out laughing. "You have the right to speak to a gorgeous radio announcer. If you can't find one, one will be appointed to whisper sweet nothings at your discretion."

Dani covered her face, shaking with laughter. "You two are completely unhinged."

"Guilty as charged," Chanice said, still grinning.

"But seriously, there's nothing wrong with a little roleplay. Could help you uncover all kinds of hidden evidence." Dot waggled her brows. "Go undercover."

Dani sank lower in her seat, her cheeks burning as she tried, and failed, to hide behind her wine glass. Her laugh came out in a little burst, somewhere between exasperation and genuine amusement.

Pressing a hand to her forehead, she shook her head, but the grin tugging at her lips refused to fade. She debated steering the conversation back to safer, more rational ground. But she loved how easily they could make her laugh, how they chipped away at her carefully maintained reserve like it was nothing.

And if she was being honest, the teasing hit a little too close to the truth.

The idea of Gavin pinning her down with that sultry stare… the way his voice dropped an octave when things got serious, low and smooth like velvet pulled tight. The look in his dark eyes after he kissed her… hungry for more.

She hadn't let herself feel this much anticipation in a long time, and that scared her more than she wanted to admit.

Because if she gave in, there'd be no hiding how much she wanted him, and no guarantee she'd be able to pull herself back out again.

She took another sip of wine, this time more to cool herself off than anything else. "I'll be relaxing at home alone tonight. Gavin's at the Garth Brooks concert tonight."

Dot waggled her brows. "Perfect. That gives you time to put on something cute and surprise him when he drops by later."

"He's not coming over," Dani started, but even as the words left her mouth, they felt flimsy.

"Oh, please, invite the man over," Chanice cut in. "You've got chemistry like a match to dry leaves. He's drawn to you like a moth to a flame, and you're here acting like it's just a warm breeze."

Dot raised her glass again. "Life's short, kid. Kiss the boy. Climb him like a tree. And for the love of lace, wear sexy underwear."

Dani laughed, cheeks flushed, and shook her head.

"You two are out of control." She paused, her smile softening. "But I love you even when you're absolutely unbearable."

Dot grinned. "That's the nicest insult I've gotten all week."

Chanice raised her glass with a wink. "Honestly, you should be thanking us for this romantic intervention."

They all laughed, the sound easy and familiar. It sliced clean through the tension that had lingered like smoke.

And Dani let herself sink into the moment, pushing away Gavin, Carl, and whatever next storm waited around the corner.

Changes Made.

Chapter Twenty-One

Golden hour light slanted through the blinds, casting long, warm stripes across the floor as Dani stepped inside.

She slipped off her sandals, the quiet of her apartment wrapping around her like a blanket, even as her mind hummed with the echoes of Happy Hour.

Dot's wild theories, Chanice's laughter, the talk of money, the teasing, especially the teasing.

They hadn't let up about how she hadn't slept with Gavin; it became the running joke of the evening.

It was all in fun, but still, it stuck with her, had her questioning what, exactly, she was waiting for.

Dropping her keys into the bowl by the door, she paused, then crossed to the kitchen and flipped on the light.

The cats twined around her ankles, meowing like they hadn't eaten in days. She scooped kibble into their bowls on autopilot, her mind replaying the teasing, the laughter, and the way Gavin's voice had curled in her ear like a secret.

Maybe it was time to stop thinking and act.

She reached for the phone on the wall and dialed the station.

A cheerful woman answered.

"WKNS, how may I direct your call?"

"Hi, this is Dani Jones. Could you connect me to Gavin Larkhurst, please?"

There was a brief pause. "He's just wrapping up the last segment before the concert broadcast. Hold one moment."

As she waited, the line filled with the easy cadence of a radio broadcast. Gavin's voice, smooth and magnetic, came through the speaker: *"If you're heading to the big Garth Brooks concert tonight, swing by the WKNS tent. I'll be there, so come say hey, grab some swag, maybe tell me your favorite summer song."*

Dani smiled despite herself. His voice and charm, even through a phone speaker, curled around her, setting her pulse racing. Then came a soft click, and the live feed gave way to the real thing.

"Dani?" he said, a smile in his voice. "Everything okay?"

"All fine," she said, tugging absently at the hem of her shirt. "I was wondering if you're doing anything after the concert."

"I was just gonna go home." His tone shifted slightly, more cautious. "Unless you need something."

His voice was warm, confident, just the right amount of playful. He sounded so easy, like this was all second nature. Meanwhile, her pulse was doing gymnastics.

It was ridiculous, but also kind of true.

The teasing from Dot and Chanice had cracked something open in her, peeled back the layers of cool detachment she liked to pretend she had. Now all she could think about was the way Gavin's hand had rested on the small of her back when he'd kissed her goodbye last week, and what might've happened if she hadn't pulled away.

She cleared her throat, heart thudding like it was trying to outrun her nerves. "Well," she said, trying to keep her tone casual,

191

"I was wondering if you might want to come over tonight. After the concert."

Silence stretched for a beat, just long enough to make her question everything, until his voice came back, warm and just a little teasing. "You sure?"

She hesitated, the question hanging there. But after Dot's raised eyebrows and Chanice's not-so-subtle smirks, it was impossible to pretend she didn't want him. And now, hearing his voice, so low and confident, with that easy charm, she felt herself unraveling, bit by bit.

Like he was already in the room with her, fingertips brushing her skin, breath warm at her ear. She knew she wanted him. There was the briefest pause, only long enough to feel him shift gears, then his voice came through, low and warm, threaded with mischief.

"Yes."

"I'll bring dessert," he said.

"And maybe a toothbrush." That playful rasp in his voice made her stomach dip. Her fingers curled tighter around the phone.

"I want you, Dani," he murmured, his voice dipping lower, slower now, like velvet sliding over flame. "Not just to flirt through a phone. I think about you… more than I should. The way you look at me, the way you laugh, the way you smile at me."

A breath caught in her throat, and she couldn't deny the little thrill that chased down her spine at the thought of him staying.

She could've come up with a dozen reasons to pump the brakes, but none of them mattered right now.

"See you soon," she said, a quiet promise in her voice.

"Count on it."

She'd spent the evening pretending to be calm, folding laundry that didn't need folding, straightening an already tidy apartment, and taking a hot shower.

She shaved with more care than she wanted to admit, then stood in front of her dresser far too long, debating underwear and loungewear like her life depended on it.

By the time she slipped into a pale camisole, thin-strapped and silky against her skin, clinging lightly to her frame, anticipation had settled in her chest. Matching shorts sat low on her hips, the hem brushing the tops of her thighs. It wasn't overtly sexy, but it felt like comfort laced with intention.

Every sound from the street made her glance at the window. She'd put on music, then turned it off. Tried reading but couldn't focus. Eventually, she flipped on the TV and let it flicker in the background. 48 Hours was airing, a special on a decades-old disappearance. She tried to focus, drawn to the puzzle of it, but even her amateur sleuth instincts couldn't compete with the low, humming energy threading through her. The hours stretched out and collapsed at once, heavy with an anticipation she couldn't shake.

It was almost midnight when Dani heard Gavin's soft knock on the door. Her heart skipped a beat, landing somewhere in her throat. For a moment, she didn't move, just stood there, staring at the door like it might open on its own.

This was real. Not a teasing comment, not a what-if. She took a steadying breath, chasing back the flutter of nerves rising in her chest. Sliding off her worn slippers, she padded barefoot across the room.

Her fingers trembled just a little as she opened the door, but her decision was made.

Gavin's familiar silhouette was framed by the dim porch light.

Humid night air, thick with salt and promise, wrapped around them both. Every nerve in her body hummed, electric and alive, as she met his gaze.

"Hey," he said, his voice low and rough. "You look…"

The camisole clung to her skin, revealing more than it covered. She'd skipped the bra, and the matching shorts were short, but not ridiculous. Comfortable. Pretty. Intentional. Her hair fell in loose waves around her face. She looked casual. Maybe even sexy, if she didn't think too hard about it.

But as she caught her reflection in the hallway mirror, a flicker of doubt crept in.

Was it too much? Too obvious? Too young?

Or worse, was she too old? The thought struck fast and uninvited.

Gavin was younger. Not by much, but enough to matter in certain lighting, in certain moments like this one. She stood there, barefoot in barely-there sleepwear, her heart thudding like she was twenty-two again and about to ruin a perfectly good friendship.

She almost laughed, almost made an excuse to change into something safer, something with sleeves.

But then she remembered the sound of his voice on the phone, the way he'd said I want you.

She steadied herself. Straightened.

Let him see her. All of her. Unapologetically.

Dani leaned one shoulder against the doorframe, her lips curved in a slow, knowing smile. "I was starting to think you weren't coming."

Gavin's gaze dipped, then dragged back up, hungry and dark.

"If I'd known what was waiting," he said, voice low, "I'd have run every red light in town."

She let out a soft laugh. Part of her thrilled at his words, at the heat in his eyes. But another part filed it under things men say when they want to be let in. Still, she didn't look away. Didn't retreat.

Gavin's mouth twitched. "Can I come in?"

She leaned a shoulder against the doorframe, crossing her arms, half to flirt, half to steady herself. "Depends. Did you bring dessert?"

He held up a small white box with dramatic flair. "Triple chocolate cake."

Her eyes flicked to the box, then back to his face. "And the toothbrush?"

His grin deepened, slow and a little wicked. "Left it in the car. Didn't want to seem presumptuous."

She arched an eyebrow. "And yet..."

He stepped closer, not quite crossing the threshold.

"This is hopeful," he said, his voice dropping just enough to tighten something low in her belly. "Not presumptuous."

There was a beat of silence, thick with heat and unsaid things.

Then she stepped aside, letting the door open wide.

"Hopeful's allowed."

Gavin stepped past her, slow and deliberate, his shoulder brushing lightly against hers. He paused just inside, then turned to face her as he closed the door with a soft click.

Setting the box on the narrow table by the door, he stepped closer, his gaze never leaving hers. His hand brushed the edge of the table as he moved, a deliberate slowness in the way he closed the space between them.

Dani felt a rush of heat flood her skin, a shiver trailing down her spine as he stopped just shy of touching her.

He lifted one hand, fingers grazing a loose wave of her hair and tucking it gently behind her ear. His knuckles skimmed the curve of her jaw as he pulled back, the touch light but loaded.

Her breath caught, pulse quickening.

Every nerve suddenly sharp and awake beneath the delicate lace and soft fabric clinging to her skin. The familiar ache of anticipation bloomed tight in her chest, making her toes curl against the cool floor.

Gavin's voice came low, barely above a whisper.

"You look like trouble." He let the words hang between them, his eyes darkening with a mix of admiration and something urgent.

Dani's smile curved, teasing, yes, but beneath it, her heart pounded with a mix of excitement and nerves.

"Maybe I'm the kind of trouble you need tonight," she said, her voice steady even as her hands trembled slightly.

Without another word, she reached up, fingers threading into his hair, pulling him down without a second thought. Their lips met, soft at first, then fiercely hungry. His hands slid around her waist, pressing against the bare skin beneath the lace.

She arched into him, feeling the heat between them flare like wildfire.

He pressed a hand to the small of her back, guiding her backward. She stumbled slightly, laughing breathlessly as he caught her against the edge of the hallway. Step by step, they moved together, a tangle of limbs and urgency, until the door to her bedroom came into view.

He opened it with one hand while the other stayed glued to her, and they spilled inside. The room was small and cozy, tucked away like a secret from the rest of the world. She pressed him against the door for a moment before they finally let themselves collapse onto the bed, the air between them electric with desire.

Soft fairy lights framed the window, casting a warm, gentle glow that softened the shadows. The bed was neatly made with crisp white sheets and a navy-blue throw folded at the foot, a contrast to the worn hardwood beneath. A few candles sat on the dresser, their wicks unlit but ready, filling the air with the faintest hint of vanilla and sandalwood.

A small stack of books, mystery novels, mostly, rested beside a glass of water, a quiet nod to the parts of herself she couldn't leave behind, even tonight.

She turned to face him, reaching for him, her hands brushing the fabric of his shirt, fingertips curling into the cotton as she nestled closer. She ran her palms down his chest to the hem, lifting.

He raised his arms, letting her peel the shirt away.

Her fingers grazed bare skin, warm and taut over muscle, and she felt the subtle hitch of his breath beneath her touch.

She took her time, letting her palms glide across his chest, mapping the dips and lines, the light dusting of hair that trailed lower. Every inch of him felt like warm steel beneath her fingertips.

Leaning in, she brushed her mouth along his jaw, tasting the salt on his skin. Her hands slid to his shoulders, then down his arms, appreciating the way strength coiled there, the kind of strength she could press against and know it would hold.

Gavin's breath hitched, and his voice dropped to a low, rough whisper just inches from her lips. "I've been thinking about this all night."

Her breath caught, a sudden warmth flooding her chest. She hesitated for a moment, unspoken nerves tangling with the ache of wanting him, and then she closed the small space between them, pressing her lips to his again.

Like a switch had been flipped, Gavin's hands gripped her waist and pulled her hard against him. His mouth found hers in a kiss that was all heat and hunger, stealing the breath straight from her lungs.

She gasped into him, startled by the sudden urgency.

Her fingers curled into his shoulders, holding on as he walked her backward, step by step, his body never leaving hers.

The backs of her legs hit the edge of the bed, and her knees nearly gave out. Her pulse thundered in her ears.

Gavin's mouth found the curve of her neck, his breath hot against her skin. "Tell me to stop," he murmured, his voice rough with restraint. "Or I won't."

For a moment, Dani couldn't find her voice.

She should have said something clever, but the truth was, she wanted this, and him, too much.

She tilted her head, eyes meeting his, wide and vulnerable. "Don't stop," she breathed. "Not tonight."

She let herself fall back, her body sinking into the covers, brown hair fanned out like a halo. Watching him through half-lidded eyes, she saw him kneel at her feet, slow and deliberate, like a man intent on worship.

His touch traced a slow path up her legs, leaving warmth in its wake. Gavin's eyes darkened as they lingered on her, something reverent flickering behind the desire.

"Did you forget something?" His grin was slow, confident, teasing.

Dani met his gaze. "I'm pretty sure I didn't."

The space between them vanished, the air thick with heat and heartbeat. Every breath, every touch, felt like a promise neither of them was ready to break.

Gavin didn't respond; instead, his actions drew a quiet gasp from her. Every movement seemed deliberate, controlled, as if he knew exactly how to unravel her. Sensations flooded through Dani, hot, immediate, as he gripped her hips and guided her into the rhythm he wanted. The strength in his touch made her breath catch; there was no question who held command in that moment.

Her first instinct was to move with him, to follow his lead, but his steady hold kept her still. The restraint sent a shiver racing down her spine. Every nerve felt alive, caught between anticipation and surrender.

"You don't have to do anything," he murmured against her skin, his voice low, carrying both a promise and a warning. "Just feel."

And she did, every part of her felt alive.

It was as if her nerves had been rewired to respond only to him. Her thoughts scattered, her breath catching as the moment tightened, drawing her deeper into it.

He shifted, pulling her closer as they moved onto the bed, holding her firmly against him. His kiss was deep and deliberate, slowing everything down even as his touch sent a wave of warmth through her.

He traced the edge of her top with his thumb before lifting it upward, each motion deliberate and unhurried. Dani's head tilted back, eyes fluttering closed as the cool air met her skin, followed by the warmth of his touch.

"You're trembling," he murmured.

Her lips parted, and for a moment, mind whirling, she almost deflected, almost masked her whirlwind of emotions with a joke.

But instead, she whispered, "I know."

Gavin leaned in, pressing a kiss just beneath her jaw. "Good," he said, wry and a little breathless.

"Means I'm not the only one out here losing his damn composure."

The unexpected mix of sincerity and sheepishness caught her off guard, and her laughter slipped out, bubbling up before she could stop it.

Gavin pulled back just enough to see her face, his own lighting up like he'd just been handed a win he hadn't dared hope for.

"I love your laugh," he murmured, eyes locked on hers, even as he pulled the cami over her head.

He sucked in a breath, his gaze raking over her like a caress. Heat bloomed across her chest as her nipples tightened under the weight of his attention, a flutter sparking low in her belly.

She wasn't as fit as she'd been in her twenties.

Softer now in places, she was well familiar with the subtle changes time had etched into her body, but under Gavin's gaze, none of that mattered.

The way he studied her, like she was something rare and breathtaking, made her feel beautiful, like he saw her and wanted her all the more.

He bent his head to her breast. Every move he made felt intentional, a promise without words. Gavin's control wasn't rushed or rough; it was steady, assured—like he wanted to savor every second of touching her and wanted her to do the same.

"Gavin, I'm naked, but you're not."

He leaned in, his breath hot against her ear. "Let me finish."

Her thoughts tangled as he drew her closer, his touch deliberate, unhurried. The warmth of his hands moved lower, finding her rhythm and matching it, guiding her breath. She melted beneath his touch, the world narrowing to the heat of his skin and the steady pulse between them.

Every sound, every shiver, every whispered breath became part of the same rising tide. The clean, warm scent of him filled her senses, and the way he said her name, low and rough, sent a tremor through her.

Light burst behind her eyes, sharp and breathtaking. For a moment, she couldn't speak, couldn't think, only feel.

She lay gasping for breath, her chest rising and falling in shallow waves as the aftershocks rippled through her limbs.

Her skin was damp with sweat, every nerve alive to the touch. The air was thick and heavy, carrying the warmth of the moment and the faint trace of him. She heard the soft rustle of fabric, the quiet clink of metal, then the dull sound of something falling to the floor.

She turned her head toward him, her cheek brushing the warm, rumpled sheets. Moonlight slanted across the bed, tracing the lines of his form as he stood nearby. Shadows lingered over the contours of his body, shifting with each slow breath he took.

Her gaze caught on him, drawn by an energy she could neither name nor resist.

The intensity between them stirred something deep inside her. She swallowed hard as heat coiled low within her, impossible to ignore.

His presence filled the room. He wasn't even touching her, yet she felt tethered to him, every breath drawn in rhythm with his. Her body seemed attuned to his in a way that made her chest ache with longing.

Gavin met her gaze, something raw and reverent flickering in his eyes.

"You okay?" he asked softly, his voice low and rough. "You seem... somewhere else."

She swallowed hard, the warmth coiling in her chest tightening into something fierce and insistent. Her fingers clenched the sheets as she met his eyes, her voice quiet but steady. "I'm here. Just trying to catch up."

His lips curved into a slow, knowing smile. "Well, I'm not going anywhere. Take all the time you need."

He lowered himself beside her, the weight of him grounding and electrifying all at once. Every touch, every glance, carried a quiet promise unspoken.

"I think I'm ready," she said with a small, steady smile.

Dani shifted closer, tracing the line of his neck with her gaze before rising onto her knees beside him.

The soft lamplight painted her skin in gold, catching on the curve of her shoulders as she steadied her breath. Her palms came to rest against his chest, feeling the strong, rhythmic beat of his heart beneath her hands.

She leaned in, their closeness a whisper of warmth and trust. With every breath, every subtle movement, the space between them seemed to dissolve, connection and longing weaving through the quiet until nothing else remained.

He clenched his jaw, letting her take the lead, and that, more than anything, made her breath catch. There was power in this, in the way he waited, in the way he looked at her as if she were something unstoppable, a force of nature.

Her hand moved slowly over him, deliberate and sure, tracing the quiet strength beneath her touch. When her gaze met his, the moment held, silent, electric. He didn't speak, didn't move, only watched her with something close to awe.

His breath escaped in a sharp exhale, the tension between them thrumming in the stillness of the room.

"You have no idea what you're doing to me," he murmured, his voice low and unsteady.

She leaned in, her lips brushing his ear. "Then show me."

His hand closed gently around her wrist, not pulling away, just pausing.

"Hold on," he said softly, eyes searching hers. "Are we good to keep going?"

Dani stilled, her pulse quickening. The question wasn't unexpected, but the care behind it made her breath catch.

"I have an IUD," she said quietly. "It's been a long time since I've been with anyone. I'm healthy." Then, softer, "You?"

He nodded. "Tested last month. I brought protection, if you'd prefer."

For a moment, they simply looked at each other, something warm and unguarded passing between them.

"I trust you," she whispered. "If you're comfortable with that."

Gavin's expression softened, his hand tightening gently around hers. "I am."

In one fluid motion, he drew her closer, holding her as if grounding them both in that moment.

She caught her breath, hands resting on his shoulders as their foreheads met, everything else fading until there was only warmth, closeness, and the quiet rhythm of shared understanding.

"God," Gavin murmured against her mouth, breathless between kisses, "you're trying to kill me."

Dani grinned, her lips brushing his. "You started it, showing up with dessert and dimples."

"Wait, you called me." He laughed, low and rough, the sound vibrating through his chest.

"The dimples were unintentional."

"Mm." She kissed the corner of his mouth. "You should be arrested for flashing them at innocent women."

Her laughter rose between them, light and unrestrained. "Is that why you're blaming me now?"

He smiled, voice dipping into a teasing drawl. "Pretty sure you climbed me first."

She laughed again, nudging her nose along his jaw. "I did no such thing."

"That's not how I remember it," he murmured, his tone softening into warmth as one hand traced a slow line up her back.

She met his eyes, breath catching, everything around them fading into the quiet pulse of shared laughter and something deeper lingering beneath it.

He froze, a low sound escaping him, and kissed her again.

Their laughter dissolved into warmth, their teasing fading into something deeper, an ache that spoke louder than words. His hands found her, steady and sure, drawing her closer as if even a breath of space were too much. With his fingers splayed against her back, he anchored her to him. She could feel his heartbeat, wild and strong, syncing with her own.

Dani's breath hitched as the closeness deepened, the world narrowing to the steady rhythm of their bodies moving together in perfect time.

Her forehead came to rest against his shoulder, her heartbeat quick and sure. He matched her pace, each touch deliberate, guiding her with quiet certainty.

The air between them shimmered with heat and connection, every breath a shared pulse of want and trust.

They moved together in perfect sync, like a match struck against tinder, sparks flaring in the quiet between breaths.

Each inhale came shallow, each exhale heavy with longing. Every point of contact felt alive, charged, their connection thrumming with unspoken meaning.

It was as if their bodies spoke in a language beyond words, one made of warmth, breath, and quiet urgency.

Their mouths found each other again, not just in a kiss but in a search, a promise that deepened with every touch.

She felt the rough brush of his stubble along her jaw, the shiver it drew from her, and she reached for him, fingers curling into his hair to keep him close.

He whispered something low against her skin, words she didn't fully catch, but felt like a spark running down her spine.

And still, they moved together, closer, tighter, until the world seemed to narrow to nothing but this moment. Him. Them.

Out of control, Dani's eyes locked with Gavin's.

There was no denying the way their bodies answered each other, the ache building like a wave she couldn't hold back.

"Gavin," she breathed, the sound half a gasp, half a prayer, and then the world seemed to break open around them.

His hand threaded through her hair, holding her close as they both gave in to the rush, a shuddering release of everything they'd been holding back.

When silence finally settled, only the soft whir of the fan remained, blending with the faint creak of the floorboards and the sleepy sigh of a cat reclaiming its place on the bed.

Dani lay beside Gavin, her leg draped over his, skin warm, heart steadying. For a long moment, neither of them spoke, they simply breathed together, caught in the quiet aftermath of something that felt bigger than either of them.

He shifted slightly, propping himself on one elbow, his gaze warm as it drifted over her face. "You're thinking too loud."

She snorted. "I'm not thinking. I'm basking."

"Oh, my apologies," he murmured, brushing a knuckle down her arm. "Please, carry on."

Dani stretched, a lazy smile curving her lips. "Highly recommend it. Five stars. Would absolutely do it again."

He laughed, turning toward her, the sheets rustling softly. "You want me to install a heat lamp in here?"

Her grin was slow and teasing. "You're handy, too? How did I get so lucky?"

Gavin pretended to ponder. "I have many hidden talents."

She curled closer, tracing an idle pattern on his chest. "That so? Maybe you'll have to show me sometime."

He raised a brow, the corner of his mouth lifting. "On the roof?"

She laughed, a warm, sleepy sound. "That kind of defeats the dungeon part of the scenario."

"True," he murmured, tracing his fingers gently along her spine. "We'll keep brainstorming."

Dani let out a contented noise, something between a sigh and a purr, and tucked her face into the curve of his shoulder. The steady beat of his heart beneath her palm, the heat of his skin, the way his arm wrapped protectively around her, everything settled.

For once, there was no noise in her head. No questions. No puzzle to solve.

Just breath and warmth and the slow drift of sleep pulling her under.

Chapter Twenty-Two

They woke slowly on Sunday, the early morning light creeping through the windows, soft and golden, brushing over the tangle of sheets and limbs.

Dani stirred first, her body warm and heavy, tucked against Gavin's chest. For a moment, she just lay there, listening to the rhythm of his breathing and the faint roll of the ocean through the cracked window.

Then he shifted behind her, his breath warm against the back of her neck, his hand finding the curve of her hip and curling there as if it belonged. He pulled her a little closer, and she smiled, eyes still closed.

"Mm, morning already?" he mumbled, his voice rough and low with sleep.

"Barely," she whispered, not moving. "Just stay like this a minute."

He hummed in agreement, pressing his nose into her hair.

"You're warm," he murmured. "Like a little sunburned furnace."

She snorted softly. "Charming."

"Didn't say I didn't like it." His fingers moved in slow, absent circles on her bare hip, the lightest brush of skin on skin.

Dani exhaled, a lazy, content sound. She shifted just slightly, letting his hand settle more firmly. "You keep doing that, and we're not getting out of bed today."

"Wasn't planning on it." He dipped his head, lips grazing her shoulder. "World can wait."

She rolled onto her back, turning just enough to meet his eyes.

They were still heavy-lidded with sleep, soft at the edges in a way she didn't often get to see. "You always this handsy before coffee?"

He grinned, slow and crooked.

"Only when I wake up next to you."

Dani laughed quietly, the sound caught somewhere between amusement and affection. She reached up and brushed her fingers through the mess of his hair.

Their lips met in long, slow kisses, unhurried and searching.

The urgency of the night before had dissolved into something gentler, more deliberate. Each kiss felt like a conversation, a quiet reaffirmation of what had passed between them.

Gavin's hand slid up the back of her neck, his fingers combing through her hair with a tenderness that unraveled her.

Dani's eyes fluttered shut, her body leaning into him instinctively, her breath catching at the warm, familiar weight of him against her.

There was no need to move quickly, no edge of desperation or doubt.

Only skin, and breath, and the soft rhythm of morning settling around them.

He pressed his forehead to hers for a moment, their noses brushing, his thumb tracing a slow arc along her jaw. She opened her eyes just enough to meet his, heavy-lidded with desire.

"You have no idea what you do to me," he whispered, his voice rough, like gravel softened by the sea.

Her breath caught at the honesty in his tone and the way it wrapped around her like heat. "I think I'm starting to," she murmured, her lips brushing his as she spoke.

His thumb stilled beneath her chin, holding her there gently, as if asking a question without words. "Say the word," he said, low and close, "and I'm yours. Right here. Right now."

She didn't look away. Didn't need to think.

The answer had been resting just beneath her skin for a while now, waiting. She tilted her face the tiniest bit closer, her breath warm against his mouth.

"Then don't wait."

It was like a switch flipped inside him.

One moment he was still and quiet; the next, he was all motion and warmth, drawing her into a kiss that stole the breath from her lungs.

Yet even in that rush, there was a quiet steadiness, a control that made every touch feel intentional, as if he were tracing the shape of something sacred.

His hands moved with purpose, memorizing her as though he were learning a language spoken only between them. His lips followed in kind, each touch a promise, each breath a whisper of devotion.

The world fell away until there was only the two of them, the rhythm of their hearts, the heat of their closeness, the slow, inevitable pull that drew them together again and again.

Her thoughts scattered like sparks, replaced by the weight of the moment, the warmth of him, the quiet power of being seen, known, and wanted.

He moved with reverent care, as though she were something sacred and only he knew how to honor her. His touch was deliberate, tracing her like a map he already knew by heart. Everywhere his hands went, her skin seemed to come alive beneath them, charged with something that felt like both longing and peace.

When his lips left hers, they lingered close, a trail of warmth that made her breath catch, her body attuned to every shift and whisper between them. Each movement carried a wordless promise, something deeper than desire.

She drew him closer without thinking, their bodies finding a rhythm that spoke more clearly than language ever could. The world beyond them faded, leaving only the quiet pulse of shared breath, the rise and fall of hearts moving in time.

It was all-consuming, and she gave herself over to it without hesitation.

They moved together in quiet harmony, breath and heartbeat finding the same rhythm. Her fingers threaded through his hair, her face buried against his shoulder as the moment built around them like a rising tide.

He held her gaze when he could, and when he couldn't, she still felt it, that wordless connection anchoring her in the storm of feeling.

When the crest finally came, it was like a breaking wave, all warmth and light and release. She gasped, a sound caught somewhere between wonder and surrender, and he followed close behind, his breath shuddering against her skin as the world stilled around them.

Their hearts beat in sync, fast and unsteady, until the rhythm slowly softened into something quiet and sure. Dani lay beneath him, her limbs heavy, her breath still catching in the calm after everything.

His forehead rested against hers, their skin warm and flushed, the space between them alive with all the things they didn't need to say.

He exhaled, a sound more like awe than words. "Jesus, Dani…"

She smiled faintly, eyes still closed. "Yeah," she murmured. "That about covers it."

Gavin brushed his knuckles along her cheek, slow and careful, as though she might fade if he wasn't gentle.

"You ruin me," he said softly.

Dani's smile deepened, something tender sparking in her chest.

She reached up, fingers threading through the hair at the back of his neck. "Good," she whispered. "We'll be ruined together."

The sun had burned off the morning fog when hunger lured them out of bed. Dani tugged on his soft WKNS t-shirt he'd left by the bed. It smelled like him, a warm mix of cedarwood, ocean salt, and whatever cologne he'd worn the day before. Familiar. Comforting. A little dangerous.

She padded out to the kitchen, the hem brushing the tops of her thighs.

Gavin was already there, barefoot in yesterday's jeans, humming something low and untuned under his breath as he sliced strawberries with the kind of intense focus usually reserved for bomb defusal or complex surgery.

His hair was still a mess, sticking up at odd angles, and there was a lazy sort of ease in the way he stood, as if the tension had bled out of him somewhere between her skin and the sheets.

Dani leaned in the doorway for a moment, just watching him, taking in the simple, quiet realness of the morning. She committed it to memory: the smell of coffee lingering in the air, the soft sound of a knife on the cutting board, the sun slanting across the floor.

He glanced up, caught her watching, and smiled.

She leaned against the doorway, arms crossed, hair still tousled from sleep.

"You know cutting fruit isn't a precision sport?"

"Careful," he said, flashing a smile. "Mocking the chef gets you decaf."

Dani made a face. "I take it back. You're a masterful chef."

He chuckled and turned back to the cutting board, his movements easy, as if he'd always been there, standing barefoot in her tiny kitchen, making breakfast.

She studied the curve of his shoulders, the quiet way he moved, the steam rising from the coffee pot behind him. Something about it all tightened in her chest. It wasn't painful, just a tiny taste of feeling.

And in that small, ordinary moment, she realized just how long it had been since she'd let herself feel something without bracing for the catch, without calculating the cost. Just a man in a kitchen, humming like it was the most natural thing in the world.

After breakfast, they walked along the beach, shoes in hand, toes skimming the tide. For a few precious hours, she let herself stop worrying about school, about Carl Rendell, about everything. She just existed, light and warm beside him, tucked under his arm like she belonged there.

By the time she left for Chanice's, for their weekly Sunday ritual of sisterhood, gossip, and the newspaper, she felt like someone else. Someone softer. Happier.

Chapter Twenty-Three

By Monday morning, under the fluorescent hum of the classroom lights, the sexy, sultry version of her felt like a dream.

The softness around the edges was already fading, slipping further away with every tick of the clock and shuffle of feet outside the door.

She was back in the world of schedules and expectations, the weekend's freedom folding neatly behind her. The air smelled faintly of dry-erase markers and stale coffee, the weekend warmth replaced by the steady buzz of routine. Desks were cluttered with half-finished projects, crumpled rubrics, and the quiet chaos left behind by Friday's last bell.

Only nine days were left in the school year, but they loomed like an obstacle course. Finalizing grades, managing disengaged seventh graders, and feeling the mounting pressure to make everything matter before the final bell rang were all part of her Monday reality.

Dani rubbed the back of her neck, already tense from hunching over desks. She tried to summon the same stillness she had felt beside Gavin.

There were students to wrangle, curriculum to wrap, and phone messages from parents with subject lines like Urgent and Concerned.

No time to pause. No time to breathe.

She moved quietly among the clusters of students, watching as they paired songs with the books they had read, scribbling down justifications for their choices.

It was a light assignment, yet still meaningful. Music had a way of cutting through barriers, exposing themes that students struggled to connect with on their own.

She stopped by Brian's group. The three boys half-heartedly flipped through crumpled copies of The Canterbury Tales while poking at each other like restless puppies.

Jonah had a highlighter tucked behind his ear, and Ben was flicking paperclips at Brian with a mischievous grin.

Dani watched Brian carefully. His usual energy was there, but something felt off. Ever since his uncle's death, Brian hadn't shown much sign of grieving. It was as if he were holding it all in, keeping the weight hidden beneath the surface while pretending everything was fine.

"Gentlemen," Dani said, folding her arms with a look more amused than stern.

They straightened just enough to feign focus.

"We're talking about The Pardoner's Tale," Brian offered quickly, nudging Ben with his elbow.

"Oh?" Dani raised an eyebrow.

"And what does medieval corruption have to do with the paperclip war?"

Ben grinned. "We needed a break."

She gave Ben the look she had perfected for silly boys, and he cleared his throat, scrambling for seriousness.

"Okay, okay. So, for The Pardoner's Tale, we were thinking "Greed" by Ice Cube."

Dani arched an eyebrow, smirking. "Interesting choice," she said, arms still folded. "Explain."

Brian leaned back in his chair, the front legs lifting just slightly off the floor. "The Pardoner's just out for money. He doesn't care about saving anyone's soul. He wants cash so he can drink and party.

And those three guys? They can't escape death because they're greedy. Ice Cube says it straight: greed messes everything up."

Jonah gave a low whistle. "Damn, bro. That was kind of deep."

Dani nodded slowly, impressed despite herself. "Good. Really good."

Brian beamed, trying not to look too pleased, while Ben threw his hands in the air like a game show host announcing a grand prize. "Boom!" he said, grinning. "Brian just solved literature."

Dani shook her head, biting back a smile as she moved on to the next group. Middle school boys were half philosophers, half goblins.

Eventually, the bell rang, and the students filtered out, eager for the sun-soaked afternoon. Dani lingered behind, organizing papers and preparing her lesson for the next day.

But the day was too perfect to stay indoors for long. When Dani finally stepped outside, warmth wrapped around her. Her feet carried her down quiet streets, past churches and through the Old Beach neighborhood. The scent of cut grass and honeysuckle floated on the breeze, mingling with the distant briny breath of the ocean. Porch swings creaked lazily in the shade, and somewhere a radio played an old R&B song that made her slow her steps just to listen.

At the corner of Baltic and 26th Street, Crandall Packing squatted like a forgotten relic, a whitewashed cinderblock building bleached by decades of sun and salt. Its painted sign, once a bold red and navy, had faded to dusty pink and gray, but the name remained legible beneath the flaking paint.

A battered loading dock stretched along one side, cluttered with wooden pallets and a rusting hand truck, while the faint hum of machinery echoed behind the corrugated metal door. Tucked around the back was a cargo van, but something about it made her stop cold: the faded license plate, the dent low on the rear panel.

She had seen this van before, heard the name, at the cemetery, weeks ago.

The memory clicked into place with startling clarity: the man with the red hair. Justin Fenz.

Dani hadn't planned to come here. She hadn't even been looking for the business.

But now, standing in front of it, something sharp and unsettled stirred in her chest, curiosity, yes, but also something darker, more alert.

Her gaze drifted to the loading dock. Stacked just outside the door were several large spools of thick white canvas.

She thought of Carl and the way they had found him.

That strange, unyielding material wrapped so tightly around his body, so dense and stiff that it had been almost impossible to cut away.

Her stomach tightened.

She should keep walking.

She knew that. She wasn't a cop, wasn't an investigator, but the image of Carl, lifeless and bound, kept rising in her mind like a question left hanging in the air too long.

Dani took a breath and stepped off the sidewalk. Her sandals scuffed against the concrete as she made her way around the building, her heart thumping harder in her chest.

She reached the door. The metal surface was cold beneath her fingertips, rough with rust along the edges and smudged with fingerprints and dust.

It stood slightly ajar, letting out a thin draft of air that smelled faintly of cardboard, machine oil, and something acrid, like hot plastic or melted glue.

From inside came the low hum of fluorescent lights and the dull thud of machinery, steady and rhythmic.

Just a quick look, she told herself. Then she could walk away and tell herself it was nothing.

She pushed the door open and stepped inside.

The air was cooler, tinged with the sharp bite of adhesive and the dust of processed cardboard. A man stood behind the counter.

He was tall and wiry, with sallow skin and sharp cheekbones shadowed by a day's worth of stubble. The air around him carried the cloying scent of cheap cologne, citrus and cloves, too strong in the otherwise industrial space. His eyes were pale and cold, scanning her with a quick, tense flick, as if he were always half a step from bracing for impact. Deep lines framed his mouth, giving him a look of permanent skepticism.

Something about him tugged at her memory, the familiar in the angle of his jaw, the way he squinted at her as if he already didn't trust what she might say.

"Hi," Dani said, her tone overly bright as her mind scrambled for something that sounded reasonable.

"I, uh, want to mail a lamp to my sister in New Jersey, but it's old and very fragile."

Even as the words left her mouth, she could feel her pulse ticking in her throat.

The lie came easily, but her focus was split, she was still trying to place him. She knew she had seen him before.

A flash of a memory surfaced: a man in a dark suit. Had it been at the cemetery? At Carl's funeral?

She wasn't sure.

She forced a smile. "I just wasn't sure if I needed to bring my own packing materials or if that's something you handle here."

The man nodded. "We can help with that. We've got bubble wrap, but there are some newer packing options too. If you want to be sure it arrives safely, we have a composite material, canvas blended with a plastic polymer. It's nearly indestructible."

He reached beneath the counter and pulled out a sample.

The motion triggered something in Dani's memory.

She knew this man. He had been arguing with Justin at the funeral.

They had left together in the same van parked outside.

She took the sample. The material was off-white, rough with a stiff, almost waxy feel, yet when she pressed it, it yielded slightly, pliable in a way that felt oddly familiar.

221

This was the material Carl had been wrapped in.

The phone behind the counter rang, sharp and sudden, and the man turned away to answer it. "Crandall Packing, this is Henry," he said, his voice already fading as he ducked into a side office.

Dani didn't hesitate. She slipped it into her pocket, her pulse quickening.

She wasn't sure what she was going to do with it; she just knew she couldn't leave it behind.

Turning to leave, Dani's hand twisted the doorknob, just as the man's voice stopped her.

"Hey, wait a minute," he called, stepping back into view. "I'm Henry Yeller. Come back when you're ready to mail that lamp. We can help."

She hesitated, turning to face him fully.

"I'm here every day, and my partner, Justin, is here at night," Henry said with a nod. "We'll make sure it gets packed right, no worries."

Justin Fenz?

Brian's father. Carl's brother-in-law.

She'd bet on it.

Dani offered a quick, grateful smile. "Thanks, Henry. I appreciate it."

Back on the sidewalk, Dani reached into her pocket, her fingers brushing against the strip of off-white material she had taken.

It was stiff, almost waxy, and unpleasantly cool against her skin.

A chill slid down her spine.

Her throat tightened even as her mind filled with questions.

What was Carl's connection to Crandall Packing?

Why had this place left her feeling like she had stepped into something dark and dangerous? And most unsettling of all: was this strange, synthetic fabric somehow linked to the way Carl had died?

The sun poured down, warm and golden, casting long, lazy shadows across the quiet street. Birds sang from the treetops. Somewhere, a lawn sprinkler ticked in a steady rhythm. The world around her moved on with easy, careless life.

But inside Dani's mind, the calm was just a surface, thin as glass and ready to shatter.

Chapter Twenty-Four

Wandering south along Pacific Avenue, Dani slowed her pace as the late afternoon sunlight poured gold across the pavement. The beach town pulsed with early summer energy. Shop doors were flung wide open, music drifted from patio speakers, and sunburned tourists trailed sand and laughter behind them. The quiet rhythm of spring had vanished, replaced by the rising hum of a season about to burst into full swing.

To her right, souvenir shops spilled onto the sidewalk with racks of airbrushed t-shirts, shell necklaces, and neon beach towels. Fuzzy reggae blared from the SunSations store, the scent of coconut oil and melted plastic wafting through its open door. Kids squealed nearby, arguing over hermit crabs.

On her left, high-rise hotels loomed, casting long shadows. Between them, Dani glimpsed flashes of ocean. Sunlight flickered like silver on the waves. A salty breeze pressed against her skin, laced with fried dough, sunscreen, and summer.

But Dani moved through it like a ghost, her body drifting home while her mind stayed tangled in the questions Crandall Packing had left behind. The scene around her was all so familiar, loud and a little tacky. She passed the shops and flashing neon signs without really seeing them, until her gaze snagged on the white numbers stenciled on a storefront: 1843. A few steps later, another, 1887. Then 1925.

She slowed without meaning to, something uneasy beginning to stir beneath her preoccupied thoughts.

CRendelf. The name from the phonebook. It had been listed at 1925 B Pacific Avenue.

Dani paused to look at the outside of the building.

Candy's Candy. A sugar-drenched assault of pastel signage and cartoon mascots decorated the exterior. Lollipops with faces, bubblegum lettering, and a grinning jellybean waved from a sandwich board. The scent of artificial strawberry and melted chocolate wafted into the street.

Above the pink candy store, the second story told a different story. Peeling paint framed the windows, their shades drawn and yellowed with age. One window was cracked open, hinting that someone might live there but didn't want to be seen.

Dani stared at it a moment longer, her pulse ticking up. This could be nothing. Another coincidence.

But then again, it might not.

Without giving herself time to hesitate, Dani stepped toward the door and slipped inside.

A bell jingled overhead as she entered Candy's Candy, and she was instantly hit with a wave of sugar, marshmallow, sour apple, chocolate fudge, and something unnervingly like bubblegum-scented hairspray.

The store looked like a unicorn had exploded. Shelves lined every wall, crammed with color: giant swirled lollipops, old-school candy buttons, and bins of jelly beans in every shade imaginable. A rotating rack spun slowly near the front counter, clipped with novelty Pez dispensers and packs of Pop Rocks. In the back corner, a small cooler buzzed beside a hand-lettered sign that read: Frozen Charleston Chews, Try One.!

Behind the counter stood a petite woman in a lavender visor and a t-shirt that read SWEET ON YOU in glittery script. Her lipstick was magenta, her earrings were plastic gummy bears, and her smile stretched wide when she saw Dani.

"Well, hey there, sugar. Just browsing, or are you on a mission?" she chirped, pulling a roll of receipts from an ancient register.

Dani smiled politely, taking in the kaleidoscope of chaos. "Bit of both. I was actually wondering about the building. I saw there's a second floor. Is it an apartment?"

The woman leaned forward, forearms resting on the glass case filled with saltwater taffy. "Oh, sure. That upstairs belongs to Cynthia Renquist. She owns the building and quite a few others on Pacific Avenue. Sweet lady, very tall and stout. A bit scatterbrained, but she keeps the lights on."

She waved vaguely upward. "Her kids use the apartment when they're home from college. Mostly it's just parties and the occasional study group that smells suspiciously like weed. If you're looking for a place to live, this is not exactly a long-term rental situation, if you catch my drift."

Dani nodded, eyes drifting toward the ceiling. "Do they stay there often?"

"Only on holidays and breaks. Haven't seen 'em in a while, though. Spring semester, I suppose. Cynthia's oldest, Brayden or Bryson, he used to run a little printing thing outta there for a while.

Flyers, posters, fake IDs, who knows." She chuckled, clearly amused. "Kids'll be kids."

"Right," Dani said, filing the name away. Cynthia Renquist. Rich, property owner, son, flyers. Parties. Fake IDs. "Thanks, I appreciate the info."

"Anytime, honey," the woman said brightly. "Have a chocolate-dipped Twizzler on your way out, it'll change your life."

Something still didn't sit right. The name in the phonebook hadn't matched Carl Rendell or Cynthia Renquist. A typo, maybe. But her gut said otherwise. A mistake wouldn't explain the tight, calculated feeling behind it. Was it a cover? Or something more deliberate, meant to obscure?

She lingered near the counter, pretending to study the display case. Under the glass, rows of rainbow-swirled lollipops stood like bright little soldiers, flanked by uneven clusters of chocolate and peanuts. Dani's eyes scanned the candy, but her mind looped back to the name, the address, the face behind the counter. Something wasn't adding up, and the sugar-sweet distraction in front of her only made the wrongness feel sharper.

"Actually," she said slowly, almost casually, her fingers brushing the edge of the counter as if anchoring herself, "I came across a listing in the phonebook for a C. *Rendelf,* at this address."

Candy's smile flickered, but she kept her tone light. "That's strange. Could've been a misprint. Those phonebooks get all kinds of things wrong."

Dani hesitated for a moment, then met Candy's eyes. "I thought it might be someone I used to know. Carl Rendell?"

The effect was immediate. Candy's smile faded, her expression softening into something closer to sorrow.

"Oh… I'm sorry, honey. Carl's gone. He passed away a few weeks ago."

Dani's chest tightened, but she kept her expression composed, tilting her head just slightly in what she hoped looked like gentle concern.

Inside, her thoughts were racing. But on the surface, she stayed calm, giving just enough sadness to seem sincere, just enough curiosity to keep the conversation going.

"Oh, no," she said, her voice low and even. "What happened?"

Candy let out a long breath and shook her head. "The newspaper said he was wanted for questioning in an arson investigation. Then they found him in the Lynnhaven River, dead."

She lowered her voice, eyes darting toward the door even though no one else was in the shop. "They think he was murdered."

Candy reached across the counter and gave Dani's hand a brief, warm squeeze. "I'm sorry you had to find out like this. Carl was a good man. Whatever happened, I hope the truth comes out."

Dani shook her head gently, offering a small, practiced smile. "No, it's okay. I'm glad you told me. I hadn't heard, and… I wanted to know."

Candy nodded, continuing, "He was close with Cynthia. Real close. Not like that, though people liked to gossip. Carl was just… dependable. Kind. The kind of man you could give your keys to and not worry he'd steal your best silver."

She glanced toward the ceiling again, this time with something more like fondness. "Like I said, Cynthia owns a good bit of the strip. This place, a couple of the apartments over on 21st, and an old T-shirt shop she's been trying to sell since Clinton took office. Carl helped her out. Collected rent, made sure the tenants weren't causing trouble."

Dani felt the floor tilt, just slightly. Carl, connected to Candy and Cynthia. To this building. To whatever was happening upstairs.

"Did he ever stay here? In the apartment?"

Candy tilted her head, thinking. "I don't think so, no. He had his own place a few blocks over."

Dani nodded slowly, her thoughts threading tighter. "Thank you," she said, her voice low. "For giving me a happy memory of Carl to hold onto."

Candy gave her a gentle smile, pressing a wrapped caramel into her palm. "You're welcome, honey. He was a good one. Not many like him left."

Outside again, the sky had shifted, the gold of late afternoon sliding into the bruised purple of early evening. The ocean glinted in narrow flashes between the hotels, but Dani barely noticed now.

She walked slowly, her mind knotted tight.

Carl had been here. Not just in name, but in function, collecting rent, walking the strip.

And that apartment upstairs. Used by college kids. Parties. Fake IDs. Maybe worse. A place people came and went without questions. A place someone could disappear into.

Dani's fingers tightened around the caramel still in her palm. Unease crept in, sharp and deliberate. Something felt off.

229

She picked up her pace toward her apartment, heels clicking sharply against the cracked sidewalk. A coldness prickled across her skin, and the sense of being watched stirred at the edges of her awareness.

A stray seagull cried overhead, but otherwise the block was too quiet for early evening in a beach town. The usual sounds of laughter, skate wheels, and music had faded, leaving only the echo of her own footsteps as she picked up the pace.

Up ahead, a figure paused near a lamppost. Dani caught only a brief profile, tall, broad-shouldered, with a heavy, uneven gait. The clunk of thick-soled boots echoed faintly as he moved, then vanished as he slipped sideways into an alley.

Something about the way he walked struck a chord. Familiar, maybe, but just out of reach. She couldn't be sure, but her gut clenched anyway.

Probably nothing. Just someone taking a shortcut. Still, the hush that had fallen over the street made her skin prickle.

She kept moving, faster now, her heartbeat syncing with the sharp tap of her heels. But the image stuck, the slope of his shoulders, the uneven gait, the slow turn of his head before he disappeared.

She couldn't shake the feeling that she was being followed.

When she reached her apartment, she locked the door behind her and kicked off her shoes, the familiar creak of the floorboards underfoot offering a strange kind of comfort. The air smelled faintly of lavender.

Shakespeare stretched on the windowsill, blinking at her in slow-motion approval. Rosalind padded over with a chirp, curling around her ankles.

Dani poured herself a glass of water, fed the cats, and let herself breathe, resting a hand on Shakespeare's warm back. For a moment, it was enough. Cats fed, door locked, lights low.

Safe.

Then she saw the blinking button on her answering machine.

Beep.

A burst of static, then a low, distorted voice: "Stop asking questions unless you want to die, too."

Click.

Dani stared at the machine, glass halfway to her lips. The chill from earlier returned in a flood, her body frozen mid-motion.

Safety, it turned out, was just an illusion.

Chapter Twenty-Five

An hour later, the phone message still echoed in Dani's ears. The low, measured voice deliberately shattered the illusion of safety she'd constructed out of routine and locked doors.

Had the man she'd seen earlier been following her?

At first, she'd chalked it up to an overactive imagination. But now, a coil of fear tightened in her chest.

Trying to breathe around it, to think, her thoughts slid away like water through her hands.

Stop asking questions unless you want to die, too.

In a shaky burst of clarity, she'd called Gavin first. His voice steadied her, even if just for a moment. Then Chanice, who didn't ask questions, just said she was coming over.

Now she was waiting, edgy and anxious. She sat rigidly on her sofa, wrapped in a throw blanket that felt thin and useless despite the warm evening.

The apartment, her sanctuary, her retreat, seemed foreign, too quiet and exposed. Every creak from the floor above made her stomach tighten. Every car passing on the street cast shadows that set her heart pounding.

She told herself she wasn't alone. Help was coming.

But when the knock came, she flinched.

She moved to the door and checked the peephole twice before opening it. Gavin's familiar face appeared, with Chanice behind him, her arms laden with greasy takeout boxes and bags.

232

"I brought enough sodium to kill a horse," Chanice said, stepping in without ceremony and heading to the kitchen. Both cats followed her.

Gavin gave Dani a quick once-over, concern tightening his features. "You alright?"

She nodded, too quickly. "Fine. I'm fine."

But they both knew she wasn't. So he let her lose herself in the cartons. Steam rose in lazy spirals, carrying the warm, savory scent of noodles, the sharp tang of vinegar from the dumplings, and the rich, meaty aroma of something swimming in dark sauce. Dani tried to focus on the food, on the mundane rhythms of company.

The normalcy of it helped. A little.

"I called Marcus," Gavin said after a pause. "He's on his way."

Dani's head snapped up.

"You didn't need to do that."

"I did." His voice left no room for argument.

She blinked, a prickle of resistance rising before she could stop it. But the set of his jaw told her it wasn't worth pushing.

She let out a slow breath, let it go.

A second knock.

More cautious this time, Dani crossed to the door. She knew it would be the police detective, but her fingers hesitated at the lock.

She opened it to find him standing there, hands in the pockets of his rumpled jacket.

He stepped inside and nodded at her, eyes scanning the room.

Chanice set out a second spread of pizza, salad in a plastic tub. Her dark curls were piled into a high ponytail, the gold hoops at her ears glinting every time she moved. She had that kind of presence

Dani had always admired. Chanice could be loud, elegant in the way of someone who had nothing to prove, her laughter ringing out like crystal struck by a spoon. When she relaxed, there was a looseness in her posture, a careless grace that made her seem untouchable. The rich bronze of her skin practically glowed against the warm lamplight, and her energy filled the room.

"Just in case noodles weren't enough," she announced, snapping open a pizza box with a flourish. "Crisis carbs. Doctor recommended."

Marcus, who'd been quietly surveying the room from inside the closed door, raised an eyebrow. His deep brown skin caught the faint shimmer of city light filtering through the blinds, highlighting a strong jaw, well-kept stubble, and eyes that missed very little. How had Dani never noticed how good-looking the detective was?

"Salad?" he said dryly, glancing at the plastic tub like it might personally offend him.

Chanice didn't miss a beat, flicking open the lid with a snap.

"It's Caesar. That makes it noble."

Marcus stepped forward, the floor creaking under his weight, and plucked up a slice of pizza, holding it halfway to his mouth as he eyed her.

"Does it come with a betrayal or just the croutons?"

"Only if you touch the last breadstick," she said sweetly, leaning just far enough across the counter to make the point.

"Which I will stab for."

He chuckled, low and warm, taking a bite and wiping his thumb on a napkin. "Noted. Defensive dining. I like that."

"Girl's gotta have boundaries," Chanice replied, spearing a piece of lettuce like it had wronged her in a past life, her fork clinking sharply against the dish.

Marcus gave her a slow smile that could have melted rubber, his gaze lingering as he set his pizza down. "I respect that."

Dani, perched on the edge of the couch with a blanket still wrapped tightly around her, watched the exchange unfold. Quick, warm, unexpectedly flirtatious—the kind of banter that danced close enough to spark without quite catching fire.

It was strange, watching them volley lines like that, as if the world outside wasn't pressing in on all of them. For the first time in hours, something almost like amusement stirred in her chest, a small flicker in the cold.

She let herself lean toward it. It didn't chase the fear away, nothing would, not tonight, but it blunted the edge, made the air feel less sharp against her skin.

Gavin sat down beside her, the couch dipping under his weight, and pressed a warm plate into her hands, noodles glistening, steam curling up to brush her face.

"Will you stay tonight?" she asked, her voice quieter than she meant it to be.

He didn't hesitate. "Of course I will. You don't have to go through this alone, Dani."

She let out a small, reluctant laugh. It felt strange in her throat, like it belonged to someone else, and she kept her gaze on the plate as she twirled the noodles, eating a bite without looking up.

The warmth of the food lingered, steadying her hands, and the rhythm of their easy voices hummed in the background, loosening something tight in her chest.

Dani sat forward, the blanket slipping from her shoulders as that looseness sharpened into resolve. Fear still hovered, but it no longer pinned her in place; it was something she could hold and work around.

A different kind of tension settled into her spine. Purpose. She needed them to know what she'd found.

Marcus noticed. "Are you ready to tell us what happened?"

"Yes," she said, her voice firmer as she set the plate down on the side table.

Chanice caught Dani's gaze and returned a knowing smile, a small but clear acknowledgment of the change.

As if drawn by the shift in energy, Roz padded quietly into the room and leapt onto the armrest beside Dani, curling up close.

Gavin slid his arm gently behind her to scratch the cat and left it lingering on her shoulder.

Dani reached into her pocket and pulled out the fabric sample.

"I walked home from school today," she began, her voice steady. "It was such a nice day, so I wandered through Old Beach and stumbled across Crandall Packaging. The day-shift worker, Henry Yeller, showed me this canvas-polymer they use as packing material. It looks a lot like what Carl's body was wrapped in."

She held the sample up, the rough texture catching the light.

Gavin reached out, running a finger over the fabric, his brow tightening. "It's hard to tell. The fabric wrapped around Carl was soaking wet and muddy."

Marcus leaned forward, eyes narrowing as he took the sample and turned it over in his hands. "If this matches, it could mean someone had access to Crandall's materials."

She let that settle for a beat before adding, "I also think Justin Fenz works the night shift there."

"Carl's brother-in-law," Marcus said, brow furrowing.

For a long moment, neither spoke. The small canvas sample lay between them on the desk, a mute accusation. Marcus ran a thumb along its frayed edge, then set it down as if it might burn him.

"Looks like you just dropped a bomb in our laps," he said quietly.

Dani exhaled. "It's not proof. But it's enough to make someone nervous."

Marcus nodded once, the weight of it settling in. "We'll need to tread carefully. If this checks out, it changes everything."

Dani sat forward, the blanket slipping slightly from her shoulders as she focused. "After I left Crandall Packaging, I started walking home but stopped at Candy's Candy. What caught my attention was the address. There was a C. Rendelf listed in the phonebook as living there. The name was so close to Carl Rendell's that I noticed it when I looked him up."

The room seemed to still, the dim lamplight casting soft, unmoving shadows across the walls. The only sound was the faint buzz of traffic below and the occasional creak of pipes in the old building.

Normally, this was background noise, but now it made her skin twitch.

"According to Candy, the owner of the store, there is no Rendelf living there, but the building is owned by Cynthia Renquist. There's an apartment on the second floor that is only used by Renquist's college kids on breaks, and she owns a lot of properties, buildings, apartments at the oceanfront. Carl worked for her, under the table, probably, collecting rent, doing repairs and odd jobs."

Chanice leaned forward, eyes narrowing with focus.

When her knee bumped the coffee table, Shakespeare, who was curled up in her lap, let out an indignant meow before hopping down with theatrical offense.

"Sorry, drama king," she muttered, barely sparing him a glance as her focus sharpened on Dani. "So, you're saying Carl was in and out of Cynthia's buildings. He had access."

"These names all have the same initials," Marcus said. "Carl Rendell. Cynthia Renquist. Caleb Raines. Now C. Rendelf? That's not random. It's a pattern."

Before Dani could respond, Chanice raised a hand, her expression sharp. "Wait. Before we go too far down the initial rabbit hole, I should tell you what I found out at the bank."

Everyone's attention snapped to her.

"After you showed me those deposit and withdrawal slips."

"What?" Marcus barked, half-rising from his chair, eyes flashing. "Why didn't you say anything sooner? You've been sitting on this for days?"

Shakespeare chose that exact moment to stretch languidly against Marcus's leg, flexing his claws just enough to make his presence known.

Marcus flinched and looked down, scowling as the cat blinked up at him with regal indifference.

"Really?" Marcus muttered, brushing him off. "Your timing sucks."

Shakespeare sauntered away, tail held high, leaving no doubt he'd just put Marcus in his place.

Dani reached over to pick up the copy of The Canterbury Tales that she'd taken from Rendell's apartment and passed it to Marcus.

He flipped through the book and found several slips.

I don't even want to know how you got this, Dani," he growled. "Keep going, Chanice."

"Well, I pulled Carl's bank account activity," she continued.

"Legally? Questionable. Useful? Definitely."

Dani leaned in, her voice low and steady, while Rosalind slipped into her lap, curling tighter into a warm, purring crescent.

Dani's fingers moved absently over the cat's fur as she asked, "What did you find?"

Chanice reached into her bag and flipped open a notebook, tapping a page with a long red nail. Before she could speak, Shakespeare leapt back onto her lap with a chirp, circling once before settling in. She absently scratched behind his ears, eyes still on the notes.

"About a year ago, Carl began depositing two grand into his account every two weeks. Then, like clockwork once a month, he'd withdraw ten thousand. Always in cash. And always in person."

"That's a lot of money," Gavin said, frowning.

"Any sign where the money was coming from?"

Chanice shook her head. "The deposits weren't payroll. No employer listed. No memo lines. Just cash, consistent amounts. Like someone was paying him off the books, and he was moving it fast."

"Money laundering?" Marcus suggested. "Or hush money?"

"Could be," Chanice said. "Or maybe he was the middleman, taking payments and passing them to someone else. But here's the thing: after Carl died, the deposits stopped, but the withdrawals didn't."

Dani blinked. "Wait. What?"

Chanice nodded grimly. "Someone withdrew ten thousand dollars from his account last month. Same branch. Same pattern. Which means either someone forged access, or Carl wasn't the only one with it."

Dani's stomach tightened. "Do you have dates?"

"I do," Chanice said, tearing out the page and sliding it across the table. "The interesting thing is that no one remembered him. I asked all the tellers, showed them the picture that was in the paper, but no one recognized him. But..."

Dani looked up at her friend as she took a breath.

"When I flagged the activity on the account, I got a few other hits. Apparently, Colton Roberts, who lives in Accomack County, and Charity Reynolds in Hampton also have accounts with similar banking habits. A few thousand every two weeks, and a big withdrawal every few months."

"More C.R. initials," Marcus murmured.

Gavin nodded. "Colton Roberts. Charity Reynolds. You think they're real people, or aliases?"

"Could be both," Chanice said. "The deposits are too consistent to be random. Someone's feeding them."

"And they're spread out," Dani said slowly. "Accomack, Hampton. That's a network."

She didn't realize she'd said it out loud until the others went quiet.

Then Gavin asked gently, "Tell us about the phone call, Dani."

She took a breath, her fingers curling slightly against her knees. "Let me go back a bit. After I left Candy's Candy, I thought I saw someone watching me, half a block away, standing there on the corner."

Her voice faltered for a second. "He looked a little like Carl Rendell."

That name hung in the air, heavier now.

"I know how that sounds," she added quickly. "But just for a second. It was the way he stood. The shape of him. I got this feeling. Like I was being watched. I didn't wait to double-check. I raced straight home."

Roz stirred as if sensing Dani's anxiety, while Shakespeare watched from across the room, tail flicking like a silent metronome.

She paused. "I was only home a few minutes when I saw the answering machine blinking."

Marcus rose and crossed the room to the small table by the wall, where the answering machine sat, its blinking red light oddly menacing.

He pressed the play button with two fingers.

The machine clicked, whirred, and then the message played.

"Stop asking questions unless you want to die, too," the voice crackled through the cheap speaker, distorted and mechanical, but terrifying.

A cold knot tightened in Dani's stomach, the words echoing louder in her mind than through the device.

Her breath hitched, and a shiver ran down her spine despite the room's warmth. Every instinct screamed to freeze, to shut down, but a stubborn part of her wanted to fight back.

"That's not a prank," Chanice whispered, voice flat.

"No," Marcus said. "That's a warning."

He removed the cassette tape from the machine, slipping it into his pocket. "I'm going to take this back to the station and log it as evidence. Maybe even clean up the audio."

Dani didn't respond right away. Her eyes were still on the machine. The blinking red light had gone dark now, but the echo of the voice was still ringing in her head.

Gavin blew out a breath. "This is bigger than just Carl. There are others with similar accounts, similar habits—and now someone's threatening Dani for poking around."

Chanice cut in, eyes narrowing. "They think she's onto them. Or worse, they think she already knows something."

Dani looked down at the paper Chanice had given her. "What if this whole thing was never just about Carl? What if I've stumbled into something much bigger?"

The room stayed quiet, the weight of that possibility sinking in.

Marcus's jaw tightened. "Do you think the call was from Justin?"

"I don't know," Dani said. "But the timing, it's not random."

Chanice's fingers tapped restlessly on the side of her salad container, her plastic fork long forgotten. "So, we've got Carl, a handyman with keys to half the town. Cynthia, a landlord-slash–real estate mogul with more secrets than leases. Justin, night-shift guy at Crandall Packaging. And now a bunch of sketchy accounts registered to people with the same damn initials. Someone in that mix doesn't want you asking questions."

Dani nodded slowly, her eyes fixed on a spot across the room. "I just wanted to know why Carl dragged me into this in the first place." Her voice lowered. "It all connects. I just don't know how yet."

Marcus gave a quiet snort, rubbing the back of his neck. "Maybe Rendell didn't mean to pull you in at all. Maybe his conversation with you at school has nothing to do with any of this."

Dani's eyes narrowed, her jaw tightening as Marcus's words hit sharper than she expected. "Maybe," she said, voice low but edged with steel, "but I'm not just going to sit back and pretend it doesn't matter."

She leaned forward, the blanket slipping from her shoulders as she met his gaze head-on. "There's something here, and I'm going to find out what. You can choose to doubt me, but I'm not backing down."

Rosalind slipped quietly from Chanice's lap, landing with a gentle thud on the floor. Her tail flicked once, sharp and deliberate, before she padded gracefully across the room toward Shakespeare, whose tail swayed lazily, dangling from Chanice's lap like a fluffy ribbon.

Marcus leaned back in his chair and folded his arms. "Look, Dani. This isn't just weird anymore. It's criminal, threats, fraud, large amounts of money. You've been targeted, so I need you to hand this over. Let the department handle it. Let me handle it."

Chanice scoffed. "Right. Because the department's done such a bang-up job so far?"

Marcus sighed and turned to Dani, his expression hardening. "You've done more than the best detectives, but this case isn't on you to solve. It's my job to take the risks. Not yours."

"Look, you're cute and all," Chanice said, sitting up straighter, her hoop earrings flashing in the lamplight, "but don't underestimate my friend."

She gestured toward Dani, her voice rising just enough to sting. "You should be thanking her for doing what the police department couldn't do. She's the reason you even have leads."

Marcus's mouth flattened into a line. "This isn't a game, Chanice."

"No," she snapped. "It's not. Carl Rendell is dead. Dani got threatened. And all you've got is a lecture?"

He stood slowly, authority drawing around him like armor. "I'm saying there's a line. Once things cross into threatening violence, there are protocols."

"Yes," Dani said quietly, rising too. "But sometimes those protocols move too slow."

Marcus met her eyes, and something shifted into reluctant respect. "You're not bulletproof, Dani," he said at last.

"I know," she replied.

Gavin spoke for the first time in a while, his voice calm but steady. "I get where you're coming from, Marcus. I do. I want Dani to be safe, too." He glanced at her. "But if you think she's just going to sit this out, you clearly don't know her."

The words caught Dani off guard, a flicker of heat rising in her chest. Until now, Gavin had urged her to step back, to keep her head down. But now he met her eyes and held them, steady and unflinching, as if to say he saw her clearly at last. Hearing him defend her and acknowledge her the way she saw herself felt like a door opening between them. It wasn't just support; it was respect.

Marcus's gaze moved from Gavin's steady loyalty to Chanice's righteous fire, and finally to Dani's unwavering resolve. He blew out a hard breath through his nose, the sound edged with reluctant acceptance.

"I didn't ask for this," Dani said, her voice even but firm, "but now that I'm involved, I need answers."

Marcus sighed, the fight in his shoulders easing as he adjusted his expectations. "Fine. But promise me you'll be smart about it. Loop me in. No more solo missions. And if anything else happens, anything, you call me first."

Dani gave a small nod. "Deal."

Marcus shook his head, though a faint smile lingered. "Fine. We'll run it like a unit, watch each other's backs, follow the leads, and no freelancing."

Chapter Twenty-Six

When the last crumbs of pizza were swept into the trash and the Chinese and salad containers were neatly stacked in Dani's fridge, the apartment felt lighter—the knot of tension loosening enough for laughter to slip through.

Roz curled up on the windowsill, her gaze fixed on the darkened street outside, while Shakespeare prowled between the chairs, ever hopeful for a scratch behind the ears.

Gavin wiped his hands on a napkin, smirking across the small kitchen. "So, Chanice, what's the verdict? Should I start coaching Marcus, or is he holding his own?"

Chanice, perched on one of Dani's mismatched barstools, gave him a sidelong look, her smile slow and knowing. "He's got charm, I'll give him that. But let's be clear, I don't get distracted by a nice smile. Friends come first. Always."

From the open doorway to the living room, Marcus grinned, one shoulder braced against the frame. "Challenge accepted."

Leaning back on the couch, Dani felt the tight weight in her chest ease. It wasn't gone, but for the first time in hours, she felt something close to relaxation.

Chanice hooked her arm through Marcus's as they headed for the door. "Walk me to my car, handsome?"

Marcus arched a brow but didn't protest, letting her steer him a few steps toward the door.

And then the phone rang.

The sound cut through the easy warmth of the room like a blade. Dani froze, her pulse kicking hard against her ribs. The last time that phone had rung, it had carried a threat that still scraped like ice against her nerves. Gavin's gaze flicked to her, taut with the same thought.

Even Roz lifted her head from the windowsill, ears angled toward the sound.

"Hey, it's me." Dot's warm voice came through the line, and the tight coil in Dani's chest loosened all at once, leaving her dizzy with relief. Her knees nearly buckled, and she gripped the phone harder.

She saw the others react too, Marcus's shoulders lowering, Chanice letting out a breath she hadn't realized she was holding, Gavin leaning back against the counter.

Dani let out a quiet, shaky laugh, pressing the phone closer as if to pull Dot's voice straight into the room.

"Hey, Dot."

"You sitting down?" The older woman's voice crackled faintly over the line.

Dani moved toward the sofa and hit the speaker button. "You're on speaker. Gavin, Chanice, Marcus—you're all going to want to hear this."

"Why wasn't I invited to the party?" Dot pouted.

"I'll tell you about it tomorrow at school," Dani assured her. "What did you find out?"

"Like you asked, I did some digging into Carl Rendell's family," Dot said, her tone sharpening as if she'd been dying to spill this. "I called a few of the ladies from my mother's mahjong group. They live for gossip, and they had plenty."

Dani's grip on the phone tightened, a small smile tugging at her lips despite the tension.

"You're telling me you've unleashed the mahjong mafia on this?" she said. "Alright, don't keep us hanging. What did they know?"

"When Carl was about fifteen or sixteen, his dad got busted and sent to prison. It was a big fraud case, we're talking investors ruined, houses repossessed, the works. His mom lost custody of Carl and his sister, Amanda. The state split them up. Amanda was fourteen when she went into foster care, but Carl was placed with a family friend."

Dot took a deep breath before adding, "That friend's been in jail for the last fifteen years for, you guessed it, fraud, pyramid schemes, every financial con in the book."

Chanice let out a low whistle, crossing her arms over her chest. "Not exactly the kind of role model anyone would hope for."

Dani's stomach tightened as she absorbed the weight of the revelation.

This toxic history could explain so much.

The fractures beneath Carl's carefully guarded exterior started clicking into place, but there were still secrets lurking in the shadows.

Marcus's voice broke through softly. "And Carl was most likely part of this family business."

Dani's mind raced. "What if the churches were just a cover? Or a place to launder the money?"

Gavin nodded slowly, running a hand through his hair.

"Maybe someone discovered the truth, or someone they'd wronged finally had enough and took matters into their own hands." Chanice frowned, biting her lip thoughtfully. "Or maybe Carl tried to break free, refused to keep playing the game, and they made an example of him."

Marcus added, "It could be a rival, or someone inside the family turning on each other. Family secrets have a way of getting deadly."

Gavin's eyes darkened. "Or maybe Carl stumbled on something no one wanted exposed, like the arson, and he paid the price for it."

The room fell quiet, the weight of possibilities settling over them like a storm waiting to break.

Marcus said softly, "Carl was most likely part of this family business."

Gavin nodded slowly, running a hand through his hair. "Maybe someone he'd stolen from had enough and killed Carl."

Dani swallowed hard, feeling the urgency coil tighter inside her. "Thanks, Dot. You did great."

There was a brief pause on the line, then Dot's voice softened. "Be careful, Dani. You're stirring up a lot of old ghosts."

"I will," Dani said, her voice steady, even if her heart wasn't.

The line went dead, and the apartment fell into a charged silence as Dani replaced the receiver. The weight of new revelations pressed down on them all.

Chanice stepped forward, her arms wrapping around Dani in a tight hug. The warmth was a stark contrast to the chill settling in Dani's chest.

"I wish I could stay tonight, but I've got a meeting at seven."

Dani managed a small smile, the tension in her shoulders easing slightly. "And it's a school night," she said softly, almost to herself.

Pulling back, Chanice looked into Dani's eyes with earnest concern. "Promise me you'll be careful."

"I will," Dani replied, returning the hug with quiet resolve.

Chanice gathered her purse from the countertop and glanced toward the doorway, where Marcus stood with a steady, serious gaze. The dim light caught the sharp lines of his face, lending him an air of quiet authority.

"Will you walk me to my car, Detective Gates?" Chanice asked.

Marcus nodded without hesitation. "Of course, Ms. Chanice."

Chanice squeezed Dani's shoulder firmly before linking arms with Marcus. Their footsteps echoed softly as they made their way to the door.

Chanice glanced back over her shoulder, a small, knowing smile playing on her lips. "Watch out for her, Gavin."

Gavin chuckled, shaking his head. "I will."

The gentle click of the door closing followed behind them. Left in the living room, Dani and Gavin exchanged a look heavy with unspoken understanding.

Exhaustion swept over Dani, leaving her pale and swaying on her feet. She sank slowly onto the couch, her head tilting back as her eyes traced the patterns of the ceiling.

Gavin sat beside her, the cushions sinking under his weight.

He stretched his arm along the back of the couch, his fingers hovering near her shoulder as if unsure whether to close the small distance. For a moment, neither of them moved, the hum of the refrigerator in the kitchen the only sound between them.

Finally, his voice broke the quiet, soft but threaded with something heavier. "You don't have to carry this alone, Dani."

Her eyes flicked to him, a trace of defiance there.

"I'm not trying to. I just… can't sit back and do nothing."

"I know that now," he said, leaning forward slightly, elbows resting on his knees. "But watching you run straight into danger" He stopped, searching for the right words. "It's like standing on the edge of a cliff, knowing I can't pull you back before you go over."

Her throat tightened. "If I stop, whoever killed him will keep working in the shadows."

"But if something happened to you" The words came quickly, almost sharp, like they'd been waiting inside him. His gaze dropped to the floor for a beat before returning to hers. "I'd lose you."

Dani's chest ached at the rawness in his voice. "I'm not trying to make you worry."

"You don't have to try," he said with a faint, tired smile. "Just… let me help. No running off alone. Not again."

She hesitated, the promise catching in her throat because she knew she couldn't keep it. Sooner or later, the need to follow a lead might outweigh the caution he was asking for.

Gavin read it in her silence and sighed, sitting back. His arm stayed stretched behind her, not quite touching, but close enough that the warmth of him was a steady presence.

Outside, the wind picked up, brushing the windowpanes with a whisper, the air growing thick and charged as a storm approached.

"Thank you for staying," she whispered, her voice trembling just enough to betray the weight behind the words. "I don't think I could be alone tonight."

Gavin's gaze softened. "I'm not going anywhere." His lips curved in the faintest smile. "But I do have to be up disgustingly early tomorrow."

Her brow lifted. "How early?"

"I need to leave here at four," he sighed. "Got to gather the latest news and deliver it to the city starting at five-thirty."

A yawn caught her off guard, slipping between her words as she chuckled. "You know, I always listen to your reports, but I draw the line at this five-thirty nonsense. Seven is much better."

"I agree," he said, his smile tugging wider, "but I don't make the rules. I just collect the paycheck and try to stay awake while doing it."

Her lips curved. "Well, if you're going to insist on ungodly hours, don't wake me up when you leave."

He caught her chin with his fingers, the faint warmth of his skin sending a shiver through her. His lips brushed hers, feather-light at first, a whisper of contact that tasted faintly of coffee.

"You're bossy, you know that?" he murmured, his breath mingling with hers.

Her pulse tripped, a low flutter deep in her chest, and she leaned in, closing the space between them. The second kiss was warmer, lingering, her senses filling with the steady rhythm of his breathing and the spicy, clean scent of his cologne. She let herself melt into the moment, into the safety of his arms, the hum of the refrigerator in the background the only reminder they weren't suspended outside time.

When he pulled back just enough to meet her eyes, she found herself reluctant to let the air between them cool. She rested her forehead against his, their breaths syncing in a slow, quiet rhythm. He brushed a stray strand of hair from her cheek, his touch deliberate, almost reverent.

"You're tired," he murmured, his voice low, steady. "Let me take care of you."

Her instinct was to tell him she'd been taking care of herself for years, but the words caught behind her teeth. Instead, she let out a shaky breath. "I'm so used to holding it together. If I let go, I'm afraid I won't know how to stop."

His thumb grazed her cheekbone, warm and sure. "Then let me hold you together."

She swallowed, wondering if this aching need to be with him would ever lessen, or if she even wanted it to.

Her walls, built brick by stubborn brick, felt suddenly fragile under the steady warmth of his touch.

"Okay," she whispered, the word slipping out like a white flag she hadn't meant to raise but no longer had the strength to lower.

A small smile of relief touched his lips, and he drew her closer, tucking her against him like she belonged there. "You don't have to be strong for me."

For the first time in what felt like forever, she didn't try to be. She let herself sink into him, feeling the steady beat of his heart under her cheek, and didn't fight the way it steadied her own.

Without a word, she curled into his side, tucking herself against him until she could feel the solid beat of his heart beneath her cheek.

His arm tightened around her, anchoring her in a way that made the heaviness in her chest loosen and her eyes flutter closed. After a long moment, he coaxed her gently to her feet, guiding her down the short hallway.

In the dim glow spilling from the living room, he helped her slip into her nightgown. Then, pulling back the covers, he guided her gently onto the bed. She sank into the mattress, her body finally surrendering to exhaustion.

Gavin stretched out beside her and wrapped his arms around her waist, holding her close.

Her head rested against his chest, where she could feel the steady rhythm of his heartbeat. She breathed in the warmth of his skin and felt the soft press of his lips against her hair.

Wrapped in the cocoon of his embrace, the shadows clouding her mind began to fade. Her eyelids grew heavier with each slow breath as she surrendered to the pull of sleep.

Chapter Twenty-Seven

Morning came far too soon. Dani stirred just enough to feel Gavin press a warm kiss to her forehead, his hand lingering on her shoulder.

"Go back to sleep," he murmured, his voice low and gentle. "I'll see you tonight."

She wanted to hold on to him, to keep him close, but the bed was already cooling by the time the front door clicked shut.

She drifted in and out of half-sleep until the clock radio clicked. Gavin's calm, professional voice woke her. His report moved through traffic and weather before landing on the line that made her sit up:

"And now, an update on a murder investigation of local church treasurer Carl Rendell. Police say they are pursuing new leads. Authorities have not yet released details, but sources suggest these may involve a connection to financial crimes. Call the tip line if you have any information."

Dani gritted her teeth, a surge of frustration tightening her chest. If only she had every piece of the puzzle, all the answers laid out in front of her, she could end this nightmare once and for all. She wanted to call that tip line, demand the truth, make it stop. But the pieces weren't hers to command.

Even as the day dragged on, the tension refused to leave her. Her morning class was restless, more interested in passing notes than reviewing for exams, but Dani could barely care. At lunch, she half-listened while her colleagues debated whether the vending machine was truly out of Diet Coke or just refusing to cooperate. Every laugh, every idle complaint, every trivial distraction bounced against the edges of her mind, only to snap back to Gavin's voice over the radio and the unsettling mention of Carl Rendell.

By the time the final bell rang, Dani was determined to keep investigating. While students spilled into the hallway in a rush of voices and slamming lockers, she was already planning her next step.

Gathering her papers, Dani stepped out into the cool afternoon air, the noise of the day fading behind her. In the parking lot, she spotted Dot leaning against her little blue hatchback, twirling her keys in one hand and wearing an expectant smile.

"Hi, Dot," Dani said, her brows knitting. What's this about?

"I noticed that look in your eye at lunch," Dot said, pushing off the car with a sly grin. "I know you're headed somewhere, and I'm coming with you."

Dani crossed her arms over her chest. "And if I said I was just going home to grade papers?"

"Then I'd call you a liar," Dot snorted. "And we'd still end up in my car. So where are we going?"

"I thought I'd go to the Kempsville Library and look through the newspaper archives." Dani's voice was casual, but her mind was already ticking through the questions she needed answered.

"Oh, fun," Dot laughed. "Hop in."

"It's the library, Dot," Dani sighed, adjusting the strap of her bag. "I think I can handle it on my own."

"Not when it involves threatening phone calls and dead men," Dot replied, eyes narrowing with a mix of worry and excitement. "Besides, I make a great Watson."

Dani shook her head, gesturing to Dot's floral-print dress and cardigan. "You're more of a Miss Marple, and you know it."

Dot grinned, unoffended. "Fine. But I'm still the one driving, Sherlock."

Before Dani could argue, Dot turned toward her Jeep, keys jingling in her hand. Dani hesitated for half a second, the memory of that last phone call prickling at the back of her neck. Dot could be overbearing, but maybe backup wasn't such a bad idea.

With a small sigh, she climbed into the passenger seat, tossing her bag at her feet. Dot slid behind the wheel, adjusted her sunglasses, and turned the ignition. The engine rumbled to life.

Minutes later, they were rolling down the road, afternoon sun streaming through the windshield. Dot hummed along to a tinny pop song on the radio, one hand tapping the steering wheel, while Dani drummed her fingers against her knee, trying to focus on the mission ahead instead of the uneasy weight of the mystery.

Dot pulled the Jeep under the shade of a maple and cut the engine. For a moment, they sat watching a few kids spill out of the building, backpacks slung over their shoulders, snack wrappers crinkling in their hands.

The building's sharp angles and green metal roof gave it an almost deliberate, model-like perfection. The late afternoon sun left long shadows across the sidewalk, and the clean white trim of the windows glittered. Inside, the fluorescent lights buzzed faintly overhead, and the scent of old paper and carpet cleaner mingled in the still air.

Dot glanced around like a tourist, taking in the stacks and the neat rows of computer terminals, while Dani made a straight line for the front desk.

A middle-aged woman, her oversized glasses magnifying sharp blue eyes, glanced up as they approached. A headband held back her graying curls, and a blue cardigan was draped over her shoulders. Her gaze shifted from Dani's focused expression to the bright, inquisitive curve of Dot's grin.

"Hi. I'm trying to find newspaper articles about church fires, and anything else related to them. Could you tell me where your local papers are kept?"

"You'll need to use the microfilm machines," the woman said, already rising from her stool. With quiet efficiency, she led them toward the back of the library. Stopping at a long, shallow drawer built into the wall, she slid it open to reveal neat rows of plastic reels labeled in thin black marker, years of newspaper files, stored like secrets.

"Here you go," the librarian said, lifting a slim plastic reel marked 1994: Local News and handing it to Dani. Then she selected another, labeled 1995, and held it out to Dot.

The microfilm itself was a thin, translucent strip, glossy and dark as night, wound tightly around a small spool.

Dani knew each frame held tiny, almost imperceptible images of text and photographs, compressed so densely that the slightest twist of the handle could make a headline leap or blur.

"You can use the machines. Just thread the film in slowly. The handle's sensitive," she warned, her fingers brushing the smooth edges of the reel with care.

The microfilm machine was a boxy, beige contraption with scuffed corners and a low hum coming from a fan somewhere deep inside. A small screen jutted up from the center like a clunky monitor, and the glass stage beneath it gleamed under the harsh overhead light. Two winding arms extended from the sides to hold the reels.

Carefully, Dani leaned over the glass stage, threading the thin, glossy strip of microfilm onto the winding arms.

Beside her, Dot held her own reel, eyes bright with curiosity.

"So, you just crank it like this?" she asked, pointing toward the winding arm.

"Yeah, slow and steady," Dani replied, keeping her fingers careful on the film. "Otherwise, the image jumps, and you lose your place."

Dot grinned. "Feels kind of like an arcade game, doesn't it?"

"If your high score is reading old church fire reports, sure," Dani said with a soft laugh.

"Every hero has humble beginnings," Dot countered, rolling her eyes playfully.

Settling onto the stool, Dani fed the reel through the spindles, adjusting the magnification knob. Blurry lines of black-and-white newsprint gradually sharpened on the screen.

Each flick of the dial whispered fragments of the past: the city council approving a Kids Cove at Mt. Trashmore, Princess Anne High School's marching band winning a state competition, a notice about the 12th annual fall festival at St. Mark's Church. The machine clicked and whirred under her fingers, as if it, too, were remembering these events.

It felt like hours passed as they scanned old issues of The Virginian-Pilot, page by page, article by article.

Headlines blurred together... property sales, obituaries, local sports scores, PTA meeting recaps. Most of it was mundane. Dot's occasional murmurs barely registered as Dani's eyes ached from focusing on the tiny, dense type.

Finally, after turning reel after reel, she paused over a small community notice tucked into a corner of the July 1994 edition:

"Kempsville Baptist Hosts Unity Revival Weekend,

special guest Reverend Wilkins from Hampton."

Nothing remarkable. She clicked forward, only to pause again in September over a letter to the editor about religious inclusion in schools. She logged it mentally, not sure it mattered.

Dani hit the jackpot, though, in the 1995 reels: Prayer-in-school debates, angry op-eds, and a few protests outside school board meetings. A photo appeared in one article that was captioned:

"Rev. Wilkins, flanked by community leaders during a rally."

Dani leaned in. Her heart skipped. In the background, almost obscured by a tree, was Carl Rendell, younger, clean-shaven, but unmistakable.

She frowned. There was no mention of him in the caption. No byline note. Just a face in the crowd.

Next to her, Dot leaned over her machine, squinting at a tiny image. "Wait—look at this."

Another photo. Carl again. This time closer, helping load boxes into a van under the headline:

"Rev. Wilkins Leads Youth Outreach Fundraiser."

Dani rubbed her tired eyes. "That's Carl." A gnawing unease twisted in her stomach. "It's a different church, but is Reverend Wilkins the same person who is ministering at The Eastern Church of God?"

Dot leaned back on her stool, crossing her arms. "That's a powerful coincidence." She flashed a quick smile, trying to lighten the mood.

"Let's keep looking for another hour, then we quit," Dani said, though her fingers itched to keep scrolling through the reels.

"I don't know." Dot tilted her head, eyes narrowing on the photo before looking back at her screen. "Maybe he was just really devoted and moved around a lot."

Dani shot her a skeptical look. "There's more to it, Dot. I can feel it."

Shrugging, Dot leaned closer to the screen. "Fine. One more hour. Let's see what we can dig up."

Ignoring the ache in her neck, Dani flipped back to 1994, letting her instincts guide her. Each frame of microfilm carried the weight of possibility—the promise that a hidden pattern might finally emerge from the mundane pages. Her pulse quickened as she moved deliberately, scanning columns, photos, tiny headlines. Dot hummed softly beside her, occasionally nudging a reel onto the spindles.

That's when Dani saw it. A headline from November, halfway down the page:

"Hampton Trinity Union Church Destroyed in Suspected Arson"

Her breath caught. She adjusted the magnification and read the small print:

Hampton, VA, A late-night fire on Sunday reduced the historic Trinity Union Church to ashes. The blaze, which broke out shortly before midnight, gutted the century-old building within hours.

"Hey," Dani nudged her friend, "look at this."

Dot leaned closer, eyes wide. "Oh, wow. That's bad."

Dani's eyes fell on the accompanying photo. A group stood amid the blackened ruins: a few deacons, some parishioners, and a tall, familiar figure.

Carl Rendell.

Only it wasn't Carl.

The caption read:

Community leader, Charles Ripel (center), stands beside Rev. Wilkins after the fire. "We won't rest until the church is rebuilt," Ripel told reporters.

Her fingers trembled on the machine's edge. She read the caption a second time, then a third.

The letters didn't change.

He wasn't just part of the story she was chasing. He was the story.

And Dani knew she'd only scratched the surface.

Chapter Twenty-Eight

The school hallway buzzed with the kind of energy that only came when summer was close enough to taste. Students cleaned out their lockers like lazy bees, more interested in weekend plans and yearbook signatures than in anything resembling the task at hand. Textbooks were dumped on teachers' desks like burdens finally cast off, and a slow trickle of library books made its way back to Mrs. Preg, who stood by the return cart like a war-weary sentry, scanning spines with narrowed eyes.

Dani leaned against the doorframe of her classroom, a thick manila folder tucked under one arm. Inside were final essays, some heartfelt, most hastily written, that she was pretending she would read over the weekend. She probably wouldn't. Her brain was full of other things.

"You look like you're about to slide to the floor in sheer exhaustion," Dot said, appearing at Dani's side with a wry smile, her glasses slightly askew.

She wore a riot of green frog-print leggings, an oversized T-shirt, and matching Birkenstocks that squeaked faintly with every step.

"Is it that obvious?" Dani asked, taking a grateful sip. "Four more days. I'm counting in hours now."

Dot laughed. "You and everyone else. I caught a kid using his science book to press flowers for his girlfriend. I didn't even have the heart to stop him."

They stood in companionable silence for a beat, watching the swirl of students move through the hall like a slow current.

"So…" Dot nudged her with an elbow. "How's it going with Gavin? I heard him on the radio this morning, sounding awfully chipper."

Dani smiled, too tired to be offended by Dot's nosiness. "He's spent every night this week at my place."

Dot sighed dramatically. "New love. I remember that feeling. Like suddenly the world has a soundtrack."

"How long have you and Arthur been married?" Dani asked.

"Thirty-two years next month," Dot said with a fond smile. "We met in college over a dissected frog and a broken Bunsen burner. Not exactly fireworks, but he brought me a clean lab coat the next week, and I fell like a brick."

Dani laughed. "That actually sounds pretty romantic."

"We've had our moments," Dot agreed, her smile fading into something softer.

"Love doesn't always start with thunder and lightning. Sometimes it's knowing someone's in your corner, no matter what. Is Gavin in your corner?"

"He's…" Dani hesitated, a small smile tugging at her lips despite the fatigue she felt deep in her bones. She stared into the swirl of her coffee for a moment before glancing back at Dot. "He's protective but also listens and supports me."

Her smile deepened. "He even brought his computer over to my apartment so I could use it."

Dot's eyebrows rose above her crooked glasses. "He sounds like a keeper."

"I think he might be," Dani said softly. The words hung in the air longer than she expected, and her heart flickered in response. It was still new, but it was starting to feel real.

"What are you two doing this weekend?"

"Oh, Gavin's working late tonight," Dani said with a sigh, adjusting the folder tucked under her arm. "So, I'm heading home to grade a few essays. I also want to go back over everything about Carl. I keep thinking if I just look at it from a slightly different angle, something will click."

Dot's expression shifted. Her smile faded, replaced by something more cautious.

She glanced down the hallway, then leaned in, lowering her voice. "You know, this might be nothing," she said, her tone suddenly serious. "But... after we saw that name, Charles Ripel, well, it just popped into my head while I was falling asleep."

Dani turned fully toward her, the background noise of the hallway fading beneath the sharp edge of curiosity. "What is it?"

Dot hesitated, her fingers fidgeting with the strap of her bag.

"It's kind of stupid I didn't think of it sooner," she admitted, her voice dipping lower. "Probably a year or so ago, I saw Carl inside First National when I was depositing my paycheck." She gave a small, sheepish shrug, as if half expecting Dani to scold her for keeping it to herself.

Dani's brow creased.

"What was he doing?"

Dot shifted her weight, stalling a moment too long. "Pacing in front of the teller window," she said at last, cheeks tinged pink.

"Like he was waiting for someone. Really agitated but trying to look casual."

Dani's fingers tapped once against her arm. "Did you talk to him? Did he say anything?"

Dot glanced away, as if she had to pull the memory out piece by piece.

"I said, 'Hello, Carl,' and he jumped like I'd caught him doing something he wasn't supposed to." She gave a quick, sheepish shrug, clearly aware she was dragging this out. "Then the teller called out to him and handed him a thick envelope."

Dani leaned forward. "And?"

"She called him Charles," Dot said, almost under her breath, as if she wasn't sure she should have mentioned it at all. "I thought it was just a mistake, maybe I misheard her, or she got his name wrong. But now?" She finally met Dani's eyes, wide with a mix of regret and unease. "We saw that picture naming him Charles Ripel, so maybe he was using a different name. And that's why he jumped when I said hi."

Dani's mind raced. Charles. So close to Carl it could slip past anyone unless they were really listening. Her pulse ticked faster. Carl hadn't wanted anyone to notice.

Dot's voice was small, almost guilty. "I'm sorry I didn't remember until now."

A flare of frustration caught in Dani's chest, not at Dot, but at the sense that the truth kept darting just out of reach. She forced her tone to stay even. "No. I think this is important," she said, the words firmer than she intended. "I'm glad you told me."

The hallway was mostly empty now, as the students waited for dismissal in their classrooms.

Dani turned toward her classroom. Her heart thudded, steady but hard, echoing in her ears. She couldn't wait to pull on this new thread and see where it led.

Three hours later, Dani was still at school.

The sun was low in the west, casting long shadows across the parking lot outside as the gloom gathered. Essays sat untouched in a neat pile beside her. She hadn't even uncapped her red pen.

Instead, she sat at her desk, scribbling notes on a legal pad.

Names. Timelines. A single question: Who was Carl Rendell?

Was he Caleb Raines?

Colton Roberts?

Charity Renyolds?

Charles Ripel?

The names swam in her head.

Dani leaned back in her wooden teacher chair, rubbing her temple. Her gut stirred uneasily.

Her eyes flicked to the clock above the door: 6:17 PM. Each second scraped through the silence like nails on glass.

But the stillness wasn't peaceful; it was waiting, watching.

A prickle crawled up the back of her neck, light as a feather but relentless, and her skin broke out in goosebumps.

A thud, sharp and heavy, rattled the windows.

She jumped, a startled gasp ripping from her throat. Her pen skidded across the floor, clattering against the tile, and a cold sweat ran down her spine.

Her head snapped to the windows, but the classroom lights reflected off the glass, swallowing any hint of the outside.

Rational thought clawed for purchase, but her pulse drummed too fast, echoing in her ears. Every shadow seemed to lean closer; every second stretched taut.

Someone was probably just locked out, she reasoned.

Maybe a teacher had left something behind, or one of the custodial crew had forgotten their key. The explanations were ordinary, harmless.

She tried to hang onto them, but they felt flimsy, like paper shields against something she couldn't quite name.

She stood, inching toward the classroom door. The hallway outside was still, unnaturally so. No footsteps. No voices. No one called for help.

She edged around the corner, eyes locking on the glass-and-steel door at the end of the corridor. From here, she couldn't see anyone, but her feet moved forward anyway, careful and slow.

She pressed the metal latch. It gave with a loud, echoing click.

The door swung open as her pulse spiked, hard enough to make her ears ring.

Nothing.

No one.

Only the early twilight bleeding into the street, stretching shadows across the cracked sidewalks like reaching fingers.

"Hello?" she called. Her voice came out smaller than she meant, snagging in the heavy air. The sound bounced off the brick walls and came back to her warped, as if someone else had said it.

The silence swelled.

Dani's throat tightened. She took a step backward, heart thudding, her instincts going wild. The air outside smelled faintly of rust and wet concrete, sharp in her nostrils. She couldn't see anyone, but that didn't mean no one was there.

Slipping back inside, she shoved the door closed, locking it with a hard snap. For a moment, she just stood there, breath catching.

Nothing had happened. Not really. And yet, she couldn't shake the need to run.

She moved quickly down the hallway, her heels tapping too loudly, the urge to flee rising in her throat like a scream.

She reached her classroom and pushed inside, closing the door behind her, trying to breathe.

The air in the room felt different now. Cooler. Thinner.

And then, movement.

Her gaze snapped to the window. Breath hitched. A man stood just outside, half-swallowed by the thickening shadows, his face pressed against the glass, features warped by grime and the harsh glare of the fluorescent lights.

He didn't knock.

Didn't blink.

He just watched.

Then, as silently as he'd appeared, he stepped backward into the twilight, dissolving into it.

Dani lunged to the window, her pulse pounding so hard her breaths came out in gasps. She shoved it open, the metal frame groaning, thick air rushing in.

She froze.

There, smeared across the bottom corner of the pane, in something dark and clotted... mud? Paint? No, thicker, tackier... were two words that made her skin prickle and her throat lock.

The air punched from her lungs.

Her knees nearly gave out, and she clamped both hands on the window frame to stay upright.

Words glistened wetly: **YOUR NEXT.**

The scream in her throat collapsed under a flood of disbelief, confusion, dread.

Not you're. Your.

The wrong spelling jabbed at her brain, absurdly out of place.

But deliberate. Sloppy enough to get under her skin, to feel personal.

Like the person who wrote it wanted her to know they weren't here to impress her. They were here to unnerve her. And it was working.

Was this connected to Carl?

The investigation?

Or something else entirely?

Her gaze swept the courtyard, searching every patch of shadow. Movement.

In the parking lot, under the flickering streetlamp, a dark pickup, maybe green or blue? rolled backward into the street. The bent front fender caught the dying light. The single working headlight swung toward her, searing her vision like a blade of white fire. She threw up a hand to block it.

And in that instant, she knew it wasn't the light she needed to fear.

It was the person behind it.

Chapter Twenty-Nine

Dani stood near the main entrance of the school, arms cinched tightly across her chest. Above her, the faint, insect-like buzz of the fluorescent lights filled the silence.

The smell of old floor wax and something faintly metallic lingered in the air. Beyond the glass doors, the sky was bruising into full night.

She'd paced the length of the atrium until her calves ached and the scuffed floor tiles blurred beneath her feet. Her hands wouldn't stop shaking, no matter how hard she pressed them into her sides. Every sound, the tick of the exit sign's light, the distant clunk of pipes, the low hum from the vending machine, made her flinch.

6:47 p.m.

It had only been thirteen minutes since she'd called the station and asked for Detective Marcus Gates. Thirteen minutes that stretched like an hour, each second thick with the question she couldn't shake: Was the man still out there?

Watching?

Counting down with her?

At last, headlights cut across the parking lot, flooding the cracked pavement like a searchlight. A white Jeep Grand Cherokee rolled to a stop. Relief fluttered in her chest, but it didn't take root. Not yet.

The driver's door opened. Marcus stepped out—tall, broad-shouldered, his suit wrinkled as though he hadn't been home in days. Dani's breath eased just a fraction, until the passenger door swung wide and another figure jumped down.

"Chanice?" Dani gasped.

Her best friend crossed the distance at a run. Dani threw the door open and met her halfway, grabbing her in a fierce hug.

"What are you doing here?" Dani's voice cracked more than she wanted.

Chanice gave a quick grin, even though her eyes were sharp with worry. "Marcus and I were heading out to dinner when dispatch paged him. I twisted his arm until he brought me along."

Dani's eyes widened. "Girl, you've left out some of the story."

Chanice smirked, about to answer, but Marcus cut in with his low, no-nonsense voice. "She'll have to tell you later. Are you okay?"

The question hit like a weight. Dani nodded automatically, then shook her head, words tangling. "I don't know. I, just come in."

For a moment, standing in the doorway with Chanice's familiar grin inches from her own, it was almost easy to forget.

But Marcus's steady stare anchored her back to the night, to the smear on the glass, to the pickup truck vanishing into the dark.

Fear, sharp and cold, surged up again, reminding her it wasn't over. Not even close.

They followed her down the hallway, the sound of their shoes echoing off the linoleum.

"Take me through it," Marcus said once they reached the classroom.

Dani drew a shaky breath and spilled it all: the bang at the door, the yawning emptiness of the hallway, the figure at the window, the words smeared across the glass.

Marcus listened without interrupting, jaw set, eyes flicking once to the dark pane. When she finished, he tilted his head slightly. "Could be mud," he murmured. "Could be something else."

"They also have poor grammar," Dani pointed out, her voice thinner than she meant.

Chanice's mouth ticked at the corner. "That'll make them easier to find. Where were you between 5:45 and 6:15? And can you use 'your' and 'you're' in a sentence correctly?"

Dani almost smiled, but the moment slipped away when Marcus pulled a flashlight from his belt, the beam cutting across the glass.

"You said you didn't recognize him?"

"No. Just a shape. A man. There was a glare. He didn't stay long."

"And the truck?"

"Dark pickup. Might be green, but it was hard to tell in the dark. Old. Bent fender. The passenger-side headlight was shattered."

He scribbled into his notebook, expression unreadable. "You think it's connected to the Rendell case, or have you pissed someone else off?"

"I don't know." Dani hugged herself, gaze darting to the corner of the window where the words still clung. "Maybe. Whoever it was knew exactly which window to write on."

He nodded. "I'm going to step outside and look around. Can you let me in when I knock?"

Dani returned his nod, eyes tracking him as he walked out of the classroom, the door clicking shut behind him.

"Did you talk to Gavin?"

"No. He's at Lynnhaven Mall for some big radio promotion," Dani replied, her voice tight.

Chanice tilted her head. "You sure you don't want to page him?"

Dani hesitated, weighing it. "I did, and left him a message. He's busy. I'll see him later."

Chanice didn't push. Instead, she gave Dani a quiet, knowing look, then said, "I was going to call you tonight. I found another name that fits our banking profile: Cynthia Marsha Rendelf. Her account was closed six years ago in Suffolk."

Dani blinked. The name landed like a cold slap.

The name was so close to Cynthia Requist's. Could it be another possible alias?

Her mouth went dry. "Rendelf," she repeated, each syllable heavy and awkward in her throat. "That's the same name I found in the phone book."

It felt like everything was connecting. And Dani couldn't shake the feeling that someone was tightening the threads around her.

Outside, Marcus scraped some of the material off the window into a small baggy, then turned his flashlight down as he walked from the window to the parking space and back. He tapped on the window, and Chanice went to let him in.

When they returned, Dani said, "Dot told me today that she saw Carl at the bank several months ago, but the teller called him Charles."

Marcus frowned. "Carl built a whole web of aliases, and the pattern is finally becoming clear. He must've assumed no one would ever notice, or follow the threads this far."

Dani's chest tightened. Carl had been right. Even someone like Marcus trained and cautious, could be pulled into the maze he'd left behind.

Chanice nodded slowly. "If Carl was controlling the money, there's someone new at the helm."

Dani's fingers tightened against her arms. "Maybe he double-crossed someone," she murmured, testing the theory aloud.

Chanice tilted her head. "Or someone duped him. You don't just walk away from that kind of scheme."

Dani swallowed, her voice thin. "Then I've been asking all the wrong questions. I was focused on Carl and not the people around him."

"So, who's around him?" Chanice pressed.

"Justin Fenz, Cynthia Renquist, maybe someone at the church… He's been with Reverend Wilkins for at least four years." Dani's voice trailed, each name tasting sour in her mouth.

Chanice's brows lifted. "That's quite a list."

"They were all connected to him," Dani said, her arms tightening around herself. "And if Carl's gone, then one of them"

"Or all of them," Chanice cut in gently.

Dani flinched at the thought.

Her thoughts spiraled, each image colliding with the next: Dot's fleeting memory, the man pressed to the window, the green truck vanishing into the darkness like it had never existed. Each piece pointed to something bigger, darker, more calculated than she'd first believed.

Her chest tightened. Her stomach churned.

Marcus closed his notebook, sliding both it and the pen into his pocket. "From the description you gave me, I believe the truck you saw was owned by Carl Rendell. It's been missing since he disappeared in May," he said. "If you see that truck again, or anyone out of place, you call the station. Not later. Right then."

"I will," Dani said, her voice trembling despite her effort to sound firm.

Marcus paused at the door. "Dani?"

"Yeah?"

He looked at her for a long second, eyes steady. "You're not just involved in this case anymore. You're part of it now."

Her heart sank, hammering against her ribs like a warning drum. She could feel the weight of it, the shift in everything she thought she knew, the sudden loss of safety she had counted on.

"I know," she whispered, barely above the hum of the fluorescent lights. But the words tasted hollow, swallowed by the echo of all she hadn't yet understood, and all she feared might come next.

Chapter Thirty

Dani unlocked her apartment and flicked on the lights, her hand still trembling around the keys. The hallway behind her echoed with the footsteps of Marcus and Chanice, following just a few steps behind.

"Let me do a sweep," Marcus said, brushing past her and motioning for Chanice to take the back.

She didn't argue; her nerves were too raw for pride.

The apartment smelled faintly of lavender and old books, scents that always made Dani feel like herself again, no matter how turbulent the world outside had become. The soft glow of a lamp bathed the living room in honey-colored light. A mug still sat on the coffee table from that morning, its rim stained with the last of her lukewarm tea.

The windows were still locked, their edges fogged slightly from the shift in evening temperature. The kitchen remained undisturbed, a dish towel draped over the oven handle just as she'd left it, the small radio on the counter silent.

Her bedroom door hung slightly ajar, the edge of her patchwork quilt just visible through the gap.

Two sets of eyes greeted her from the back of the couch.

Shakespeare blinked once, slow and unconcerned, before hopping down with a soft thump to wind himself around her legs. Rosalind, perched on the armrest, stayed curled in a loaf shape, her tail twitching once as if in judgment.

Dani bent to scoop Shakespeare up, pressing her face into his warm fur, the low purr grounding her for the first time all evening.

"Hey, you two," she murmured. "Thanks for holding down the fort."

She carried him to the kitchen, grabbed a treat from the tin, then paused to listen. Still quiet. Still safe.

But the comfort of home now felt like a thin sheet stretched over something deeper, something stirring beneath.

After a few minutes, Marcus emerged from the hall. "All clear."

Dani exhaled, tension bleeding from her shoulders. "Thank you. I mean it."

Marcus nodded, watching her closely. "You sure you'll be okay?"

"Gavin's coming over," she said. "He's finishing the radio event at Lynnhaven, but he should be here soon."

She tried to sound casual, light, even as her voice snagged on the edge of exhaustion.

"I'll stay," Chanice said, arms already crossed, voice firm.

"You don't need to be here alone, not after what happened."

Marcus looked between them, silent but clearly reading the room.

Dani shook her head gently, though her heart swelled at the offer.

"Chanice, I'm fine. Really. I'll lock up after you, and Gavin's coming over soon."

"I don't care if Gavin's bringing a SWAT team," Chanice said, flopping down on the sofa and crossing her long legs. "Some creep shows up at your window, and now you're just what? Gonna cozy up with your cats and grade essays?"

"I'm not cozying up with anything," Dani said, reaching down absently to brush the cat's head. "I'm going to do some digging on the computer Gavin loaned me look into the names we've found."

Her chest tightened. Chanice would never go back to her date with Marcus if she thought Dani needed her. "I need to be able to think, to breathe, to process."

Chanice's jaw tightened. "And what if he comes back?"

"I'll call. I swear to God, I will. First sign of anything weird, I'll call you." Dani tried to hold her gaze steady, but despite her bravado, she could feel the tremor in her own voice.

Chanice didn't budge. Arms crossed, shoulders squared, she looked like she could stand there all night if it meant keeping Dani safe.

"Please," Dani said more quietly now. Her throat ached with the word. "If you stay, I'm just going to pretend I'm not scared. If you leave, I have to actually deal with it. You know me."

That gave Chanice pause. Dani saw it in the flicker of her eyes, the hesitation and calculation as she weighed her stubborn instinct to protect against Dani's plea.

Marcus cleared his throat, breaking the silence.

"She's right, Chanice. Guarding isn't the same thing as helping. If Dani says she needs space to think, we ought to respect that."

His gaze softened as it landed on Dani. "But you better hold to that promise. First sign of trouble, you call."

At last, Chanice sighed and pointed a warning finger in Dani's direction. "You better not be lying to me, or I'll haunt your ass."

Dani managed a smile. "I wouldn't dare."

"You still keep that baseball bat under your bed?"

"Of course."

"Good." Chanice glanced at Marcus, then back at her. "Call and leave a message on my machine when Gavin gets here. And I mean when his foot crosses the threshold, not a minute before."

"I will."

Marcus gave her arm a quick squeeze before following Chanice toward the door. "Don't make me regret siding with you," he muttered.

Dani locked the door behind them, checked it twice, then stood there, forehead resting against the cool wood.

Her pulse finally began to settle, but she stayed like that, listening to their footsteps fade before pushing away.

The apartment felt too quiet, the silence broken only by the faint ticking of the kitchen clock. Her stomach gave a low growl.

As if on cue, Shakespeare circled her legs with an insistent flick of his tail, eyeing her as if she'd been holding out on him.

"Alright, alright," she muttered.

Her school clothes felt stiff, like they carried the weight of the day, but she didn't bother changing yet. She pulled open a cabinet, shook kibble into bowls, the soft clatter filling the space. Rosalind padded in, tail high, and Shakespeare abandoned his theatrics for his dish.

Only after their bowls were full did she realize how empty her own stomach felt. She grabbed a sleeve of crackers from the counter, ate three in quick succession, then set the rest aside for a glass of water. It wasn't much, but it was enough to keep her from shaking.

Finally, she crossed to her desk.

The clunky beige computer tower gave a low whir as it came to life, the power button glowing a dim amber. The monitor blinked to green, then rolled through its sluggish start-up screen, pixels crawling into focus as though they needed convincing.

She clicked open Netscape Navigator, the blue ship's wheel logo rotating lazily, as though it were straining at sea. Then she double-clicked the dial-up connection icon.

First came the soft static click.

Then the sequence: a stuttering *screech krk-KSSHH-shhhk*, followed by a series of high-pitched digital chirps, like robotic birds having a meltdown.

WeeeEEEEE-ahhh-eeeeee-kkkchhhhhh. The shrill handshake between machines trying to connect across invisible lines.

It was a sound that had once felt like magic.

Now it just scraped across her nerves.

The AltaVista homepage finally blinked onto the screen: a plain white background with a blocky blue logo, a single search box in the center.

Connected.

Dani flexed her fingers, exhaled slowly, and began to type.

She typed::

Fires church Virginia 1980 to 1997

Minutes passed. Dead ends. Broken links. Generic summaries. The fires seemed to vanish into obscurity online, erased from memory.

Her stomach tightened, fingers cold against the mouse.

At last, a link produced something more than dead ends and hollow summaries: a scan of an old print page, yellowed and crooked, as though the paper itself had been fed through a tired scanner. The headline from 1987 wavered in digitized black.

**Two local churches damaged in suspicious fires.
Investigation ongoing.**

Chesapeake, VA – March 15, 1987

Authorities are investigating two suspicious fires that caused extensive damage to New Vine Ministries and Pine Ridge Mission Church in Chesapeake. Both incidents occurred late at night, destroying significant portions of the sanctuaries and community halls.

Local officials noted the unusual timing of the fires: in both cases, the blazes started shortly after financial records had reportedly been requested from the churches' boards. Longtime volunteer Amanda Rendell, who has been active at both congregations, assisted church staff during and after the incidents, helping to coordinate relief efforts.

No arrests have been made, and investigators continue to review evidence. Church leaders have expressed shock and concern for the safety of their congregations, while promising to rebuild and continue services.

Dani froze. The name, Amanda Rendell, pulsed on the screen.

Carl's sister.

Her maiden name.

She scrolled back up, rereading the report. How old would she have been? Late twenties?

The implication was chilling: Amanda had been active at both sites when suspicious fires occurred. Whether through coincidence, oversight, or something more deliberate, her volunteer work was now a thread Dani couldn't ignore.

Adjusting her angle, Dani changed her search.

Amanda Rendell Chesapeake Virginia religious volunteer 1980 to 1997

A few more hits popped up: an obituary for a distant relative, a mention in a church newsletter archive, but none tied her to the suspicious fires or any larger network.

Dani's jaw tightened. The computer hummed, the modem's steady squeal filling the quiet room. She rubbed her eyes, leaned back, and decided to change gears again.

Cynthia Renquist AND Carl Rendell

The screen blinked, whirred, and slowly churned. Finally, a jagged scan of a newspaper page appeared: The Virginian-Pilot, Business Section, July 12, 1996. The font wavered, the formatting uneven, but the words were clear enough.:

Cynthia Renquist:
Tidewater Philanthropist and Private Investor

Cynthia Renquist has long been recognized as one of the most influential women in Tidewater, though she prefers to maintain a low profile. Conducting her public and financial affairs through her nephew and legal proxy, Carl Rendell, Renquist has built a reputation for discreet yet impactful involvement in the region's philanthropic, religious, and business communities.

Sources indicate that Renquist supports a number of local religious and community organizations, often channeling resources through trusted family members or administrative proxies.

Among these beneficiaries are The Eastern Church of God and Hampton Trinity Church, two congregations noted for their active volunteer programs and community outreach. Family members, including her niece Amanda Fenz, have reportedly played roles in administering these initiatives, though such involvement remains largely behind the scenes.

While her influence is far-reaching, Renquist maintains deliberate anonymity, rarely appearing in public and preferring to let the results of her contributions speak for themselves. The discreet nature of her support has earned her both respect and curiosity within Tidewater's philanthropic circles, as observers continue to speculate on the scope and impact of her work.

Dani clicked "Disconnect", and the modem gave a sharp click. She powered off the computer, then sat for a moment, staring at the blank screen.

She pushed back from the desk, dragging a notepad and a pack of pens toward the center of the table.

Tapping a pen nervously against the paper, she began sketching lines and circles, trying to force the swirling thoughts in her head into something tangible.

At the center, she wrote Carl in block letters.

From him, she drew lines outward: one to Cynthia Renquist, another to Amanda Rendell, then branching toward other names they'd uncovered: Caleb, Colton, Charles, Charity, Marsha, each one scrawled in hurried ink.

Beneath them, she started a second cluster: Churches: Eastern Church of God. Trinity. Calvary Light Fellowship. Vine Ministries. Pine Ridge Mission.

The names sprawled across the page like a web, lines crisscrossing, looping back on themselves until the paper looked more like a map of infection than a family tree.

Each line carried possibilities: influence, oversight, secrecy. Dani added question marks next to some of the churches, unsure whether Amanda had known about any larger scheme, or whether Cynthia's money had been clean, or part of something darker.

She drew arrows looping between family members, marking roles and connections as they appeared in the articles she'd scrolled through.

A star by Amanda's name. A triangle by Cynthia's. Carl's name underlined twice, heavy and threatening.

Shakespeare leapt onto the table, pawing at the paper. Dani swatted him gently aside, scribbling faster.

The diagram grew messy, a tangle of lines and shapes, but for the first time, she could see the structure lurking beneath the chaos: a network of influence, family, and hidden power that stretched farther than she had dared imagine.

And at the center of it all, she saw not Carl, not Amanda, not even Cynthia, but the money binding them together.

Her pulse kicked hard. If she kept tugging these threads, she knew there'd be no turning back.

When the phone rang, she jerked so violently her knee smacked the desk. The sharp pain hardly registered over the sound, harsh, insistent, drilling through the apartment like a siren. For a beat, she just stared at it, breath snagged in her throat, until the second ring snapped her into motion.

She snatched up the receiver. "Hello?"

"Ms. Jones?" The voice was low, clipped. Official.

Her stomach dropped.

"This is Officer Taylor with the Virginia Beach Police Department. Detective Gates and Doran need you to come to Little Island Park. We have a development in the Rendell case."

Her grip tightened on the phone. It didn't make sense.

Marcus was on a date with Chanice.

"Detective Gates was just at my apartment. What's happened?"

"Detective Gates is en route to the park and asked us to call you. Police recovered a green pickup registered to Rendell. There was an old book in the glove box: The Canterbury Tales."

Dani's chest seized. The Canterbury Tales?

Her mind shot straight to The Pardoner's Tale, the story Carl had stormed into school about. Greed. Betrayal. Death. It couldn't be a coincidence. But why call her? The police didn't pull in English teachers to look at old books. That wasn't procedure.

Unless Marcus thought there was something in the book meant for her.

A message. A warning. A confession.

A shiver coursed through her, cold as ice water down her spine.

She forced her voice steady.

"You want me to come all the way out there? To the park?"

"Yes." Taylor's voice was flat and serious. "You'll want to see this."

Her free hand was already on her keys. "I'll be there."

Chapter Thirty-One

The road to Sandbridge twisted like a ribbon of shadow, the streetlights thinning out until darkness pressed in from both sides. Dani kept her headlights on high, the beams cutting through salt-flecked mist as she made her way toward Little Island Park. It was just past 10 p.m.

The night held a heavy stillness, the kind that made every sound sharper, from the grind of her tires on asphalt to the restless pound of her own pulse.

A thin fog had settled over the road, curling and coiling like smoke as she drove.

It clung to the treetops and drifted across the asphalt in pale, shifting ribbons, making the familiar road feel alien. Every curve and shadow seemed uncertain, forcing Dani to slow, her grip tightening on the wheel.

She passed the burned-out husk of the Eastern Church of God. The charred frame stood like a smoky skeleton against the misty sky, but Dani didn't pull over. She didn't need to; the image had etched itself into her memory.

The car dipped slightly as she crossed a bridge near the marsh. A thin fog curled around the guardrails and drifted across the road, muting the edges of the headlights. Something flickered in the haze, and Dani instinctively tapped the brakes. A bobcat stood in the middle of the road, lean and elegant, muscles coiled beneath a coat the color of moonlit sandstone.

Its feral eyes locked onto hers for a second before it melted back into the fog-shrouded underbrush, leaving the road empty and eerily silent once more.

Predator and prey, she thought, watching the shadows close in behind it. Everything out here tonight was either one or the other.

Dani's throat tightened. She had paged Gavin before leaving, she wasn't reckless enough to skip that. But even as she'd sent the message, she'd known she would still have to face this on her own. He was still tied up at the mall, finishing the radio event. By the time he returned the equipment to the station and made it to her apartment, she would already be out to the park and back again.

And Marcus's request had felt too urgent to put off or ignore.

She exhaled, barely realizing she'd been holding her breath, and loosened her grip on the wheel. It's fine, she told herself. Marcus would be there, and other officers were already on the scene. She wouldn't be in any danger.

Turning onto Sandbridge Road, the landscape shifted. The wild edges gave way to the hush of half-filled beach houses. Porch lights glowed like distant fireflies. A few cars sat in driveways, early renters hoping for a quiet escape before summer roared to life.

But quiet wasn't the same as peace.

Maybe it was a message.

A signal, daring her to notice.

Or maybe the book itself held something: a hidden note, a pressed page, a clue embedded in the text.

But why trust her, of all people, to find it?

Yet the police wouldn't summon her for no reason. There had to be something they thought only she could understand or recognize, something tying Carl and the book together.

Her thoughts followed her as she turned into Little Island Park's gravel lot. The wide parking area yawned open ahead, nearly deserted.

She spotted the battered green pickup almost immediately, its dark shape muted by the rolling fog that hung low over the lot.

A few unmarked cars were clustered nearby, their outlines ghostly in the haze. Dani slowed to a crawl, her eyes sweeping the mist-shrouded lot, alert for movement, police, headlights, anything.

Beyond the dunes, faint pinpricks of light drifted in and out of view. Flashlights, slow-moving and deliberate, sent bobbing beams slicing through the fog like will-o'-the-wisps. The mist caught each arc of light, briefly illuminating patches of sand before swallowing them back into the thick gray haze, leaving the world around her eerily blurred.

Dani parked and shut off the engine. The sudden silence pressed in.

Stepping out of the car, the sound of the door shutting echoed across the lot, muffled and softened by the thick fog clinging to the ground.

A soft wind rolled in from the ocean in low, damp breaths, brushing her face with the scent of seaweed and salt.

She made her way toward the boardwalk, following the lights, her footsteps dull against the worn wooden planks as she climbed onto the raised path.

The fog curled around the supports and railing, drifting in ghostly tendrils that made the lights feel further away, almost as if the world beyond the boardwalk had vanished entirely.

The beach facilities loomed to her right: two dark bathhouses with doors chained shut for the night, and a low, squat building that held the lifeguard storage.

All of them looked deserted, like forgotten relics left to weather the winter. A loose door rattled softly in the wind, the sound cutting through the fog and the quiet of the night.

Somewhere out there, the tide whispered its secrets against the shore.

The boardwalk opened out to an overlook, and the dunes gave way to wide, empty sand. The flashlights were closer now, maybe thirty yards off, ghostlike, blinking in and out of view behind swaying banks of sea grass.

No voices carried on the wind. Just the distant hush of waves, the whisper of sand shifting, and the groan of the overlook boards beneath her feet.

To the left, she spotted two figures moving with purpose across the beach. Dani squinted.

A flicker of relief passed through her, though the fog curling low over the sand made everything look unreal, half-shapes shifting in the mist. She lifted a hand and called out, her voice trembling slightly.

"Hello? Hey, over here!"

The figures paused, heads tilting in her direction, but the haze made them hard to read. One was tall, broad-shouldered; the other trailed behind with a slight limp. Were they Marcus and his partner? Dani couldn't be sure.

She took a tentative step forward, voice tighter than she meant. "I, I'm coming," she said, the words swallowed almost immediately by the fog and the rush of the waves.

Then she saw movement to her right.

A figure emerged from the shadows at the edge of the overlook, tall and thin, the brim of a police hat just discernible through the thick fog.

He stepped forward soundlessly, his outline blurred in the dim light.

"Evening," he said. His voice was low, steady. "Are you Danica Jones? I'm Officer Taylor."

Dani stopped short, her pulse hammering. "Yes, hi."

Her stomach tightened. The darkness, the fog curling around him, made it hard to really see his face, only the sharp angle of a jaw, the faint tilt of his head. But there was something oddly familiar about him. She squinted, trying to make sense of what little the dim light revealed, but the hat shadowed his eyes.

"Thank you for coming all the way out here," he said. His mouth opened into a smile, but it didn't quite reach his eyes.

He wasn't unfriendly, exactly, but hollow, practiced. He stepped closer, and Dani caught the faint scent of citrus and cloves drifting from him, sharp and unexpected in the damp night air.

"Detective Gates wants you to look at some clothing we found and some boots—to see if they look familiar."

She paused, her heels digging into the sand. "Clothes? I thought it was a book?"

The policeman gave a small nod, already turning toward the path that led away from the overlook and into the dunes.

Fog swirled thick around them, curling in lazy tendrils that obscured the lower part of his body. "We found them after I called you. Just this way. It won't take long."

She glanced once more over her shoulder. The distant flashlights looked like ghostly halos floating farther away, but others flickered ahead like lures in the dark.

She squinted through the fog, straining to pin down the familiarity, but the shadows twisted his features, and the mist softened the edges.

The angle of his jaw, the tilt of his head, the easy way he moved, and that scent. The citrus and cloves tugged at a memory she couldn't quite grasp.

Her mind clawed for a face, a voice, a moment, but each attempt slipped away like smoke.

And yet, she didn't turn back.

Every instinct urged her to retreat, to call out to Marcus, to race back to her car. But something sharper and insistent tightened in her chest.

Curiosity, the need to know.

If she walked away now, whatever thread she sensed, whatever the police thought she alone could recognize, would vanish.

So, she took another tentative step, then another, letting the fog swallow her up.

Chapter Thirty-Two

The sand was deep and loose beneath her feet, tugging at her ankles with every step until her calves burned and her breath came ragged.

The fog pressed low and heavy, curling around her legs, blurring the ground ahead, making every stride feel as if she were moving blind into a gray, shifting tide.

Officer Taylor moved ahead with surprising ease, barely seeming to struggle, his long legs cutting a clean path through the dune grass. He didn't look back.

A pulse of doubt slid through her chest.

What was she doing, following a man she barely knew into the fog, away from the safety of her car, away from the other officers? For half a breath, she considered turning back. But no, this was a police investigation. Marcus had to be nearby.

But the longer they walked into the night, the more she had to force the reassurance into place and cling to it like a lifeline.

"How much farther?" she asked, her voice tighter than she intended, edged with the strain in her chest and the unease that coiled sharper with every step.

"Not far," Taylor said. His tone was casual, almost bored.

She glanced back down the beach. The cluster of flashlights looked like distant stars now, dimming into the dark.

A sharp kee-rah cut the silence. Dani flinched, her heart jolting. A night heron, she told herself, though in the dark it sounded more like a warning.

Before she could settle, another cry split the night, louder and disturbingly close to a woman's scream. Dani froze, breath catching as the sound echoed over the dunes.

"What was that?" she asked, her voice thinner than she intended.

He didn't slow, didn't look back.

"A fox," he answered quickly, in a clipped tone.

She wished she could read his face, see if there was a flicker of unease in his eyes or the twitch of a smile at his mouth.

The darkness and fog swallowed the details, leaving her with only his voice and the unsettling calm that seemed to coat it. She swallowed hard, her pulse hammering in her ears, and forced her feet to keep moving.

"You sure we're going the right way?" she asked. "I thought the lights were"

"They were," he said, cutting her off. "They've moved."

The answer didn't settle her.

If anything, it made the darkness seem thicker, the fog heavier. Dani rubbed her arms, suddenly chilled. "Feels like the whole place is watching."

Taylor stopped walking. His silhouette wavered in the dim light, the flashlight tilting just enough to slice his face into shadow beneath the brim of his hat.

Dani squinted through the mist. She could see the line of his jaw, the slope of his shoulders, the way he carried himself, but the details that might make him familiar remained just out of reach.

Her mind reached for a memory, a hint, a face she thought she knew, but it slipped away, swallowed by the fog.

"It is." There was no smile in his voice. No reassurance. Just a simple, eerie acknowledgment.

She swallowed hard and kept moving, but now every crunch of sand beneath her feet sounded louder. Every flick of grass felt like it could hide teeth.

And the flashlights ahead kept getting smaller.

The wind picked up, lifting fine grains of sand that stung her cheeks and eyes. It whistled through the tall grasses with a sound like whispering voices, too soft to understand but too persistent to ignore. The fog swirled around her legs, curling and twisting with the gusts, clinging in pockets that blurred the dunes and scrub ahead.

Behind her, something moved, a rustle in the brush, or maybe the sudden flapping of wings. The mist wrapped around her like a living thing, thickening in the shifting shadows, making each step feel slower, heavier, more uncertain.

She tried again. "You mentioned finding clothes. Why would they be left out here?"

Taylor didn't answer right away, just kept walking.

"Evidence turns up in strange places. People think the ocean swallows things, but the tide always gives it back."

That wasn't an answer. Not really.

Her gut clenched, and she slowed, pressing a hand to her side to steady her ragged breathing.

The ache in her calves had climbed into her thighs and hips, each step heavier than the last. The dune grass was taller now, brushing against her arms, scratching her skin as she pushed through.

Sand had worked its way into her shoes, crunching with every step, and the fog thickened around them, softening the edges of the world.

Just ahead, a low fence marked the edge of a narrow path. It was splintered and half-buried in the sand, but Dani caught the stenciled letters as Taylor's flashlight swept over them.

Back Bay National Wildlife Refuge.

The wildness of the terrain, the way everything felt untamed and vast, marked the place immediately.

Out here, the ocean met marshland and forest in ways that made maps useless. The refuge stretched for miles toward North Carolina, full of tangled trails, blackwater creeks, and hidden swamps where you could vanish without a trace.

There were no lights or houses. Only a visitor's center, but it was surely locked for the night.

She stopped cold, fog curling around her ankles. "We're in the refuge," she said, her voice taut.

Taylor paused ahead of her and turned slowly. He stood just beyond a low rise, his silhouette framed by the stars. The brim of his hat obscured his face, casting a shadow where his eyes should be. "Yes," he said. "We are."

Dani's skin prickled.

The fog pressed cold and damp against her legs, curling around them like living tendrils. The lights around them had vanished, swallowed by the night. The air felt thick, almost suffocating, and every step forward seemed to drag her deeper.

Something was wrong.

"I'm not going any farther," she said, her voice sharp and tense, teeth clenched, cutting through the hush. "Take me back to the overlook. I want to speak to Detective Gates."

Taylor didn't move. Not a step. Not a flicker of acknowledgment.

The fog thickened between them, swirling like smoke, making him seem more shadow than man. From somewhere in the mist came a distant rustle, like dry reeds bending, then a faint, hollow scrape.

Dani's stomach coiled tight with unease.

The night itself felt deliberate, watching, and the oppressive silence pressed against her like a living weight.

She turned, heart hammering, lungs burning as she fought her way back through the loose sand, the thick, damp grass, and the rising wind that lashed at her face with icy fingers. The fog pressed low, curling around her legs, soaking into her clothes, blurring everything beyond a few feet. Each step sent grit and sand spilling over her shoes, whispering against her skin like the quiet hiss of ghosts.

Snap.

A twig? No, a heavier branch, snapped sharply.

Her stomach plummeted.

A sudden flutter erupted from the grasses to her right.

A bird startled into flight. Its wings sliced past her face, wet and cold, spraying mist and sand, then vanishing.

There was another rustle from the left. Closer this time, deliberate, purposeful.

Dani spun away, a scream trapped in her throat, her heart hammering so hard that she could feel it against her skull.

The wind whipped sand into her eyes and scraped across her cheeks. The tang of salt and wet earth filled her nose, sharp and choking.

A shadow lunged, slamming into her side, throwing her off balance.

Her fingers scraped against the rough dune grass. Panic flared hot and electric through her veins.

Her ears rang with the rush of blood and the hiss of wind as the scream she hadn't yet released clawed upward.

Everything spun, smell, touch, sound, sight, until there was only terror and blackness swallowing her whole.

Then everything stopped.

No sound.

No wind.

No breath.

Only dense, pressing, absolute black.

As the night swallowed her whole.

Chapter Thirty-Three

The first thing Dani felt was the cold bite of tile against her cheek, sharp and unyielding. Then came the pain.

A deep, hammering ache at her temple, like someone was tapping relentlessly from the inside out.

She groaned and rolled onto her side, her head swimming with nausea.

The sour, damp smell of the air hit her next.

Metallic. Blood. She tasted it before she even touched her temple.

Her face was slippery with it.

Her eyes fluttered open.

The room solidified around her in jagged fragments, each edge sharper than the next. Cinderblock walls coated in peeling institutional green, a cracked mirror hanging crooked above a rust-stained sink.

Two open stalls yawned like dark mouths, a single closed door behind her.

The wind rose outside, whispering threats she couldn't name. Her chest tightened as the room closed in around her. Dani sat up slowly, every muscle screaming in protest.

Her fingers brushed over the rough, sticky blood on her face. Panic prickled around the edges, but beneath it all was a slower, colder dread, curling in her gut.

She tried to make sense of where she was. A bathroom, obviously, but where? How had she gotten here?

Her memory was fractured, holding glimpses of sand, fog, and shadows. Fear unlike anything she'd ever known threatened to consume her.

She curled herself tightly against the wall, knowing she was trapped, alone, and completely vulnerable. Panic rose, sharp and hot, and she forced it down, teeth gritted.

Then voices.

Men.

Just beyond the door.

"Why the hell didn't you stick to the plan?" one snapped.

Dani froze, her chest tightening. That sharp, biting, angry tone struck something deep inside her. Recognition shivered through her, so strong that it made her throat go dry.

She knew it.

Her mind reached for the name, but fear shoved it back.

Not possible, she told herself. It couldn't be. He was dead.

Her mind recoiled, scrambling for an explanation, but there was none, only the sound, angry and alive, slicing through the stale air. Nothing about this room, or this night, made sense.

"Did you want me to shoot her right there on the beach, with cops sniffing around already?"

That was Taylor, his voice steady, annoyed but not shaken.

Her whole body went cold.

"They found your truck," Taylor said, quieter this time.

Silence stretched on the other side of the door.

Her thoughts tangled. If the police had found Carl's truck, then the lights she'd seen on the beach hadn't been a trick of the fog. They were real.

Real officers. Real help. She should have been walking toward them, not away.

Taylor had pulled her the other direction, deeper into the dark, into the dunes.

A cold clarity bled through her confusion. He hadn't led her to the investigation. He'd led her away from it.

"You think I don't know that?" the other man snapped, his voice cutting sharp through the thin walls.

Dani's stomach dropped. That voice, it was impossible.

It couldn't be.

"I was this close to being in the clear," he went on, his voice taut with fury. "Three accounts shut down clean. The Cayman transfer was ready for the other two. But then the bank starts sniffing around. All because of her," his words spit like venom, "digging where she didn't belong. Sticking her nose in."

Her pulse thundered. It was real. The voice was real.

Carl Rendell.

Alive.

Her breath caught hard in her throat. She had seen his lifeless body. She had stood at his funeral. And yet, he was here.

Just feet away.

"You should've left sooner."

The words came from a third man, low and steady, cutting through the thin walls like a blade. Dani's stomach twisted. There was another man out there.

"I should've had more time," Carl snapped, his voice rising to a ragged shout. "But Wilkins wanted her cut, and then that body you two planted showed up too soon and blew the whole thing wide open."

A loud bang on the door made Dani flinch.

She scrambled back toward the wall next to the sink, head throbbing, vision tilting. No phone. No window. No weapon. Just the sickly buzz of the overhead light, the stench of damp tile, and that thin door separating her from three men who hated her.

Desperate, she scanned the room again, her eyes catching on a small mound tucked beneath the sink. Sand. Coarse and damp, like it had been swept there hastily and forgotten. Probably left by a custodian mid-task, someone who never came back to finish the job.

It wasn't much, but if it came to it, it might buy her a second.

Dani's hands shook violently as she crawled forward, every movement sending jolts of pain through her body. She scooped up a handful of sand into both palms, the grit digging into her skin.

Heart hammering in her throat, she pressed herself flat against the wall, gasping, eyes darting wildly around the room, every nerve screaming to get away.

The doorknob rattled, turning slowly, deliberately, and the door creaked open.

Three figures stepped inside.

Justin Fenz was the first to enter. He was easily recognizable with his red hair, pale skin, and sharp jaw. His resemblance to his son, Brian, was unmistakable.

Behind him, a shadow moved into the flickering light. The police hat and uniform couldn't hide the cold eyes and sallow skin. In the light, Dani immediately recognized Henry Yeller from Crandall Packing. She'd never imagined seeing him here, breathing the same air, standing in the same room. Her chest tightened, a tremor of panic crawling up her spine.

Then the last figure stepped forward.

Carl Rendell. Heavyset. His gray hair tangled around his shoulders, beard uneven and longer than she remembered.

The air seemed to thicken around him, every step deliberate, each movement radiating a dangerous calm. Dani's stomach knotted, bile rising as her eyes locked on his face. The man she had researched, whose death she had accepted, was here, breathing, watching, closer than she ever imagined possible.

Her hands trembled uncontrollably, and she pressed herself harder against the cinderblock wall, wishing she could disappear into it.

Every instinct screamed to run, but the room offered no escape. Her pulse roared in her ears.

She could feel the weight of his gaze, heavy and accusing, cutting through the dim fluorescent light, and it was suffocating.

"Awake already," Carl said, his voice smooth, deliberate, like the toll of a bell. "Good. Time is a luxury we cannot squander."

Dani's throat tightened, words trembling. "Why... why are you doing this?"

He lowered himself slowly before her, deliberate, hands hovering over her like a priest. "Danica Jones," he murmured, each syllable sacred. "I chose you. An old school marm, her youth gone."

His finger traced a slow line across the wound at her temple, and Dani's skin crawled beneath the pain. Goosebumps rose along her arms, every nerve screaming.

"You were my alibi," he continued. "The innocent, sanctified in the eyes of all. And yet, bound to my purpose."

It felt like he was using her blood to mark her. Her heart hammered as she pressed back against the tile, trying to escape the precision of his touch.

Carl leaned close, lips near her ear. "The altar was prepared long before the fire. Prayer does not pay the bills; faith must be balanced with sacrifice. Every coin, every blessing, every trust."

Her stomach twisted. They believed in him, the parishioners, the choir, the families. Every smile, every handshake, every Sunday service, they trusted him.

Carl leaned in, eyes glittering, voice low and venomous. "And don't think I wasn't protected," he said, gesturing with a loose, manic sweep of his hand. "Reverend Wilkins? Always with a kind word and a smile. You never suspected her complicity. Every word, every blessing, it was all part of my plan."

Dani froze. Her stomach lurched. The minister she knew? She was helping him?

"Justice," he whispered, low and velvety. "The fools thought it was God's work, but I planned their ruin. And now... you are part of it, too. My alibi while my sons lit the fuse that brought the pious to their knees."

Dani's eyes darted to Justin and Henry. His sons, literally or metaphorically? She barely had time to wonder.

She didn't see any weapons, but they didn't need them. She was outnumbered, trapped, and at their mercy.

Her fingers clenched the gritty sand in her palms, the rough grains biting into her skin, grounding her even as panic clawed like icy talons through her chest, twisting her stomach into knots and tightening her throat until it felt impossible to draw a full breath.

Carl straightened, hands folded like a twisted priest in mid-prayer. His eyes bored into hers. "When we met at the school, were you afraid of me? Or did you already see through the mask I wore?"

Dani swallowed hard, her mind racing despite the icy grip of terror.

Every step he took, every twitch of his hand, every tilt of his head, it was all deliberate, rehearsed. I have to remember it all, she thought, heart hammering.

And also count the tiles, the spaces, the distance to the door. Her fingers dug into the gritty sand, the rough grains a tiny anchor against the rising panic clawing through her chest.

He smiled, a cruel, knowing curl of the lips.

"This wasn't the first time you used someone as an alibi. Or burned a church," she said, voice cracking. "You, you've done this before. Picked the faithful, the ones who'd never suspect, used them to cover your tracks."

Keep talking, Dani told herself. Maybe, maybe there would be a chance to throw the sand in his eyes, make a run for the door.

"No," he said dryly. "And it won't be my last. After we get rid of you, Rio de Janeiro. Churches are awaiting the Minister of Finance."

"But people loved you," Dani whispered. "Respected you. They spoke at your funeral."

Carl's laughter exploded, booming and manic, echoing off the tiled walls. His grin stretched wide, eyes glittering like broken stained glass. He leaned in, shoulders squared, posture solemn yet terrifying.

"Who? Samuel?" he sneered. "I paid him to spin those little bedtime psalms. So touching, wasn't it? Me, perched on church steps at dawn, haloed by morning light, coffee in hand. So humble, so pious."

He crouched slightly, bringing his face close. The heat of his breath smelled faintly of smoke and incense. "All lies, my lamb. Every word. I was handing Sunday's plate to Justin for collection."

Justin shifted, scowling, fists tightening.

"Every blessing? Straight into our pockets. That's how you run a church. Make 'em feel holy while you bleed 'em dry."

Dani's voice wavered. "What about your sister, Amanda? Was she part of it?"

Her stomach twisted. She needed to know.

If Amanda had been involved, Carl's reach was total. No one could be trusted—and what would happen to Brian?

Carl's laughter cut sharp, a sermon of madness.

"Amanda? No, poor lamb. Too timid. Too scared. Faithful… but useless."

"We need to get moving," Henry said quietly, shifting his weight, hands tightening at his sides.

Nodding, Carl leaned close to Dani, breath hot, fingers twitching.

"Now you," he whispered, voice low and deadly, "kneel, little one, and become like the church I raised in ashes."

Dani froze, her body trembling, the gritty sand biting into her palms. Kneel? Her mind screamed no, but every instinct urged her to survive. If she gave him that, she might only be speeding her own death. Her fear twisted tighter, bile rising, throat raw, but she forced herself to take a shallow, steadying breath.

No. She wouldn't kneel. Not yet. Not while there was even the smallest chance to turn this around. She needed more time, more distraction, any opening to get out.

She forced her voice out, shaky and brittle. "I, I saw you on the beach after you disappeared."

Carl's smirk curled slow and venomous. "I know you did, you idiot. Every step, every laugh ruined your little date, didn't I?"

He had been watching her. Every moment. Every laugh. Dani's chest tightened further. She felt exposed, stripped of control, trapped under his gaze.

"Why?" she croaked. "Why would you want me to see you?"

"Because, Danica," he murmured, low and oily, "the best trick isn't showing the truth...it's letting someone think they've seen it. And you? You saw exactly what I wanted."

"You waved. You signaled someone," she stammered.

His eyes darted to Justin and Henry. "The signal to feed my body to the sea, so that I could be reborn. And you? You found the fruit of our labor a week later."

Dani pressed herself harder against the cinderblock wall, fighting off the panic that threatened to overwhelm her.

Justin shifted behind Carl, arms crossed. "Time to finish this."

Carl waved him off, obsession glittering in his eyes. "No, she should know the liturgy before the final act."

He crouched, leaning closer, voice dropping low.

Dani felt the heat of it press against her. "You're going to burn, Danica. Not for God, not for justice, just for me. Every breath, smoke. Every heartbeat, a candle snuffed."

"I've already prepared my new self. Carla Rechel. Pure, untraceable, rising from your ashes." His voice dropped further, almost breathless. "You'll burn while the doctors change my features, so Carla can rise."

Dani's head filled with thoughts of survival. She couldn't die here in this bathroom. She had to fight to survive. Somewhere in the back of her mind a horrifying thought took shape: Carl wasn't just going to kill her.

He would emerge as Carla after surgery, and keep going, ruining people's lives, siphoning off their money, and burning their churches.

The fluorescent lights flickered, casting shadows of his madness across the walls. Dani's fingers clenched the sand in her palms, the gritty grains grounding her.

She would not kneel.

Chapter Thirty-Four

"What about them?" Dani asked, nodding toward Justin and Henry, her voice tight but loud enough to draw attention. "Are they going with you?"

Carl's lips twisted into a slow, sharp smile. "Why would they?"

His gaze flicked to Justin and Henry, sharp and calculating, like a predator measuring its prey.

Justin's voice cracked, tense. "You think you can just walk away and leave us here?"

Henry's fists tightened at his sides. "You wouldn't even have a plan without us. Don't get cocky."

Carl straightened, letting their words bounce off him like stones against steel. He smirked, unconcerned, with Dani pressed against the cinderblock wall behind him, fingers digging into the gritty sand, knuckles white, heart hammering. Every detail of his posture screamed control, from every twitch of his shoulder to the slow narrowing of his eyes.

"Oh, I know exactly who's indispensable," he said, his voice low and laced with venom, each syllable a blade. "And it's not who you think."

He stepped back deliberately, turning his full glare on Justin, leaving Dani in the shadows.

She counted his steps, noted the distance, the shift in his weight, her pulse pounding. The cinderblock scraped against her back as if reminding her of the walls closing in.

"All those new identities, the documents, the papers, you'd be nowhere without us," Justin shot back, stepping closer, red hair catching the light.

"The print shop above Candy's Candy? That was us, Carl. Not you. Every fake passport, every account, every new face, it's all our work. And when it comes to blood on the floor, suddenly you're just gone."

Henry squared up next to him, jaw tight, fists clenched.

"You're too arrogant to admit it, Carl. But without us, you're nothing. Every detail, every escape route, every identity, we built them. You'd be in prison without us."

Slowly, deliberately, Carl straightened, raising his head to focus entirely on the two men in front of him.

Dani's heart slammed in her chest.

This was the miracle she'd been waiting for.

The men's attention was locked on each other, every muscle tense, every sneer directed at the other. The path to the door was clear.

Dani pressed herself flat against the wall, grit in her palms, eyes scanning the lane behind them. One move. One chance.

That was all she needed.

Carl chuckled, shaking his head, lips curling into a twisted semblance of reverence. "Ah, my two little generals, squabbling over scraps. Such devotion... such faith misplaced."

No one was watching her. The men were completely focused on each other.

Her eyes flicked between the two men, measuring the distance, calculating the split-second opening. Her entire body screamed: run. Strike. Survive.

Hands raised slightly, like a preacher, Carl continued, taking another step closer to the other men. "I could watch this sermon of pride and vanity all day."

Dani's chest heaved. Every heartbeat felt like a drum pounding against her ribs, each pulse a countdown. A sharp breath filled her lungs, steadying the terror clawing at her throat as she launched. Time seemed to stretch into an awful, slow glide.

She took a sudden, deliberate step to the side, catching Carl's eye. His head snapped toward her, pupils narrowing, drawn by the movement.

Before he could react further, Dani's arms shot out, sand spraying in shimmering arcs. Her hands smashed into his eyes, the gritty grains biting and blinding him. He hissed, stumbling back, clutching his face, fury and pain twisting his features.

She shoved him hard, and Carl staggered back, a strangled shout leaving his throat. His weight slammed into Justin, then Henry, sending both men crashing into the open stalls behind them.

Every nerve screamed.

But instinct was louder. She yanked the door open and fled toward the red EXIT sign ahead of her.

Time snapped back into reality as Dani scrambled toward the door.

The air tasted of dust and adrenaline, and every second stretched like a knife.

One step. One motion. One chance.

Behind her, curses rose, sharp, angry, disoriented. The slap of shoes followed a beat later.

They were coming.

Dani burst through the doors, stumbling outside into the darkness, the murky glow of a half-moon barely illuminating the narrow path.

Her chest heaved as realization hit.

She'd been in the Back Bay Visitor Center restrooms.

Without stopping to think, she darted around the side of the building, skidding across the dirt road, sand and gravel kicking up under her feet, before reaching the boardwalk that led toward the dunes.

The path wound around low shrubs and scraggly grass, eventually spilling out onto sand. Her lungs burned. Her legs screamed. She forced herself to duck low and move fast, weaving into the shadows cast by the dunes.

The beach lay open ahead, quiet and vast, the ocean's hiss in the distance.

Behind her, the sound of a door slamming open cut through the night.

"Find her!" Carl's voice was jagged and furious.

"Fan out!" Justin barked.

"She couldn't have gotten far," Henry yelled.

Crouching between the dunes, she barely breathed.

She couldn't stay here. She needed to go.

Following the slope of the dunes and staying low, Dani broke into a desperate run. Her feet sank and slipped in the loose, powdery sand, each step sucking away speed, but adrenaline pushed her forward, legs burning, heart hammering like a drum in her chest.

If she could just make it back to Little Island Park to her car,

A sharp crack split the night air.

Were they shooting at her?

She threw herself sideways into the coarse, dew-damp grass, chest heaving, sand sticking to sweat-slick skin.

Another shot.

Something, a bullet?, hissed past her. Too close.

Heart in her throat, Dani scrambled forward, hands tearing through the rough, bristling blades of sawgrass, cutting her palms and arms. Each step sank into loose earth, each breath ragged, tasting of salt and fear.

Behind her, Justin's voice roared, full of fury and menace. "You can't hide from us."

He was close.

Clouds parted, and the moonlight caught something ahead: a weathered structure rising from the dunes, planks gray with age, edges splintered and worn by wind and waves. A faded sign swung, creaking on rusted hinges, the overlook.

A wooden platform perched above the water, offering a narrow bridge over the sand to Little Island's parking lot. If she could just reach it...

The scent of the sea grew stronger as the incline steepened, the ocean wind tangling her hair, lashing her face.

Shadows twisted across the sand, making the dunes seem like dark, jagged waves frozen in place. Each movement forward was a gamble, each glance behind a reminder of how close they were.

The wooden rails of the overlook glinted in the silver light—a promise of height, of cover, of survival.

Another shot shattered the night, but she didn't glance back.

She couldn't.

Instead, she launched herself up the slope of the final dune, half-crawling, half-running. A stitch stabbed her side.

Her vision tunneled.

The park was just ahead.

Filled with lights. Movement.

Voices.

She ran harder.

Chapter Thirty-Five

The sand shifted beneath her feet with every desperate step, but Dani didn't stop. The boardwalk loomed ahead. Beyond it, she heard voices, people. Safety.

Her breath tore from her lungs as she scrambled up the last rise of the dune, legs screaming. She tripped up the steps, nearly pitching forward, but her hands caught the rail, and she hauled herself onto the boardwalk.

"Help! Over here!" Her voice cracked, hoarse but urgent, the cry carrying across the dark, echoing over the surf. Flashlight beams cut through the shadows, jerking wildly in her direction.

Dani's heart lurched with salvation. She broke into a run down the walkway, the wooden planks rattling under her pounding steps, every slam of her shoes a plea to keep moving, keep breathing, stay alive.

A man with a flashlight stepped forward. "Dani?"

Marcus.

He ran to meet her as her legs buckled beneath her, catching her just before she collapsed.

"Dani, are you okay?" he asked, arms steadying her.

"I-I think so," she gasped. "They're back there, Carl, Justin Fenz, and Henry Yeller. He called me. Told me he was Officer Taylor. Told me you wanted me to come. They shot at me."

"Dani!" The shout cut through the dark.

Her breath hitched at the sound of his voice.

Then she saw him.

Gavin.

Stepping into the light, his pale face taut with worry, jaw clenched hard. Relief surged through her, sharp and sudden, grounding her racing heart.

He was here.

"Gavin!" Her voice cracked as she stumbled down the boardwalk. "I'm sorry, I should've waited for you. I thought,"

He reached for her, his hand firm on her arm, steadying her as her legs threatened to give. "Shhh, it's okay. You're safe now. I've got you."

For a heartbeat, the terror loosened its grip.

Dani sagged against him, drawing in his steadiness like air. But behind them, the night was not silent. The crunch of sand. Shouts, closer now.

"You two stay here," Marcus ordered, as he and Pete Doran swept their flashlights methodically over the rolling dunes, the narrow beams cutting through the thick darkness like twin searchlights.

Pete's hand hovered near his holstered gun, fingers twitching with tense readiness as his eyes locked onto a flicker of motion. "There's movement to the south. Three figures."

Ghostlike silhouettes appeared at the top of a dune before vanishing behind a ridge, their movements jagged and frantic.

The sharp crackle of police radios broke the silence as the detectives called out coordinates and confirmed positions, their voices clipped but urgent in the night air.

Relief hit Dani like a blow, stealing what little strength she had left. Her legs sagged, and she stumbled before sinking into the cold, grainy sand, the world tilting as exhaustion claimed her.

Gavin caught her gently, lowering her to the ground and holding her.

His voice was low, urgent. "Dani, look at me. Did they hurt you?"

She nodded numbly, one trembling hand brushing her throbbing temple. "Carl hit me. I woke up in the visitor center bathroom. He stole the money, all the accounts, the aliases, they were his. They burned the churches. They were going to… they were going to burn me. He's trying to disappear, become someone else."

Her breath came in quick, shallow bursts, her heart hammering like a trapped animal. Panic clawed up her throat, making her vision blur and the world tilt, each sound sharp and distorted. She gasped, desperate for air.

"Okay, okay," Gavin murmured, his voice steady, an anchor in the storm of her adrenaline-fueled terror. He wrapped her hands in his, warm and grounding, squeezing just enough to remind her she wasn't alone. "You're safe now. Breathe with me, okay? In and out."

She tried to follow, mimicking his rhythm, even as her chest hitched and her thoughts spiraled. Gavin didn't rush her; he just held her, eyes locked on hers, steady and unshakable, until the worst of it began to ebb.

A medic's flashlight swept across them, voices murmuring in the background. Someone pressed gauze gently to her temple, but

Dani barely registered the touch. The only thing that mattered was Gavin's voice, his presence anchoring her in a world that had almost slipped away.

Slowly, he helped her to her feet, the EMTs hovering close but fading to shadows at the edges of her vision. The cold metal of her car pressed against her back as he leaned her there, his hand lingering at her elbow, steadying her.

The dunes stretched out around them, ghostly under the half-moon's glow. Wind tugged at her hair, carrying salt and sand, but all she felt was the warmth of his nearness, the unspoken promise in the way he didn't let go.

Her knees wobbled, but she matched her breaths to his, slow, even, certain. In that fragile rhythm, surrounded by chaos and darkness, she let herself lean into him, just enough to believe she might be safe.

A shuddering exhale escaped her, the trembling ebbing for the first time since the dunes. Gradually, the sharp edges of her panic dulled, replaced by a fragile, trembling calm. She still felt raw and vulnerable, but the crushing weight of fear began to lift.

Nearby, Pete spoke into his radio. "We've got eyes on suspects. Three males, armed. Repeat, armed. We need perimeter teams in the Wildlife Refuge, immediate intercept."

Behind them, more lights cut through the dark, flashing red and blue along the dunes, voices rising over radios. The salty breeze tugged at Dani's clothes, whipping around her and Gavin as reality sank in: the cavalry had arrived.

Time passed.

Radios crackled with bursts of movement. Units coordinated, searchlights swept the dunes.

Dani sat curled into herself, Gavin's arm around her shoulders, his presence the only thing keeping her grounded as the adrenaline slowly ebbed into exhaustion.

Then a voice came through, firm and clipped.

"Suspects in custody. I repeat, Rendell, Fenz, and Yeller are in custody. No resistance. Transporting them to the station now."

Dani lifted her head, heart stuttering. For a moment, she couldn't believe what she'd heard.

Marcus approached, tucking his radio back into his shoulder harness. "They doubled back toward the service road. We had a perimeter already set up to look for you. They walked right into it." He crouched beside her, his voice gentler now. "We've got them. It's over."

Dani nodded, slow and heavy.

The words felt far away, drifting around her like echoes, but she clung to them anyway.

When they finally stepped back, Marcus was there again, a tired smile softening his face. "Go home. We'll get your statement tomorrow. Get some rest. You've been through hell."

"You ready?" Gavin asked, his voice low beside her.

She looked at him, then nodded. "Yeah. Let's go home."

Chapter Thirty-Six

Gavin didn't say much on the drive. He kept one hand on the wheel and the other resting lightly on Dani's knee, a quiet tether that helped her pull herself together.

She stared out the window, her mind a blur.

Every time she closed her eyes, she saw Carl's smile, heard Henry's voice, felt Justin's shadow looming over her.

Her scalp throbbed, and her arm ached where Carl had twisted it. Her whole body felt wrung out.

When they reached her apartment, Gavin helped her inside, locking the door behind them. She moved as if she were underwater, shaky and uncertain, as he guided her to the bathroom with quiet purpose, then turned on the shower before stepping back.

"You okay if I stay?" Gavin asked gently, his voice barely above a whisper.

Dani nodded. "Please."

He stepped closer, careful and slow, giving her space to pull away if she needed to. She didn't. Her eyes met his, tired, red-rimmed, but steady. She trusted him.

"Let's get you out of these," he said softly, touching the hem of her torn, sand-covered shirt. "You've got scrapes all over."

She raised her arms in consent, and he peeled the fabric away with careful hands. There were red marks along her shoulders, and a bruise was already blooming across her ribs.

His jaw tightened, but he said nothing. Not yet. He helped her step out of the rest of her clothes, then turned on the shower, steam curling into the room.

Once the water was warm, he held her hand as she stepped in. Dani stood beneath the spray, eyes closed, letting it run over her as if it could rinse away the pain and fear.

When her legs swayed, Gavin was there, wrapping her in a fluffy towel and drying her off with quiet care.

He knelt to gently press his lips to the shallow scrapes on her knees, then stood and brushed a soft touch across a bruise blooming on her shoulder, just light gestures that reminded her she wasn't broken, that she was safe.

Dani caught his hand. Her throat ached with the words, but she pushed them out anyway, barely louder than a breath.

"I'm sorry I didn't page you. I should have."

His thumb brushed over her knuckles—slow and grounding.

"Hey," he said softly. "You don't have to be sorry. I'm just glad Marcus called me when the police found your car."

Tears burned hot at the back of her eyes. "But if I had," her voice cracked, "you wouldn't have had to"

He shook his head, the movement a blur at the edge of her vision. "No. Don't do that. Don't carry more than you already are. I would have come, no matter what."

The edges of the room blurred, her grip slackening as sleep pulled at her. Gavin squeezed her hand. "I'm going to wake you every couple of hours, okay? Because of the concussion."

Dani managed the faintest nod, her eyelids already sliding closed as she curled into his body.

The steady warmth of his hand around hers, the certainty that he would be there even in sleep, loosened the last frayed knot inside her. Her whole body softened, breath shuddering out as she whispered, "I love you."

Then the scent of something warm drifted in from the kitchen, waking her.

Toast, maybe, or soup left to simmer?

Her stomach stirred at the smell, even as a dull throb pulsed through her temple and every muscle felt bruised and heavy.

The light coming in through the curtains seemed too bright, making her eyes water, and a faint ringing buzzed in her ears.

When she shifted under the blankets, the room tilted slightly, and nausea curled at the back of her throat.

A weight pinned her down, warm and vibrating softly. Shakespeare curled there like a sentinel, his purrs deep and steady, his green eyes half-lidded but alert.

By her hip, Rosalind was tucked tightly against her side, her small body curled protectively, as if keeping guard.

The sight of them brought a sudden tightness to her throat.

They'd always known when she needed a hug. And now, they comforted her without words: You're home. You're okay.

She exhaled slowly, one hand coming up to stroke Shakespeare's fur. For a moment, she allowed the stillness to wrap around her and let the soft purring fill the void inside her.

And then it all rushed back: the bathroom floor slick beneath her palms, Carl's voice curling in her ear, the bite of sand ground into her fist.

The sharp crack of gunshots. Running until her lungs tore.

Gavin's face filled with worry.

A soft knock on the doorframe pulled her free of the images. Dani blinked, wincing as the room swayed.

Gavin stood there, hair tousled, wearing the same shirt from last night, sleeves shoved up to his elbows.

"You're up," he said quietly, stepping in. "I didn't want to wake you."

"Was I hit by a truck?" she croaked, managing a half-smile.

Gavin gave her a careful look, his eyes searching hers for anything fragile, then came to sit beside her on the edge of the bed, setting the plate on the nightstand.

"Are you hungry? I made grilled cheese and heated up a can of tomato soup. It's not gourmet, but it's warm."

She smiled faintly, her voice still hoarse. "Help me out from under the cats, and I'll come eat with you."

Gavin leaned in, eyeing the two furry sentinels. "Shakespeare looks like he'd bite me if I tried."

"He'd never. He's a gentleman," Dani murmured, shifting just slightly.

The big gray cat let out a grumble of protest, and Rosalind curled tighter by her hip. She blinked one eye open, assessing the disturbance.

Gavin reached down gently, slipping a hand under Shakespeare's belly. "Alright, buddy. Let's negotiate."

He lifted the cat with exaggerated care, earning a flick of the tail and a theatrical sigh from the big cat. "That's right," Gavin muttered, placing him at the foot of the bed. "You've done your shift."

Dani laughed softly, just a breath, but it felt good.

Rosalind allowed herself to be nudged away, flopping down on a pillow.

Gavin offered her his hand. "Your turn."

She took it, wincing a little as her sore muscles complained. "Everything hurts."

"I know," he said quietly, helping her sit up, steadying her as she swung her legs over the edge. His hand lingered at her back, warm and steady. "But you're upright. Let's get you some food and some painkillers."

She leaned into him for a moment, just to feel the solidness of his presence. "Thank you."

"Any time," he said with a smile. Dani reached for a sandwich but paused, her fingers hovering over the plate on the kitchen bar.

Sunlight spilled through the window, catching the crumbs and casting long shadows across the tiled floor. "Is it over?"

"For now," Gavin said, leaning against the counter beside her, his hand brushing hers as he reached for a glass.

"You'll still have to talk to the police, give a full statement later today. But yeah, they're in jail."

Dani took a bite, chewing slowly, trying to focus on the warmth spreading through her stomach rather than the cold memory clawing at the back of her mind.

She glanced out the window, watching the light shift across the street outside before looking back at him.

"He was going to have plastic surgery and become Carla Rechel and scam more churches in Rio," she said, her voice low.

Gavin's eyes softened. He rested a hand lightly on hers across the bar.

"But you stopped him. You kept people safe," he said. "Seriously, what you did matters."

Dani let her hand linger under his, feeling the quiet steadiness in his touch. For the first time in hours, the tight knot of tension in her chest loosened, even just a little.

Dani set the sandwich down, her appetite waning again. "I keep thinking if I'd just done what you said and let it go…"

He shook his head, voice low but firm. "Then he'd still be out there, Dani. Scamming people."

Tears stung her eyes. "I'm sorry, I"

"Hey." Gavin stepped closer, bending slightly at the knees so their eyes met. He reached out and gently took her hands. "No regrets. You survived. That's what matters."

It struck her how much he'd changed over the last few months, shifting from demanding she stop investigating to respecting her need to see things through. Even now, bruised and dazed from everything, with her head still throbbing and her muscles tense, she felt safe and accepted.

He brushed a loose strand of hair from her face, then drew her gently into a hug. Dani rested her forehead against his chest, her body sagging slightly, the concussion making every movement feel heavier.

After a moment, he lifted his head just enough to press a soft kiss to her temple, then let his lips trail down her cheek and neck. "Do you remember what you whispered to me last night?"

She nodded, her voice barely above a whisper but steady. "I do."

"Tell me again," he urged softly.

"I love you," she breathed.

"I love you, too," he replied, pressing a warm kiss to her temple.

Chapter Thirty-Seven

Dani drifted on the edge of sleep, her body curled into the corner of the couch, a blanket tucked under her chin. The late afternoon light spilled through the windows in warm streaks, dancing across the floor in soft amber tones.

The television was on, some nature documentary murmuring about ocean currents and coral reefs, the volume low.

Shakespeare sprawled across the top of the couch like a sleepy gargoyle, while Rosalind watched from the windowsill. The house was quiet.

There was a gentle tap-tap on the front door, and Dani flinched awake. Her heart gave a panicked lurch before her brain caught up. She was home. Safe.

She sat up slowly, pushing a hand through her hair.

"Gavin?" she called, her voice still thick with sleep.

He wasn't in the room.

The knock came again, followed by Chanice's voice from the other side of the door.

"Dani?" came a familiar voice. "Let me in."

Dani went to let her friend in, managing a tired smile. "Hi."

Chanice swept in, her eyes going wide. "Girl, you look like hell."

Dot appeared, carrying a Tupperware container and a tote bag slung over her shoulder. "She means that in the most loving way possible." She swept past to stuff things into the fridge.

"I do," Chanice added quickly, rushing over and kneeling beside the couch. "But seriously, are you okay?"

"Gavin told you?"

"He called me," Dot said, closing the fridge door and coming back. "And I called Chanice, who threatened his life if he didn't let us in to check on you today."

Dani gave a soft laugh and leaned back, comforted by the sight of their familiar faces. "I'm not sure where he is, but I'm okay. Just tired. Sore."

"The newspaper said shots were fired," Chanice said, her expression softening as she reached for Dani's hand. "I'm so glad you're okay."

Dani's throat tightened unexpectedly, and she hugged Chanice, then gathered Dot in, too. "I'm glad you're both here."

Another knock interrupted them, this time louder and more official-sounding. Dani tensed again, her nerves still a live wire under the surface.

"I'll get it," Dot said, already halfway to the door.

She opened it to reveal Marcus, freshly pressed and serious in a navy suit and tie, a notepad tucked under his arm.

"Hey," he said, giving a small nod as his eyes swept the room. "Sorry to barge in, but I need Dani's statement so I can finish the paperwork."

"Of course," Dani said, brushing sleep from her eyes and trying to sit up straighter.

Before anyone could respond, a door opened down the hallway, and Gavin appeared, damp and distracted, a towel slung low around his waist, hair dripping from the shower.

Four heads turned in unison.

Dot arched an eyebrow, admiring his abs and muscled legs. "Well, hello."

Gavin froze mid-step, blinked at Marcus, then at the others, and sighed, running a hand through his wet hair. "I'll, uh, get dressed."

"Don't rush away," Dot called as he turned into the bedroom. "You're adding some interesting color commentary to this police interview."

Chanice grinned wickedly and elbowed Dot. "Is he your new bodyguard, or are you running a spa back there?"

Moments later, Dani sat cross-legged on the couch, wrapped in a soft throw blanket. The mug of tea Dot had made was warm between her palms.

Chanice sat on the floor near her feet, Dot curled up in the armchair, and Marcus had claimed a spot on the other end of the couch, the notepad resting against one knee

Fully clothed now, Gavin hovered on a stool by the breakfast bar, arms folded loosely, giving Dani space but staying close. His eyes never strayed far from her.

"Take your time," Marcus said gently, "but I need you to walk me through what happened, starting from the phone call you received."

Dani sipped her tea, the warmth grounding her as much as the cat curled in her lap. "I got the call around 9:40. I was home, waiting for Gavin, when I got a call from Officer Taylor, well, Henry Yeller pretending to be a police officer."

Marcus nodded grimly, jotting something down.

"He said you needed me at Little Island Park, that you'd found Rendell's truck and an old copy of The Canterbury Tales in the glove box."

"That sounds fake as hell," Chanice muttered, frowning.

"Right?" Dani gave a weak laugh. "But it didn't occur to me at the time. I said Marcus had just been here a few hours before, but Taylor was insistent, so I went."

Dot shook her head. "Classic murder-mystery setup. Lure the heroine out into the night with Chaucer."

Dani smiled faintly.

"When I got there, the truck I'd seen at school was parked with a few other cars, but no one was around. I saw flashlights down the beach and thought it was Marcus and Pete, so I went down the path to the overlook."

Marcus leaned forward. "When did Yeller approach you?"

"I saw two men and called out, but Yeller came from the other direction. This time he said you wanted me to look at some clothes and boots you'd found down the shoreline." She paused, tightening her grip on the mug.

"It wasn't until we passed into the Nature Preserve that I realized something was off. I said I wanted to go back. That's when another man came out of the bushes and hit me."

Chanice's eyes flared. "He knocked you out?" The words came out sharp, but her expression faltered almost immediately, guilt flickering across her features. "God, Dani… I kept pushing you to keep digging, and now," She broke off, shaking her head, her voice quieter. "I never should've put that on you."

"Hey," Dani said softly. "This isn't on you. One second I was running from Yeller; the next I woke up on a bathroom floor inside the refuge. Carl made his choices. You didn't."

Silence fell over the room for a beat, broken only by the low hum of the heater and Rosalind's faint snore from the windowsill.

She continued, recounting everything: Carl's confession, his plan for plastic surgery and a new identity; how Justin and Henry had set the church fire while she'd provided Carl with an alibi; how Amanda Fenz was innocent, but Reverend Wilkins was not.

Dot's eyes widened. "Wow, that's a lot to process. I can't believe you kept your head through all of that, especially with a concussion."

Chanice reached over, giving Dani's hand a gentle squeeze. "You're a hero. You saved people, Dani."

Dani's voice trembled slightly as she continued, "They were going to kill me. I threw sand in Carl's face and knocked him into Henry and Justin. That gave me enough time to run."

She turned to Marcus and then Gavin. "I don't know what would've happened if you hadn't been there."

Dot leaned closer, eyes steady. "You were so brave, Dani."

"You saved yourself," Marcus said. "We were just the backup."

Chanice nodded, smiling softly. "Exactly. You made it out. That's all that matters."

"What happened to them?" Dot asked Marcus.

"All three men were arrested trying to leave the refuge. We found evidence in Justin's car that ties them to the church fires and recovered several guns."

"I can't believe you went out there alone! What were you thinking?" Chanice's head snapped toward Dani so fast it made Dot flinch.

Dani's gaze flicked to Gavin as if hoping he'd answer for her. "I want to say I thought Marcus needed me," she said, voice tight, "but honestly… my curiosity got the better of me."

"Oh, girl," Chanice started, voice rising with outrage. "We are gonna talk about this."

Before she could launch into full lecture mode, Gavin crossed the room in three quick strides and settled on the armrest beside her, slipping a comforting arm around her shoulders.

He drew her slightly against him, letting her feel the steady warmth of his presence. "You're safe," he said, voice low but firm. "That's what matters. Everything else we'll handle together."

He brushed a loose strand of hair from Dani's forehead, then rested a hand lightly on her shoulder, anchoring her.

A quiet reminder that he was there if she needed support.

His other hand stayed free, relaxed at his side, giving her room to shift, to stand, to make her own choices. "You've been through hell," he murmured, "but I trust you. I've got your back. Always."

Dani felt the weight of his steadiness without feeling confined, a rare combination of safety and freedom that made her smile.

Chanice opened her mouth to argue, but Marcus slid off the couch and dropped to the floor beside her, catching her wrist and pulling her gently down into his lap.

"Easy, tiger," he said with a crooked smile. "You're scaring the witness."

Dot let out a startled laugh. "What is happening? Why has no one told me about this?"

Chanice, wide-eyed, blinked down at Marcus. "You did not just distract me with a cuddle trap."

"I did," Marcus said unapologetically. "And it worked."

Dani leaned into Gavin's side, the brief burst of tension dissolving into the absurdity of her friends.

But soon the laughter faded, and silence settled over the room again.

"I still can't believe how far Carl took it," Chanice said. "All the fake identities, accounts, and arson."

Dot leaned forward, brows furrowed. "What kind of person does that? That's not just fraud. That's psychopathy."

"It's greed," Dani said softly. "Pure greed. But dressed up in redemption. He made it sound noble. But it was just about money."

Gavin sighed, his brow furrowed. "There's something else that still doesn't sit right with me. Why keep up the act? Why fake his death at all?"

Dot nodded. "He could've just disappeared, new name, new face. But instead, he went through all that trouble to fake being dead. What's the point?"

Marcus rubbed the back of his neck. "The body we found obviously wasn't Carl. But we identified it as Carl because it was his cousin, Denny Rendell. They were close in age, same build, same jawline. No wallet on him. The water had blurred the features enough that it looked like a match. It wasn't until the dental records came back yesterday that we knew for sure it wasn't him."

"Denny?" Dot's voice wavered, the color draining from her face. "I, I knew he was missing, but everyone assumed he'd just run off. Lord, I told myself he'd landed some new job out west or found a girl. I never…" She broke off, one hand pressed to her chest as if trying to steady her racing heart. "I never thought he'd end up like this."

Marcus nodded, his voice low. "Denny's been blackmailing Carl for years. Knew all his fake identities and was probably in on some of the early scams. We found all of his notes and ledgers in a safe in his house this morning."

Dani tightened her grip on the blanket. "Carl killed him to tie up loose ends."

"Looks like Justin and Henry did it. And that sample you took from the packaging store? It was a match."

"So, two birds with one stone," Gavin said. "Stop the blackmail and get a fresh start."

Dani exhaled slowly, eyes drifting to the floor.

"He didn't want anyone chasing him or his next identity," Marcus said, looking up. "Did he say why he targeted churches?"

"Not directly, but people trust churches," Dani said bitterly. "No one questions the minister or the man who helps run a church."

There was a long pause. Then Dot asked, "You said he came to school to see you for an alibi, but it feels like he was modeling himself after Chaucer's story."

Dani blinked. "You're right. The Pardoner's Tale. 'Radix malorum est cupiditas.'"

"Translation, please," Chanice asked from where she was still curled in Marcus's lap.

Dani looked at each of them. "The Pardoner tells his tale to shame people, to make them give him their tithes by warning them that avarice is the root of all evil. But the Pardoner is corrupt, spending the money on women and alcohol instead of giving it to the church."

Dot shook her head. "The similarities are striking."

Dani's gaze drifted downward, tracing the lines of the floor as her mind churned. It was familiar, the lies, the manipulation. The way Carl twisted faith for profit, how easy it is for people to look away until it's too late. She swallowed hard, the memory of Carl's smirk as he spelled it out so calmly.

And yet... she survived. She acted. She didn't let him win.

Chanice reached up to squeeze Dani's hand. "I'm just glad you're safe now. You outsmarted them."

Dani managed a faint smile. "I think I just got lucky."

"No," Marcus said, rising with his notes. "You paid attention. You read people better than most cops. Even though I wish it were otherwise, you never quit."

Gavin pressed a kiss to the top of Dani's head, his arm snug around her waist.

Outside, the late afternoon light had turned gold, the sun dipping low enough to touch the trees.

Her friends were here. She was home. Against all odds, she'd survived.

Epilogue

The late afternoon sun streamed through the open windows, casting golden patterns across the living room. Outside, children's laughter carried through the thick, humid July air. The house smelled faintly of sunscreen and freshly cut grass, the unmistakable scent of summer settling in, a reminder that school was out and the long days stretched unclaimed before them.

Dani stretched out on the couch, her skin warm from the day's sun, a soft smile tugging at her lips.

Gavin settled beside her, his hand finding hers with that familiar ease. His fingers traced gentle circles on her sun-kissed skin, light and teasing against the bare arms exposed by her breezy sundress.

Dani leaned into him, soft yet deliberate, until their bodies pressed closer, warmth mingling between them in the golden summer light.

Her airy sundress swayed with every movement, making the tiny daisies on the pale yellow fabric dance.

Shakespeare and Rosalind lounged nearby, lazily batting at the curtains as a breeze fluttered in, cooling the room. Dani reached out, fingers curling around Gavin's hand, squeezing gently.

He'd been right. After the rest and relaxation of the past few weeks the long, lazy mornings, sun-drenched afternoons, and the slow pace of summer break, she felt strong. Whole. With school out and no deadlines pressing down, the weight that had pressed hard on her chest, lightened and became manageable.

Gavin's voice dropped to a low murmur, teasing. "You know, I could get used to this sunshine, you in that dress, and me stealing all your attention."

Dani smirked, turning her head just enough to catch his eye. "Is that a challenge, or a promise?"

He grinned, fingers tightening just a little around hers. "Depends on how willing you are to let me prove it."

They were supposed to be heading out to a concert, but the world outside the apartment didn't seem to exist. Dani laughed softly, the sound warm and inviting. "You're lucky I like a little trouble."

His chuckle vibrated against her ear, low and easy, as he leaned in close. Their foreheads touched, a slow, teasing closeness that made her pulse quicken.

Gavin's fingers brushed hers, fingers tangling briefly, holding on just long enough to make her notice.

Dani's sundress swirled lightly around her knees as she leaned into him, their shoulders brushing, breaths mingling. Every glance, every soft laugh, was tinged with an urgency that was entirely theirs

Gavin's fingers tangled in Dani's hair as he pulled her close, lips brushing hers with a slow, teasing touch. The soft fabric of her sundress dipped, exposing a good bit of creamy breast.

The night, the concert, the world beyond the room faded. In that moment, there was only the quiet closeness, the shared warmth, and the anticipation of everything yet to come.

He shifted to taste her, tugging the fabric down further to expose her nipples.

The promise of the night, the music, the crowd, faded away beneath the heat of their touch. Every glance, every whispered word, every soft laugh carried the weight of something deeper, something urgent and tender all at once.

Gavin's hand slid from her arm to the small of her back, pulling her closer until there was no space left between them. Dani's breath hitched, fingers curling into the fabric of his shirt as his lips traced a path down her neck, soft and warm, sending shivers rippling through her skin.

He whispered against her skin, "You are so beautiful."

Dani's lips curved into a slow smile. "You're pretty good looking yourself."

Their eyes locked, a silent promise passing between them, deeper than words. The world outside faded until there was only the heat of skin, the taste of breath, and the quiet hum of summer settling around them.

Just as Gavin pushed up Dani's sundress to find her wet and needy, a sharp knock broke through the quiet. Dani tensed, then laughed softly.

"Ignore it," Gavin grunted, but she was already on her feet, smoothing the fabric of her sundress as she moved toward the door.

Her pulse still raced, a tingle lingering along her skin. Part of her wanted to stay, wanted to melt back into him and ignore the world.

But the knock came again, and curiosity pulled her forward. It would only take a second, and as she moved, she felt Gavin's steady, warm, and grounding presence behind her.

The heat of his body teased her back just enough to remind her he was there, safe and patient, letting her take the lead.

At the door stood a teenager, maybe fourteen or fifteen, with a mop of unruly brown hair that fell into his anxious eyes. His clothes were worn, a faded t-shirt and sneakers scuffed at the toes, but his posture was hopeful, shoulders squared despite the tremor in his hands. He clutched a notebook with dog-eared pages.

"Ms. Jones? My grandma says we can trust you. Something bad is happening at the new Seatack Rec Center. She wanted me to ask for your help."

Dani's eyes flicked to Gavin who stood beside her now. His nod and the faint, confident curl of his lips told her everything.

She opened the door wider, and the boy stepped inside, clutching his battered notebook as if it contained the world's secrets.

Gavin's hand brushed hers. Her pulse quickened, a thrilling knot of anticipation twisting in her stomach. She took a slow breath, tasting the tension between them and feeling it sharpen her senses.

The boy's voice trembled. "Someone's been sneaking in at night. No one knows why."

A shiver ran down Dani's spine.

The summer air drifting through the open door felt sharper somehow, a whisper of danger brushing her skin. Her pulse raced.

Whatever was waiting at the Seatack Recreation Center, she knew they would face it together, but she couldn't shake the sense that someone was setting them up.

About the Author

M. Jayne LaDow, author of *The Marchfield Series*, blends her love of storytelling with years as an educator to craft mysteries full of secrets, suspense, and unexpected twists. When she's not exploring quiet towns that hide dark truths, she can be found on the beaches of Virginia or plotting her next twist with her mischievous cats. She lives in Virginia Beach with her husband, children, and a lively collection of furry and scaly companions.

Books

By M. Jayne LaDow

One Night Stands and Lesson Plans
Learning Goals and Dancing Poles
Pop Quizzes and Stolen Kisses
Tardy Pass, No Questions Asked

By MJ Long

Pippa, The Pipefish
Villains Incorporated and other one act plays

Acknowledgements

Every story begins with whispers, subtle hints, fleeting ideas, and hidden truths that lead a writer down unexpected paths. To those who have shared their insights, offered guidance, or simply believed in the journey, thank you for lighting the way through the shadows.

To Jim, who taught me everything I know about dangerously charming radio announcers, and how their voices could probably convince the entire small town to ignore a body in the library.

To my kids, Megan and Miles, whose brilliant ideas are only rivaled by their mischief, which I strongly suspect would land them as prime suspects in any cozy mystery (but they'd be too clever to get caught).

To my sister, Liz, who can turn the darkest nights into absurdly bright escapades, usually involving questionable snacks and laughter loud enough to wake the neighbors, who are, of course, suspicious characters.

To my friend Lauren, who has braved every brainstorming session, plot twist, and caffeine-fueled panic attack with the resilience of a trusty sidekick who knows better than to open the creaky door first.

To Suzanne, my author buddy, who prevented me from hiding under a rock, confessing to crimes I didn't commit, or becoming the eccentric recluse everyone in town whispers about.

To Lea Audrey and Patti, once pen pals, now trusted co-conspirators, who never doubt I'll emerge from the chaos clutching the right clue (and maybe a scone).

To all my students, who unknowingly supplied me with more material, mysteries, and red herrings than they'll ever realize — especially those brave souls who survived reading *The Pardoner's Tale* with me.

And to Nancy, my friend, who endured the chaos of teaching in the late nineties, years so turbulent and strange they make any fictional mystery look positively quaint.

Finally, to the readers who chase secrets, linger on cliffhangers, and fall for flawed, passionate hearts: this story exists because of your curiosity and courage. May you always find delight in the mysteries that lie just beneath the surface.

Coming Soon

Budget Cuts and Midnight Lust

When budgets clash, sparks fly—and not just from the Bunsen burners.

PE teacher Emma Sinclair and science teacher Max Harrison have been Marchfield Middle's most legendary rivals. She's all whistles and winning attitudes. He's all lab coats and logical theories. And now they're stuck sharing what's left of the school's pathetic budget for both Field Day AND the Science Fair.

As if their forced partnership wasn't combustible enough, they've been saddled with Captain Wigglesworth, an overly chatty parrot who has zero filter and a talent for revealing everyone's secrets at the worst possible moments.

Between dodgeball disasters, explosive experiments, and one opinionated bird, Emma and Max discover that their heated arguments might actually be hiding a different kind of chemistry altogether.

But can two people who've built careers on competition learn to play for the same team? And more importantly—can they survive middle school matchmaking courtesy of 200 curious twelve-year-olds and one meddling parrot?

Budget Cuts and Midnight Lust **is a laugh-out-loud enemies-to-lovers romance where the real education happens after school hours.**

Coming in May 2026